POSEUR

a novel by
Rachel Maude

poppy

LITTLE, BROWN AND COMPANY
New York   Boston

Poppy
Little, Brown and Company
Hachette Book Group USA
237 Park Avenue, New York, NY 10017
Visit our Web site at www.pickapoppy.com

First Edition: January 2008

ISBN-10: 0-316-06583-8
ISBN-13: 978-0-316-06583-2

10 9 8 7 6 5 4 3 2 1

CW

Printed in the United States of America

Book design by Tracy Shaw

For my parents

The Girl: Janie Farrish
The Getup: Cream cashmere cardigan, vintage Black Sabbath t-shirt rags tank, yellow silk Miss Sixty flats, silver bangles, and *it*

It was still there when she woke up, hanging neatly on the back of her closet door. *It* was still the same bright green—like a new leaf, like a traffic light set to go. *It* was the most spectacular thing she owned, and if some other sixteen-year-old girl had owned it, it would have been the most spectacular thing she owned too.

But some other sixteen-year-old girl didn't own it. Janie did.

She'd found it at one of Jet Rag's legendary dollar sales, forever sealing Janie's opinion that Jet Rag was, and always will be, the best vintage clothing store in the universe. Not that she'd been to every vintage clothing store in the universe. She didn't have to. Jet Rag was right there on La Brea Boulevard, a mere twenty minutes away from her house on the other side of the hills, and a mere minute away from the La Brea Tar Pits. All of L.A. is divided by those who cruise La Brea for the tar pits and those who cruise La Brea for Jet Rag. If you go for Jet Rag, chances are you're sixteen, beautiful, and impossibly unique. If you go for the tar pits, chances are you're six or sixty or really, really lame. (So there's a black swamp in the middle of Los Angeles that burps up dinosaur bones. You can't *wear* dinosaur bones. And if you can't wear something, what's the point?)

Every Saturday morning, the Jet Rag staff dumps an enormous load of clothes in the middle of their cracked-asphalt parking lot and people seriously riot over them like those peasants in the French Revolution. Every piece of clothing costs exactly one dollar. Depending on what you find, a dollar ranges from *incredible deal* to *insane rip-off*. And since the deal-to-rip-off ratio is like a hundred to one, the rioting makes perfect sense. Everyone there wants to find *it* first.

Par example: Janie's best friend, Amelia Hernandez, found a mint condition, vintage wool houndstooth Yves Saint Laurent jacket. YSL jacket + $1.00 = incredible deal. On the flip side, Janie found a "Pinky and the Brain" t-shirt with bloodstains on it: Pinky and the Brain + bloodstains + $1.00 = insane rip-off. Janie was so grossed out, she actually puked up some of the orange juice she'd had for breakfast. Which meant the next person to pick up the shirt would have blood *and* barf to contend with.

But the Jet Rag dollar-sale isn't for the faint of heart. The Jet Rag dollar sale is for die-hard, hard-core fashionistas: the hippest of the hip, the slickest of the slick, the sickest of the sick.

Well, and homeless people.

That summer Amelia seemed to have all the luck. In addition to the Yves Saint Laurent jacket, she found a sexy little Western shirt with mother-of-pearl buttons, a pair of blue suede kitten-heeled boots, and — the crème de la nonfat creamer — a vintage Sonic Youth "Goo" t-shirt that Janie had a sinking feeling was from the original nineties tour. Not that she wasn't happy for Amelia. (She was even happier when the t-shirt turned out to be eighteen sizes too big for either one of them to actually wear.)

By the end of August, Janie still hadn't found anything. She was just about to surrender, to throw her empty-handed hands in the air, when she spotted *it*.

It — to be specific — was a vintage green cotton miniskirt by none other than Mary Quant, the number one designer for such sixties fashion icons as Mia Farrow and the British supermodel Twiggy. Janie was beginning to think she looked like a sixties fashion icon. Maybe that sounds egotistical; it's not. It's not like guys fantasize about Twiggy, even if they do know who she is, which of course they don't. Why would they? In her heyday, Twiggy looked like a cross between an alien and an eleven-year-old boy. Seriously, who'd want to take the shirt off of that? No self-respecting guy at Winston Prep, that's for sure.

Janie knew firsthand.

She had always gotten straight As, and now, as she was beginning to discover, her grade average also applied to her bra size. Janie's boobs, if you could dignify them with that term, were the great tragedy of her life. They were absolute traitors to the cause. Not that the cause was such a big deal — just her happiness, her dreams, her very will to live.

If it hadn't been for her legs, she might have been forced to do something drastic. Her legs — long and smooth and track team—

toned — were her saving grace. Who cared if her bra looked like a pair of eye patches? She could pull off a miniskirt like nobody's business. Which was why she was so happy to find it. That is, until she went home and tried it on.

Then she was ecstatic.

Janie felt like the kind of girl who zipped around London in an Aston Martin with Jude Law. The kind of girl who inspired older Italian men with cultivated taste to tip their hats in appreciation. The kind of girl who knotted silk scarves under her chin and hailed cabs in New York City while enchanted tourists snapped pictures (just in case she was famous).

She felt like the kind of girl she wasn't.

It'd be one thing if girls like this didn't exist (Janie could just tell herself she was holding herself up to some impossible standard), but girls like this did exist. And what was worse, she went to high school with them.

That bit about Italian men? Actually happened to Petra Greene. The New York City cab story? Straight from the life of Melissa Moon. And London? The Aston Martin? With Jude without-a-flaw Law? Just another blip in Charlotte Beverwil's everyday existence.

But we'll get to them later.

This year would be different. This year Janie would show up at school wearing *it*. And *it* would redefine her, force all of Winston to pause and reevaluate their previous misconceived notions. *It* would banish forever their memory of her as an entering freshman; in a world of double 66 Gucci totes and monogrammed Kate

Spade organizers, Janie had arrived sporting an ink-stained Everest backpack. In a world of eyebrows tended to biweekly by professional "browticians," Janie had arrived with two self-plucked "tadpoles" on her face (or so she was informed by the appalled Charlotte Beverwil). In a world of flawless complexions, Janie had arrived with a spackle of zits on her cheeks, chin, and chest. At Winston Prep, acne was widely perceived as a *historical* malady, like smallpox or polio. No one actually *got* those things anymore . . . did they? Janie's new, elite peers eyed her with suspicion, like she'd just rolled in from some contaminated Third World country.

It was the acne that did her in. At the end of ninth grade, Janie Farrish's chin ranked number two on the Winston yearbook's "don't" list. (Tommy Balinger — who streaked the Winston vs. Sacred Heart girls' badminton championship wearing nothing but two shuttlecocks on his nipples — made number one.)

But today was the first day of tenth grade, a whole new beginning. Janie's eyebrows were smooth and arched, her ink-stained backpack long disposed of. Best of all, her complexion was perfect: clear and fresh and sun-kissed. For the first time in years, Janie could see her actual face: her neat, strong nose and defined jaw line, her extra-high cheekbones. Her upper lip, fuller than her lower lip, perpetually pouted. And her enormous gray eyes, shadowy with lashes, looked soft and shy. Sometimes — when the sun was shining and she'd had a good amount of sleep, when sweet songs played in her head and her bangs fell the right way, when the sky rose like a peaceful blue parachute and the world was on her side—Janie realized she was pretty. But the feeling was so fragile and new, the slightest setback made it disappear. The sun ducked behind a cloud, her bangs flipped the wrong way—and that was it. She felt ugly again. Which feeling was the right one? She honestly couldn't tell.

Janie plucked her new green skirt from the plastic hanger. She pulled it past her trim knees, shimmied it up around her thighs, lined up the seams, and zipped. Her "new" rags tank (she'd scissored the sleeves off her Black Sabbath t-shirt the night before) slipped down her right shoulder, exposing a bright turquoise bra strap. She turned to face the mirror, greeting herself with her best self-assured smile.

She was ready.

Even though he woke up forty-five minutes late, Jake Farrish was already dressed and eating breakfast before his twin sister. Jake didn't waste too much time constructing his look, if that's what you chose to call it. His mom preferred to call it his "look away."

Not that her opinion mattered.

Jake pretty much wore old cords, faded seventies cowboy shirts, black Converse, and his gray United States of Apparel hoody with the Amnesiac pin every day. His hair he rewarded with his greatest investment of time — a whole five and a half minutes. (Who knew the distribution of one dime-sized blob of wax required so much attention?) When he was done, he inspected himself from all angles, furrowing his brow like James Dean. Not that Jake looked like James Dean. With his mussed black-brown hair, porcelain skin, and flushed cheeks (interrupted only by a trilogy of beauty marks), Jake resembled a brown-eyed Adam Brody. Of course, Jake *hated* that comparison.

"I do *not* look like that guy!" he'd insist every time his sister put in the Season One DVD of the tragically canceled *O.C.*

"Don't look at me," came Janie's reply. "*I* think you look like Summer."

The Farrish kitchen was small and square, and the appliances old and broken-down. Not that their mother used those words. Mrs. Farrish preferred the term "temperamental," as in "temperamental appliances require special treatment." Jake and Janie were warned to be "gentle" with the dishwasher, "careful" with the microwave, and "mindful" of the freezer door. If Mrs. Farrish had her way, the twins would tip-toe around the kitchen like it was a mental ward. She acted as if slamming the refrigerator door would drive the toaster to suicide.

By the time Janie entered the kitchen, Jake was well into his second bowl of Cheetah Chomps. "Hey," she said, staring into the fridge and doing her best to look casual. She could feel her brother assessing her outfit the way overprotective brothers sometimes do. Jake was fundamentally hypocritical when it came to female fashion. The equation went something like this:

Girl + Miniskirt = Smokin'

Girl + Shared Genetic Material + Miniskirt = Repulsive

She opened the fridge, letting her straight brown hair fall like a curtain across her face. Janie would not look away from the fridge until Jake said something. She sort of hoped he'd tell her she looked like a slut. Then she could just toss her hair back, arch one cool eyebrow, and thank him for the compliment.

"Dude," he began at last, "did you know cheetahs can achieve speeds of up to seventy miles per hour?"

Janie slammed the fridge shut. What kind of guy reads the back of a cereal box while his sister, his own *flesh and blood,* was tricked out like a wanton whore?

"Wow, Jake," she scowled. "What an amazing and fun fact."

"Whoa . . . ," he continued, hunching over his cereal like a caveman. "One of its natural predators is the eagle. How awesome is that? Like the eagle's all . . . *bwa!* And the cheetah's all, I don't *think* so!"

With that, he unleashed a mighty eagle-cry and karate-chopped the air for a full fifteen seconds. Janie watched him, doing her best not to crack a smile. She folded her arms and asked the inevitable.

"Um . . . are you retarded?"

"Yes," he replied. He scooted his chair back and pointed at his sister with his spoon. "What are you doing dressed like that? You look like a skanky-ass ho."

"Come on"—she grinned, tossing him the car keys—"we're gonna be late."

The Girl: Petra Greene
The Getup: Still in her pajamas (oversized SAVE THE
UNICORNS t-shirt)

On the other side of the hill, in the ten-bedroom Beverly Hills
estate her mother dreamed up as a "tasteful fusion of Mount
Olympus and Versailles," Petra Greene was sleeping through her
alarm. Again. She made the mistake of setting her radio clock to
Mazzy Star, whose monotonous, dreamy tones only served to
plummet Petra deeper into an REM state. If it hadn't been for
her sister Isabel's sudden, piercing screams, she may never have
woken up.

"What's going on?" Petra yawned upon entering the kitchen.
She wiped some invisible sand from her wide, hazel-green eyes
and stretched, pulling the frayed elastic from her honey-blond
hair. Her unleashed ponytail spilled to her waist in a chaos of tan-
gles, some of which were dangerously close to dreads. Still, even
at 7:28 a.m., with no makeup and little to no sleep, Petra Greene
looked like a goddess. If the Victoria's Secret supermodel Laetitia
Casta had a little sister, Petra would be it. (And Laetitia would be
the ugly one.)

Lola, the Greenes' tireless nanny, was on her knees, wrestling
six-year-old Isabel into a tight, navy blue pinafore. Four-year-old
Sofia, obedient and already dressed in her own pinafore, watched
her sister with quiet fascination. The Greenes adopted Isabel and

Sofia from an orphanage in China when they were just two years and four months old, respectively. To hear her parents tell it, "You can't save the world. But if you can provide two *terribly* unfortunate little girls the opportunity to grow up in a stable, loving environment, then why not?" Petra had to laugh. Sure, her parents were loving and stable — if you compared them to the beleaguered staff of an underfunded Chinese orphanage. Compare them to anyone else, however, and they were who they were: complete and utter nutcases. Her mother was clinically depressed, but she was small potatoes compared to Petra's father, who was, according to Mrs. Greene, a sociopath. "Imagine if Pinocchio not only ignored Jiminy Cricket but slowly fried him to death under a magnifying glass," her mother once explained to a bright-eyed, nine-year-old Petra. "*That* would be your father."

To make up for her insane parents, Petra became particularly devoted to Sofia and Isabel. Even when they screamed their heads off, she was a pillar of unconditional love and patient support.

"She no like the new uniform for school," Lola explained with a heavy sigh. Isabel let out another earth-shattering scream.

"Come on, Iz." Petra crouched to the floor. "Let me see. . . ."

Lola sat back as Isabel turned toward her older sister, red-faced and clenching her fists. In addition to the navy blue pinafore, Isabel wore a white button-down shirt with a starched lace Peter Pan collar. Her immaculate white socks folded neatly above her patent leather Mary Janes, and her stick-straight black bob was held in place by an argyle headband.

"She *have* to wear," Lola explained, half to Petra, half to Isabel. "Is rule."

"No!" Isabel cried, stomping her foot.

"Isabel," Petra began slowly, "are you the kind of girl who's rude to people?"

"No . . . ," Isabel replied with considerably less force.

"Then apologize to Lola."

"Sorry, Lola," Isabel muttered to the floor. And then, working herself up again, she whimpered, "I wan . . . I wann-wear my . . . Sponge! Bob! Shirt!"

"I know, Iz . . . ," Petra sighed. "But you have to wear the uniform. You know that."

"But YOU don't," Isabel pointed out, her face puffing at the injustice.

"You're right. That doesn't seem very fair, does it?" Sofia and Isabel shook their heads. "Okay," Petra frowned. "Let me put on my thinking cap." She reached for her oversized sunflower print coffee mug and placed it on top of her head. Sofia giggled while Isabel sniffed, wiping her nose. Petra closed her eyes, as if to summon the thinking cap gods.

"I've got it," she announced, and swiftly removed the coffee mug.

"What?" Isabel asked.

"*I'll* wear a uniform to school too," Petra explained. "Except I don't have one, so you guys will have to make it for me, okay? You can pick out *whatever you want*. And I won't argue and I won't scream and I won't cry because . . ." She paused for effect. "It's my *uniform*. And I've *got* to wear it."

"We can pick out whatever we want?" Isabel's eyes widened.

"That's right."

An expression of pure delight broke across her six-year-old sister's face. "Come on!" she ordered, pulling Petra by the hand. "We have to get you dressed *now* or you'll be late for school!"

Janie and Jake shared custody of their mom's old Volvo, a black 240 DL sedan. The car, like the Farrish twins, was born sixteen years earlier, which meant *technically* they were all the same age. However, as Jake explained to his parents on the eve of his and Janie's birthday last year, one human year is *actually* the equivalent of seven for a Volvo.

"Like a dog," Janie had chimed in.

"Exactly." Jake lay a supportive hand on his sister's shoulder. "According to my calculations, you're about to bequeath to us a one-hundred-twelve-year-old mode of transportation."

"I mean, is that safe?" Janie continued. Her brother tilted his head and pressed his lips together as if to say *I'm not so sure*.

They knew it was a long shot, but maybe their parents would do something cool. Like enable their loving children to arrive at Winston *in style*. For once.

"Like a cute new MINI Cooper?" Janie suggested.

"No!" Jake blurted, shooting her the Death Glare. "What she meant to say," he corrected, returning a modified gaze to their parents, "was a Mercedes CLS 600."

"I'll look into it," Mrs. Farrish replied. But, of course, she didn't. Neither of them did.

Their parents were actually kind of selfish, when you thought about it.

The commute to Winston took twenty to thirty-five minutes, depending on traffic. The first five minutes belonged to Ventura Boulevard, the San Fernando Valley's main drag. Jake sped down the wide, four-lane street, and Janie watched the slender trunks of palm trees whip by. The early morning sky was the gray of wet cement, and the streetlights were still on. The twins passed by DuPar's Coffee Shop—where Valley kids gather on weekend nights—and stopped at Laurel Canyon Boulevard. To their right, in front of the Wells Fargo bank with the mosaic tile mural of "The Old West," a bunch of people protested the war. To their left, in front of the Coffee Bean & Tea Leaf, a bunch of people protested the protesters.

Janie looked out the window and sighed. If only they could take a right, she thought. They could get on the 101 South and head over to the Los Angeles County High School for the Arts that Amelia attended. In eighth grade, Janie and she made plans to apply to L.A.C.H.S.A. together. Amelia would apply for music, Janie would apply for visual arts, and together they would start new lives as Tortured Artists. But then Janie and Jake were awarded academic scholarships to Winston Prep, the impossibly exclusive private school in the Hollywood Hills. Winston was an opportunity she could not — according to her education-obsessed parents — turn down. And so Janie and Amelia, who'd gone to the same schools since second grade, went their separate ways. Amelia took a right where Janie took a left. While Amelia got to be the Tortured Artist, Janie just got to be tortured.

As they pulled into Laurel Canyon, Janie faced ahead. As usual, their Volvo was last in an endless line of cars coursing uphill like the interlocked teeth of a shiny new zipper. Every time Jake eased on the brakes, the black Volvo released a low, moaning noise like a dying whale. After three dead whales, Janie flipped on the radio. In a matter of seconds, the noise was replaced with "I Will Remember You," by Sarah McLachlan, which was, in their humble opinion, a trillion times worse.

"I will remember poooop . . . ," Janie crooned.

"Will you remember peeee . . . ?" Jake crooned back.

Jake slid in the new Franz Ferdinand CD, ending their sophisticated duet. Janie loved Franz Ferdinand. The driving beat made her want to spin around and dance and cheer, but the lyrics made her want to lie down, stare at the ceiling, and cry. Maybe because their music pulled her heart in opposite directions, Franz Ferdinand reminded her of Paul Elliot Miller.

Oh, Paul. Would she ever see him again?

The Volvo continued to wheeze up the hill, passing the dramatic ruins of a house that collapsed in the mudslides the year before. Janie thought it looked cool—all those huge slabs of broken concrete, crumbling plaster and shattered glass in the grass. Like a modern art sculpture, she thought. Unfortunately, Jake thought the same thing:

"Ah yes," he announced. "My *pièce de résistance.*"

When they reached the top of the hill, Jake turned right, taking the car down Mulholland. Janie leaned back into the cracked, tan vinyl seat, remembering the lyrics to that old R.E.M. song her parents liked: "If I ever want to fly . . . Mulholland Drive . . . I am alive."

Michael Stipe could feel alive all he wanted. Janie, on the other hand, felt something else. She felt, suddenly, inescapably, *on her way to Winston Prep*—the exact *opposite* of alive. Janie pulled at the hem of her miniskirt, letting it sink in for the first time. She took a deep breath. She wasn't nervous. She was fine.

But then her brother took a sharp left. Were they really on Coldwater Canyon already? The Volvo sailed across a dip in the road, and Janie gripped the sides of her seat. She was going to be sick.

"Wait," she squawked.

"What?" Jake replied, still staring straight ahead.

"We need to go home."

"What?" He scrunched his forehead. "Why?"

Wasn't it obvious? She was Clashing! With a capital *C.*

Clashing with a capital *C* is different than clashing with a lowercase *c.* Lowercase *c* clashing is, like, wearing gold earrings with a silver necklace. Or leopard print with zebra print. Or black pants with navy blue socks. At the end of the day, lowercase *c* clashing is just sort of ugly. And just sort of ugly isn't the end of the world.

Clashing with a capital *C*, on the other hand, is. Because Clashing with a capital *C* is when what you're wearing doesn't match *your entire life:* Laura Bush in a string bikini, Marilyn Manson in yoga pants, 50 Cent with a parasol.

Janie Farrish in a bright green micro-mini.

Her early morning rush of confidence vanished like a hallucination. Why oh why had she decided to wear this skirt? What had she been thinking? Even if she did have nice legs, micro miniskirts were the uniform of attractive people, not her! Janie stared down at her upper thighs in horror. She looked like a complete and utter poseur.

She turned to her brother with pleading eyes. *Please, God. Pleasepleaseplease make him understand.*

"I," she began. She was calm. She was rational. "I kinda just realized . . . I can't wear this."

"What?"

"I need to go home and change."

Jake looked closely at his sister, his eyebrows furrowed with concern. Janie exhaled, basking in her brother's sympathy. He could be really great when he wanted to be.

Then he burst into laughter.

"Jake!" She pushed his shoulder. "I'm not joking!"

"I know," he continued to laugh. "That's what makes it so funny."

Janie watched in horror as Winston Assembly Hall came into view, peeking through the branches of the school's trademark weeping willows. Winston Prep was comprised of one large U-shaped stucco building and some small neighboring bungalows. The main structure used to be an apartment complex, and not just any apartment complex, but an old-school 1930s Hollywood Spanish-style complex. The central quad featured terracotta tiles and stucco walls. Staircases spiraled down from classroom doors. There were wrought-iron banisters, multitiered fountains, and classical archways. From a distance, the school looked like a gigantic, peach-colored wedding cake. Up close, it looked like a Mexican prison.

At least it did to Janie.

Jake put on his blinker. Janie's heart jumped up, somersaulted, smacked itself unconscious, and splashed into the icy pool that was her stomach.

"What are you doing?" she gasped.

"Parking," Jake replied, shifting the clutch.

"You're parking in the *Showroom*?"

"Uh . . . yeah." Jake responded, as if that made perfect sense. As if they hadn't always parked underground. Janie felt a little woozy. She'd always been a little scared of heights, and the Showroom was her highest peak yet. Even if it was, technically, ground level.

Clashing with a Capital C

case # 213

☆ Paris Hilton in a Nuns' Habit ☆

The Showroom was Winston's crowning glory (in addition to their stellar academic reputation, of course). It featured cars most people only dream about. These were drive-into-the-sunset cars. Speeding-through-the-Alps cars. Escaping-in-a-hail-of-gunfire cars. Seriously. Most kids at Winston were so rich, cars were just another accessory, as accessible (and in some cases, disposable) as gummy bracelets. From BMW to Mercedes, Porsche to Ferrari, Hummer to Prius—no brand went unrepresented, no engine went un-revved.

The Showroom was called the Showroom because it was the only level of school parking located outside. Which meant your car was on display. And if your car was on display, then you were too. Which probably meant you liked to be looked at. More importantly, people liked to look at you, which could only mean one thing. You were popular.

Popularity at Winston was easy to spot. There were obvious clues, like beauty, confidence, and style. And then more subtle ones. *Par example,* popular girls tend to attach their keys to purple squiggle bracelets. And they almost always have small, white wads of gum between their perfect, smiling teeth. And they call each other chica, bitch, and slut — and then they hug, squealing like they've won some kind of award.

Which, in a way, they have.

Popular guys were easier. Popular guys were just guys popular girls happen to like.

There were exceptions, of course. Some kids were popular because they were impossibly talented. Or impossibly funny. Or impossibly cool.

But not impossibly dumb, Janie thought as her brother pulled into one of the coveted Showroom spots. She sank deep into her seat, willing herself to disappear. He couldn't possibly mean to park here for real, right? Jake turned the engine off, unbuckling his seat belt. *He's worse than impossibly dumb,* she realized as he opened the door. *He's clinically insane.* Janie watched in stunned disbelief as Jake got out of the car. Of course, stunned disbelief was nothing compared to the spine-numbing paralysis she felt next. When he lifted his hand and waved. And Charlotte Beverwil, leaning on the hood of her mint condition 1969 cream-colored Jaguar, waved back. And *smiled*.

That's when she realized: her brother wasn't dumb. He wasn't insane.

Somehow, when Janie wasn't looking, Jake had become popular.

The Girl: Charlotte Beverwil
The Getup: Silk Blumarine dress with grapevine
pattern, yellow Marni headband, plum-colored Marc
Jacobs knit leggings, black patent-leather Chanel flats

With her winter cream skin, unruly espresso-dark hair and almond shaped pool green eyes, Charlotte Sidonie Beverwil most closely resembled the "Tiffany" supermodel Shalom Harlow. Except while Shalom Harlow measured in at six feet, Charlotte stood a full foot shorter. Fortunately Charlotte had long legs that, she argued, gave her the "illusion of height." It was true, in a way. She *did* seem a lot taller than she was. But it had nothing to do with her legs. She looked a lot taller than she was because she *said* she looked a lot taller than she was.

And you didn't argue with Charlotte Beverwil.

For the first day of school, she chose a feminine dress to wear over knit leggings and ballet flats. She hoped the dress, which she'd embroidered with an intricate pattern of interlocking grapevines, would remind Jake of their summer together. Jake and Charlotte had gone to school together for over a year, but they hadn't really met — that is Charlotte hadn't *cared* to meet — until that August.

Charlotte was supposed to have spent the entire month of August in Brugge, a quaint little port town in Belgium. There, amid crumbling buildings and murky canals, she would perfect her sewing in an exclusive embroidery class taught by Belgian nuns.

But after just four days of pinpricked fingers and a nine o'clock curfew, Charlotte couldn't take it anymore. She called her dad and — after a thirty-minute begathon — arranged her escape. She laughed every time she remembered the nuns rushing outside as Daddy's Augusta 109 luxury helicopter descended upon the roof of a neighboring brewery. The whirring blades whipped the pristine garden into a frenzy — uprooted their precious petunias, exploded their prim white roses. As Charlotte ran toward the aircraft, the blizzard of petals whirled like confetti, toasting her newfound freedom. The nuns stood by and watched in shock, clutching their habits and their hearts.

As the Augusta lifted into the air, Charlotte sank into one of the supple leather chairs and sucked sweetly on a Bloody Mary. She was on her way to Northern California, Napa Valley to be exact, where her father was starring, directing, and producing the film adaptation of *Dead on the Vine,* the Pulitzer Prize–winning Depression epic by the famous recluse author Benjamin Nugent. Everyone said it was "unadaptable." Daddy was out to prove them wrong.

When she arrived, her father took her on a brief tour of the vineyard, kissed her on the forehead, and told her to "stay in trouble." After dabbing the kiss off her forehead with a Bioré wipe, Charlotte took a moment to look around. The vineyard surrounded a beautiful ranch house with a wraparound porch and a hammock. She instantly declared the hammock her spot, perching inside like a dainty spider in her web. (No wonder the cute production assistants hovered around like gnats.) Hundreds of scenery actors, called extras, dotted the hills like cattle. They were there to mime the harvest. While the extras practiced looking starved and dejected, prop guys went around with clusters of phony grapes, hanging them from the vines. Charlotte let her hand drop from the edge of the hammock to the Spanish tile floor. If only it really was 1931. How *romantic* would that be? Sure, a lot of people were poor — but not movie stars. People always went to the movies, no matter how hard things got. Charlotte nestled into her web and sighed. The Beverwils would have been just fine.

"Yo."

Charlotte fluttered her green eyes open and frowned, annoyed. Who said "yo" in 1931?

"Would you, um . . . like an ice-blended cappuccino?" A dark-haired guy around her age extended a trayful of Dixie cup–sized beverages and cleared his throat. She frowned again. As far as historical accuracy, "ice-blended" was almost as bad as "yo."

"Thanks." Charlotte nodded, accepting the offer. Historical accuracy be damned. She loved ice-blendeds even more than she loved the Depression. She took a long sip and — maybe it was the caffeine — it instantly hit her.

Cappuccino Boy was remarkably handsome.

"I'm Charlotte." She extended her tiny hand.

"I know." Cappuccino Boy grinned, slapping her hand high-five style. "We go to the same school?"

"What?" Charlotte squinted into the sun. "Oh my god, *Jake Farrish?*"

He smiled—and why wouldn't he? *Charlotte Beverwil knew his name.*

"Yo," he said again.

"You look . . . ," she began, struggling to sit up. But her hand slipped through the netting and hit the floor. Charlotte started to slide. She was not a natural klutz, but she knew when to pretend otherwise. As the hammock threatened to flip, she let out a little gasp. Jake put down his tray and rushed to assist her.

Just as she knew he would.

"There." He righted the hammock and held Charlotte's hand as she stepped to the floor. She leaned into him in an effort to steady herself. As she looked up into his dark chocolate eyes, her heart surged toward her throat.

"You look . . . ," she began again.

Jake shrugged, endlessly proud of himself. "I kinda grew this summer."

But it wasn't only that. His face, which used to look like a bad case of diaper rash, was perfect—smooth and luminous and slightly flushed at the cheeks. And his *hair*. Last year, he went around with a shamelessly long and ratty ponytail. But now his brownish-black locks were cut short and cutely mussed. No doubt about it. Jake Farrish had gone from metal head to *drop dead.* As in *gorgeous.*

"What are you doing here?" she asked, fingering the delicate chain around her neck.

"I'm helping my dad. He's in craft service."

"Oh?" Craft service is basically catering for the movie industry, which meant Jake's dad spent his days preparing mass quantities of coffee, BBQ chicken breasts, and pinwheel veggie platters. "What do you do there?"

"Slave to the blender, baby," he smirked. "Iced mochas, iced cappuccinos, iced nonfat sugar-free vanilla cappa-schnappa-rhinos. . . ."

"Margaritas?" she asked.

Jake grinned. "Those too."

So Charlotte followed him to the opposite end of the set, where the craft service truck was parked. She sat on the edge of the tailgate, kicking her feet like a five-year-old while Jake crushed ice by the sandwich bar. When it comes down to it, movie sets operate under the same hierarchy as the *Titanic:* first class, second class, craft service. Charlotte flushed with excitement. This meant she was like Kate Winslet's character, Rose, and Jake was like Leonardo's Jack! *Plus romantique et tu meurs!*

Charlotte hardly left that tailgate for three weeks. And then, after the last night of shooting, she and Jake took a long walk through the vineyard. It was one in the morning, and the moon was bright and full. The grapevines were bathed in a silvery light and the churned soil was warm beneath their feet. And she could smell it: the grapes, the soil. She could even smell the moon.

"Charlotte . . . ," Jake said. He plucked a leaf from a vine. Even in the dark, it was green.

"Yes?" Charlotte breathed.

He stepped toward her. The wind moved a piece of her hair across the bridge of her nose. She stared at the ground. If she could pretend to be a klutz, then she could also pretend to be shy.

Jake reached for her hand. The sound of crickets filled the dark, their chirps evenly measured, as if to mark the seconds of a countdown.

"Here," he said, handing her the leaf. He looked her in her eyes. "This is for you."

And then that was it.

But Charlotte made a vow: it wouldn't be for long.

Charlotte heard Jake's car door click, swing open, and close. As she would not allow herself to look directly (way too obvious), she closed her eyes. Maybe she could trick her brain into thinking she was blind and develop supersonic hearing. Then she could just *listen* to his hotness.

"Charlotte," he beckoned. She opened her pool green eyes at the sound of his voice, fluttering all five million of her ink-black lashes.

Too bad she was wearing sunglasses.

"Hey," Charlotte replied (like she'd only just noticed him). Jake walked toward her, a silhouette haloed by sun. *A perfect eclipse,* she thought, proud of her analogy. Plus, it reminded her — she could really use some gum.

"*Qu'est ce qui se passe?*" she asked, crushing a tiny white square between a flawless row of pearly teeth.

"No, I . . . no spare change," he apologized, pretending to search his pockets. "Sorry."

Charlotte laughed. "*Qu'est ce qui se passe* means 'what's up.'"

"*Sure* it does." He raised an eyebrow. Then folded his arms like Mr. Clean. Charlotte smiled. *Just the man to take on Miss Dirty*.

"Jake!" Anna Santochi shrieked, emerging from the nearby locker jungle. "Omigod! Your *hair*!" But Jake barely lifted his hand to wave in response. He was too busy staring at Charlotte, who stood there, shaking her gum like a maraca.

"Wanna piece?" she asked, once Anna turned and headed for the drinking fountain.

"Okay," he replied. Charlotte decided she liked nothing more than to watch Jake chew. He had three small beauty marks along his jaw and one above his eyebrow. She connected them like stars in a constellation, navigating his face like a sailor in search of direction. Jake looked at her and smiled, disappearing a single star into the crease at his mouth. Charlotte sighed, resigning herself. She was hopelessly adrift. She was doomed at sea.

"You know" — Jake pointed to his mouth — "this stuff has saccharine in it. Causes cancer in rats."

"Do I look like a rat to you?" Charlotte smirked.

"That *would* explain the impulse to leap on your car and scream like a girl," he remarked.

"Whattup, gorgeous!" Someone called in greeting. Probably Jason. Or Luke. Or . . . who cared? Whoever it was, Charlotte ignored him.

"Maybe we should quit gum chewing and take up smoking," she suggested, her eyes fixed on Jake.

"Excellent plan."

Charlotte cupped her manicured hand to her mouth. (Anything can be feminine — even acts of expectoration.) When she was done, the gum sat in the shell of her palm like a pearl in an oyster. After a moment's hesitation, she leaned over, sticking the minty wad firmly to Jake's skinny-yet-toned arm.

"What" — he looked at his arm — "was that?"

"I'm putting you on the patch," she explained solemnly. "For your saccharine addiction."

"Awesome," Jake responded with an amused grin. "I'm such a badass."

Charlotte looked down, feeling proud. All around her, the Showroom rioted with noise: with first day *omigods and shutups* and *noways* and *youlookamazings* and *haveyouseenyouknowwhos*. Doors slammed, lockers rattled, hands slapped, girls shrieked, radios blared, hydraulics hissed, sub-woofers woofed, sidekicks chirped, trunks kuh-klunked, sneakers squeaked, book bags jostled, keys jingled, engines rumbled, brakes squealed, and someone, somewhere, bounced a basketball: *buh-boom, buh-boom, buh-boom, buh-boom* . . .

But it couldn't compete with Charlotte's beating heart.

Jake and Janie Farrish were "scholarship kids"—an anomaly at Winston. They were also "new kids"—another anomaly. For the most part, Winston recruited students in kindergarten and kept them all the way through twelfth grade. Which isn't to say relationships began in kindergarten. Dr. Spencer, Bronwyn Spencer's mother, had delivered fourteen of the sixty students in the sophomore class *alone*. At one time their mothers had sat in her waiting room, probably even next to one another—perusing the same *People*s, sipping the same Evian, fingering the leaves of the same potted ficus. "Why shouldn't our children attend the same school?" they were fond of saying. "They were clusters of *cells* together!"

Some cliques start at birth. Winston's start at conception.

Charlotte, however, was born in a hospital outside Paris. Her mother had wanted the privacy; that's how famous she was. She was "Georgina Malta"—you might remember her as that incredibly hot chick from that Chris Isaak video. Or was it that Meat Loaf video? It hardly mattered. When it came down to it, she was famous for being Georgina Malta-*Beverwil*.

Wife to Academy Award–winning actor, producer, and director William (aka "Bud") Beverwil.

Triathlete Bud (aka "Bod") Beverwil.

Avid Art Collector Bud (aka "Bid") Beverwil.

Legendary Playboy Bud (aka "Bed") Beverwil.

Okay, so her dad was a Hollywood icon. That hardly counted for glamour, not in Charlotte's book. For one: her hayseed parents were from *the Midwest,* thereby denying her the Parisian lineage she rightfully deserved. For *two*...well, there was no for two. For two you have to move past one.

And she would never move past one.

There was no way around it: Charlotte was a die-hard, hardcore, hard-hitting Francophile. She was Paris Bueller. She was Frenchenstein. Everything she touched went the way of *oui:* her books (Colette, Voltaire), her drink (Orangina, Perrier), her music (Air, Phoenix, the pensive Eric Satie), her good habits (bicycling, *aventure amoureuse*), her bad habits (cigarettes, *ennui).*

And then, of course, there was fashion.

Charlotte liked to think of herself as the style child of Marie Antoinette and Jean-Luc Godard. Which is to say, she *adored* cigarette pants and pencil skirts, skinny belts and pearls. *Lived for* lace collars and tiny puffed sleeves, knotted silk scarves and ballerina flats. And, of course, she *absolutely worshipped* Chanel.

And how does this relate to Jake and Janie?

When you're this obsessed with France, even insults adhere to theme. Which is to say, Charlotte was responsible for Janie's highly unfortunate Winston nickname. Not that she ever took the credit. She didn't have to. Who else could have come up with it?

"Who did you say she looked like?" Laila Pikser asked as they warmed up at the bar. Laila was kind of a ditz, but her arabesques were positively perpendicular.

"It's a *what,* not a *who,*" Charlotte explained, keeping her eyes to the wall-length mirror. "I said she's the human version of *Centre Pompidou.*"

"Who's Sandra Pompidoo?"

"The modern art museum in Paris," Charlotte sighed, pinning a renegade curl into her loosely coiffed bun. "The ugliest, weirdest, stupidest building in the world."

"Oh," Laila sighed, extending her long leg to the bar. "Can't you just say she's ugly and weird?"

"Bo-ring," Charlotte sang.

"That girl Janie's in my mother's French class," Kate Joliet announced mid-plié. Kate's pliés were a sorry affair, but her French was flawless. Madame Joliet, Kate's mother, taught Beginning French at Winston. "She told me she thought she was 'quite beautiful.'"

"No, she did not."

"She said she had delicate features and a neck *comme un cygne.*"

"Like a *swan?*" Charlotte choked in translation. "Do swans get acne? I forget."

"That's what I said!" Kate (who always said what Charlotte said) declared.

"Maybe they get acne but the feathers cover it," Laila suggested.

"Anyway," Kate continued, ignoring Laila, "my mom got all pissy and was like, she's just going through an awkward stage . . . *try to be kind*." She groaned and tipped her head back in despair.

"Quit checking yourself out in the ceiling mirror, Kate," Charlotte instructed.

"I am not!" Kate gasped and stamped her satiny foot. Laila cackled with delight. "Shut *up*, Laila!"

"Seriously," Charlotte agreed. The girls grew quiet, flexing their toes. Occasionally they needed a moment to hate each other. This was one of those moments. To make it less obvious, they watched Mr. Hans push the upright piano from one end of the room to the other. The piano's tiny wheels chirped like crickets and the wood floor creaked from the strain. From the looks of things, the three girls found the goings-on of Mr. Hans positively gripping.

"You know what?" Charlotte said, ending their sixteen-second silence.

"What?" Kate asked, her relief palpable (she hated it when they weren't talking).

"I don't buy it."

"What don't you buy?" Laila paid *very close attention* to what Charlotte did and did not buy.

"Awkward stages," she sniffed. "I don't believe in them."

And seriously, why should she? It's not like *she'd* ever experienced one. Not personally. Neither, for that matter, had any of her friends. In terms of stages, they'd graduated from *Gerber Baby* to *Adorable Toddler* to *Beautiful Child* to *Stunning Young Woman*. And

Charlotte fully expected to stay in *Stunning Young Woman* for another 35 years *at least*.

She was sure of it: awkward stages were a myth of some kind. Kind of like unicorns. Except unicorns were pretty.

"That girl *wishes* she was going through an awkward stage," she observed, arranging her arms into a halo. "Even if the pimples *did* go away, she'd still be attractively challenged."

"I know," Kate agreed. "Unfortunately for her, she's just — awkward."

"A total pompidou," Charlotte confirmed.

"Pompi*don't*," Kate tittered in reply.

Anyone who grew up in L.A. knows something about the La Brea Tar Pits, and this is what they know: The pits are gigantic swamps of disgusting black goo called "tar." Every day blobs of tar rise through the earth's crust, gurgle into ancient cracks and crannies until — at long last — they break the surface, creating a swamp or "pit." When water collects on the surface of the pit, some species, such as elephants, confuse them for drinking holes.

Long ago, as the elephants wandered around to cool off, they became lodged in the goo. The goo — like quicksand — swallowed them up. Over time, their elephant bones turned into objects called fossils. These fossils stayed inside the tar for thousands of years — like pineapple chunks in a Jell-O mold.

Janie, like most Angelinos, learned about the tar pits during a second-grade field trip. Her tour guide had a ponytail and addressed her as "ma'am"—even though she was eight. He led her class to the edge of a tar pit, which was fenced off. There was a life-size statue of an elephant in the middle of the swamp. "Here we see the nature of tar *in action*." The guide gestured to the statue. "This poor guy is trapped!"

"But he's not *real*," second-grade Janie pointed out.

"Yes, ma'am, he is," the guide informed her. The class pressed their faces to the fence and murmured. They were unconvinced.

"If he's real, why doesn't he move?" Janie asked.

"Because he's a smart elephant," the guide went on. "He knows that if he tried to escape, the tar would pull him down even farther. So he decided to stay completely still. No wonder he's survived so long!"

The elephant = Me
The tar pit = Winston Prep

As she got older, Janie realized the guide was just playing around. But she took his lesson to heart. Which is why—seven years later, on the first day of her sophomore year at Winston Prep—Janie stayed inside the Volvo. She decided to stay completely still. As long as she was a statue, she was safe from disaster.

A few minutes into her vow never to move again, Janie's cell phone rang. She'd programmed the ring to *The Virgin Suicides* theme by Air. Janie let the phone ring long enough to imagine herself as Kirsten Dunst—so miserable, so blond. Keeping the rest of her body frozen in place, she moved her hand toward the phone. She wondered how many inches into the tar that would cost her.

"Hello?"

"Janiekins!" Amelia squealed on the other line. Janie flinched at her best friend's intonation of cheer. Way too *Bring It On* Kirsten for her current mood.

"Hey." Janie pushed one finger to her vintage heart-shaped Lolita sunglasses.

"How's the first day?" Amelia asked in an exaggerated whisper.

"Well . . . I don't exactly know yet."

"What do you mean?"

"I haven't left the car."

"O-migod."

"Amelia," Janie confessed. "I think I'm, like, an elephant."

"What?" The voice on the other line scoffed. "You're the skinniest person I know."

"No, you don't understand. Remember that field trip we took in second grade? Well, I *realized*. Winston is a tar pit. Which makes *me* the elephant. Which *means* . . ."

"Okay, stop right there," Amelia ordered. "You officially sound insane."

"I'm not insane," Janie replied in a calm tone. "I'm trying to *survive*." She heard the sound of Amelia slapping her forehead.

"I'm really sorry," Amelia groaned. "But this kind of behavior calls for drastic measures." And then, before Janie could tell her best friend she was *just kidding*, Amelia screamed at the top of her lungs.

"Paul!"

As the sound of that name filled her ear, Janie gasped into the phone. "Amelia, no!"

"Paul!" she called out again.

"No, no, no!" Janie panicked. "Don't do this — I *hate* you!"

"What?" Paul Elliot Miller's gravelly voice surfaced on the other line. He sounded confused.

He also sounded gorgeous.

Paul's nose was delicate, lightly freckled. His nostrils, ever-so-slightly flared, gave him the haughty-yet-vulnerable quality of an English Lord — a *cute* English Lord, not one of those pasty, chinless ones. Paul had one bluish green eye and one greenish-brown eye, just like Kate Bosworth (a comparison Paul did not enjoy). He also had a small silver piercing in his left eyebrow and another one on the right side of his lower lip. His hair, like his moods, forever changed color, from silvery white to electric green to ink-stain blue. And still. No amount of piercings, eyeliner, bad posture, or Manic Panic could disguise the obvious truth: Paul Elliot Miller was a pretty boy. He could not, despite his efforts, look any other way. He even paid his friend Max to punch him in the face—right there in the parking lot of the Whole Foods in Brentwood—and despite a broken nose and a black eye, Paul's face healed without a trace of permanent damage. Yes, there was the hairline scar across his upper lip—but that was (embarrassingly) from chicken pox.

Besides, the scar only drew attention to his luscious swollen mouth, which was (despite the nonstop profanity it spewed) the prettiest thing about him.

For a long time, Amelia kept the undeniable fact of Paul's beauty a secret. Whenever he entered conversation, she kept the details strictly business. "Paul thinks he's God's gift to the guitar," Amelia would say with a roll of her eyes. Or, "Paul's work ethic totally sucks." Or, "Paul has this new obsession with the Pixies, which is doing really cool things for our sound."

Not until the two girls had run into him on Melrose did Janie finally discover the truth. "Why didn't you tell me he was so *cute?*" she gasped, once she and Amelia were alone.

Amelia made a face, like *are you kidding me?* "I can't look at the guys like that," she stuck out her tongue. "They're like my *family*. Besides," she added after a considered pause, "I wouldn't want to do anything. You know. To risk the band."

Janie shook her head in slow disbelief. Sometimes it was hard to believe Amelia's discipline. It really was.

Since the Melrose encounter, she'd seen Paul only twice: once when he swung by Amelia's house to look for his keys, which he found behind her nightstand, and once when Janie sat in on band practice. Of course, she asked to sit in again, but Amelia demurred. A few days later, when Janie asked again, her best friend sighed. "It's kinda hard to focus with other people around." Amelia's confession came as something of a shock (since when was Janie "other people"?). At the same time, she understood (what did she know about being in a band?). So Janie made do with what she had. She rationed her memories of Paul the way Pilgrims rationed corn to last the winter. Every night, as she gazed at the moon and star glow-stickers on her ceiling, she'd choose *just one detail* to think about. Monday: the way he hooked his lost keys to the silver chain at his narrow hips. Tuesday: the way he sucked the small hoop piercing on his full lower lip. Friday: the way he lifted his threadbare black t-shirt to scratch the taut stretch of skin above his square-studded leather belt. Just when she was down to her last two or three memories, just when she thought she was about to starve to death, Amelia put him on the phone.

"Hello?" he growled a second time. Janie could hardly breathe. After her period of depravation, the mere sound of Paul's voice was serious sensory overload.

"Hey, Paw!" she croaked, before literally biting her fist. Hey, Paw? *What?* "How's art school? Do you guys, like, wear berets?"

"Who *is* this?" he asked, sounding confused.

"Uh . . ." For the life of her, Janie could not remember.

"Hey," Amelia grabbed the phone back. "It's me."

"OhmygodIhateyou!" Janie exhaled, covering her eyes with her free hand.

"Whatev," Amelia replied. Janie practically *heard* her roll her eyes. "That was to remind you. Life outside of Winston. It exists!"

"What a relief." Janie scowled.

"You can do one of two things right now," Amelia continued. "You can remain in the vehicle like a good law-abiding elephant. Or you can take a risk. You can walk across the Showroom like you *own* it. Which you *will* because you have *changed*. In the words of William H. Shakespeare — *all the world's a runway,* and it's about time you, Janie Mae Farrish, took your part and freakin' *played* it! Yeah! Are you *with* me?!"

"Okay. That seriously grossed me out," Janie replied.

"Tell me you'll walk across the Showroom like you own it!"

"Fine."

"Like you mean it!"

"Fine. Yay! I own it!"

"That's the spirit!"

Janie smiled. As deeply annoying as Bring-It-On Kirsten was, she kind of did the trick. Janie hung up the phone with a strange feeling. And the feeling propelled her fingers to the door, her feet to the ground, and all five feet ten inches of her out of the black Volvo and into the world. She looked around: the leaves drenched in sun, the cars smooth as glaciers, the banners — WELCOME BACK FALCONS! — bobbing blue balloons, glinting green glitter.

She felt *positive*.

It sort of made her want to gag.

It also made her shut the door behind her.

The Girl: Melissa Moon
The Getup: Black velour Juicy Couture pants, silver
Jimmy Choo stilettos, pink and black D&G t-shirt,
Bvlgari diamond studs

Melissa Moon glided her platinum Lexus convertible down Sunset Boulevard, blasting CD-Seedy's latest album-gone-platinum: *Mo'tel*. Damn, she loved this album. *Mo'tel* was the first album to truly address the built-in conflicts of growing up half black, half Korean in South Central, Los Angeles. In her favorite track, "Gimme All Your Love, Gimme All Your Money," Seedy describes the night his black father met and fell in love with his Korean mother (during a routine robbery of her family's liquor store.) Some people found it offensive. Melissa, on the other hand, thought it was genius.

Not that she was biased.

In addition to being the world's most controversial rapper-cum-producer, Seedy (aka Christopher Duane Moon) was also her dad. For the Moon family, rap was about as traditional as Bing Crosby at Christmas. Not that they listened to Bing Crosby at Christmas, preferring Seedy's holiday album: *Chestnuts Roasting and I Open Fire.*

Melissa laid into the gas with the strappy toe of her metallic Jimmy Choo stiletto. The convertible picked up speed, transforming her Japanese Hair Straightened hair into a thousand lashing whips. She flinched, pulling it back into a ponytail.

"Whooooooo!" someone called from a passing Escalade. Melissa was used to it. Her face had launched a thousand SUVs.

With her sultry eyes, dusky complexion, and Angelina pout, Melissa had the kind of beauty people liked to call "exotic." But she loathed the term. It was like, exotic according to *who?* Some milk-fed white guy with a picket fence up his butt? Early on in their courtship, her boyfriend, Marco Duvall, made the mistake of saying she looked "foreign." Her immediate response was, "Look, *I'm* the one who grew up here. If anyone 'looks foreign,' it's *you!*"

Marco had recently moved from Tucson.

Roots were important to Melissa. Even though she lived in a Bel Air palace, she wasn't about to let the general public forget where she grew up: South *Central,* people. In a *duplex.* And then she'd put a hand on her hip, daring you to judge her. To her endless disappointment, no one ever did. But come on, they weren't crazy. Her dad had Melissa tattooed on his *fist.* We're not talking her name, either. We're talking her entire baby picture.

Melissa came to an intersection at Sunset Boulevard and North Beverly Drive and pulled to a stop. She removed her Christian Dior sunglasses, exhaling cinnamon breath on the tinted-pink lenses. A sudden wolf-whistle penetrated her left eardrum, but Melissa knew better than to pay attention. Unfortunately for her, her dog did not.

"Emilio Poochie, no!" Melissa cried as her tan-and-cream toy Pomeranian leapt into her lap. "In the back, *now!*" Within two seconds, Emilio sat quivering in the backseat, his army green driving goggles slipping off his tiny face. Melissa sighed, sinking her venti cappuccino into the cup holder. She leaned over and popped open the glove compartment, straining to locate her lint roller. By the time she did, the Lexus was straddling two lanes.

Melissa kept one hand on the wheel and went to work on her black Juicy pants. She liked to think of herself as the style child of J.Lo and Condoleezza Rice. Which is to say as much as she was about ghetto glam, she was also about Commanding Worldwide Respect. Which is exactly what Juicy pants accomplish — when they aren't covered by dog hair.

She lifted her chin to the rearview mirror once her task at hand was completed. "I'm sorry I yelled, baby. Forgive me?" Emilio put his paws on the back of her black leather seat and licked her diamond-studded earlobe. Of course he forgave her.

He was a dog. But he wasn't stupid.

By the time the Lexus glinted onto Winston Drive, Melissa's Juicys were in top form. Marco hated those Juicy pants. He compared them to a "Beverly Hills lawn at night": black, immaculate, and impossible to break into.

Not that he said that out loud.

"MuhLISuh!" his baritone voice hollered across the Showroom. Melissa half-waved her cappuccino hand, cranking the wheel with the other. Marco loped toward her, his bulging arms and muscular back straining the fabric of his I'D RATHER BE IN BUCARAMANGA t-shirt. A rawhide necklace grew taut against his thick, strong neck. His hundreds of springing soft brown curls, which all the girls loved and Marco hated, were crammed into a plush, forest green Kangol hat.

"Wait up!" he panted, trotting alongside the Lexus.

"Can you *not* see my eyes are on the road?!" she snapped, nearly plowing into a girl in a bright green miniskirt. She screamed as the car jerked to a halt, inches away from the girl's bare thighs. The girl wavered and lost balance, planting her barely-clad butt on the hood with a loud *whump*.

"Are you okay?" the girl squeaked.

"Get offa my car," Melissa replied. "Please."

The girl sprung to her feet as if the Lexus were a hot plate. Not that Melissa noticed. The sudden stop had triggered a cappuccino explosion, the effects of which were still seeping into her brand-new D&G t-shirt. Melissa stared down at the spot, and from the look on her face, you would have sworn it was blood.

She wasn't the only one.

"Omigawd-uh!" a high-pitched female voice squawked, sounding the alarm. Marco froze as a soft flapping filled the air — soft, but terrifying — like a flock of winged monkeys. He turned around, bracing himself. Sure enough, six or seven girls in flip-flops were headed straight for him. They arranged into perfect V formation, with Deena Yazdi, Melissa's self-appointed best friend, at the head. Over the summer, Deena had streaked her jet-black wavy hair in red, copper, and blonds. The majority of the highlights fell on either side of her attractive, if somewhat horsy, tanned face. Her nose-jobbed nostrils were tiny and pinched—as if they perpetually sensed something foul. Her eyes, lined with the usual smoky Chanel eyeliner, bulged out with exaggerated concern.

"OmiGAWD-uh!" she squawked a second time. (In times of stress, Deena kind of sounded like an evangelical preacher.) "What happen'd-uh?"

"It's okay," Marco explained, waving her off. "She almost hit this girl."

"Who?" Deena peered around. Apparently, the girl had already fled for her life. "Did you *see* what she did to Melissa's shirt?"

"To Melissa's *shirt?*" Marco gaped, incredulous. Deena narrowed her eyes.

"You—are so—rude."

"She almost hit someone and you're talkin' about a shirt!"

"That is not the point-uh!"

Marco was about to tell Deena what she could do with her "point-uh," when Melissa stepped out of her car. He stepped back, taking in the whole picture.

"Damn," he murmured, shaking his head. "You look fine."

"No," Melissa pointed out, "I have a stain."

"Yeah," her devoted boyfriend indulged an eyeful of her coffee-spattered double-Ds. "Your stain is *fine.*"

She rolled her eyes, holding out her keys: "Just . . . park the car, okay?"

"Here." Deena presented Melissa a small bottle of Fiji water. "Maybe you can still get it out?"

"No way," Melissa pursed her lips. "This shirt is dry clean only."

"That sucks-uh!" Deena exclaimed, her face crumpling at the injustice of it all. Until she remembered the vanilla latte in her right hand. "Wait." She plucked off the lid and (making sure Melissa saw her) dumped the contents all over her bright white Theory tank top.

"Deena — you are crazy!" Melissa gasped.

"As if I'd let you go through this alone," her best friend declared with pride. In the face of that kind of logic, the V-Formation had no choice but to follow suit. One by one, they dribbled their Doppios, capsized their capps, and slopped their sugar-free chais. Their t-shirts steeped like tea bags. Their padded bras plumped like sponges. Together they squealed, each at a pitch higher than the last, until they achieved OPTIMUM FREQUENCY, that decibel level unique among girls, though typically reserved for ice-cold pools and flirtatious games of "tag." Still, despite their volume, they might as well have been invisible.

Melissa stood in the center of it all and clapped her hands to her mouth. She shook her head, not making a single sound.

But she was the one to watch.

Glen Morrison stood at the Assembly Hall entrance, strumming James Taylor's "Fire and Rain" on his buttercup-yellow guitar. Students streamed by like salmon heading upriver. On the occasion one deigned to notice him, Glen dipped his head in greeting. Then he'd shake his floppy gray hair from his eyes and smile.

He maybe had to do this twice.

In 1967, Glen and a bunch of other hippie parents founded Winston Prep as a "non-traditional alternative" to other private schools in Los Angeles. They sat in a "non-hierarchical" circle and discussed their "non-biased" vision. In terms of education, Winston stressed a "non-stress" approach. Instead of exclusivity, Winston offered *creativity*. Instead of competition, Winston offered *conversation*. Winston nurtured the heart as well as the head. Winston *cared* about *caring*.

Their vision survived about as long as a quart of milk. Forgotten in the back of a van with no air-conditioning. In Death Valley.

Nevertheless, Glen strummed on.

Assembly Hall consisted of one enormous, ballroom-sized space. Sunlight streamed in through tall French windows, and the leaves of the weeping willows shimmered behind the glass. There were no chairs to sit on or desks to hide behind. Everyone, students and teachers alike, sat on the smooth, brushed concrete floor. For all appearances, students sat wherever they liked. If you paid attention, however, you'd notice everyone sat in the same spot every day. A strict seating chart was in place — and your spot on the floor, just like your spot in the lot, depended entirely on your social ranking. But while parking spots had to do with what you drove, floor spots had to do with who you were. And who you were was defined by *what you wore*. And, of course, how you wore it.

The least popular Winstonians sat in the center of the floor, known as "Ground Zero." The goal was to sit as far from Ground Zero as possible. The farther you got, the more popular you were. The most coveted seats on the floor were those at the outermost point—in this case, a seat against the wall. A wall seat was a clear sign to the student body that you'd made it.

Melissa and her friends sat along the sunniest part of the East Wall. East Wallers looked like they spent their lunchtime hot-tubbing with Snoop Dogg. East Wallers wore form-fitting, brand-name clothes that sparkled when they walked. East Wallers were all sass. Basic Rule: if you can't match your stilettos to your nail jewels, *sit someplace else*.

Charlotte and her friends sat on the west side. West Wallers were the so-called "indie darlings" of Winston Prep. West Wallers looked like they spent lunchtime gallery-hopping with Sofia Coppola and Chloë Sevigny. West Wallers dressed in understated yet expensive fabrics: silk, cashmere, sheer cottons. West Wallers were all class. Basic Rule: if you can't pair vintage capris with couture flats, *sit someplace else*.

Janie and her friends sat toward the back, near the middle: this was No Man's Land. Nomanlanders looked like they spent lunchtime, well . . . eating lunch. Nomanlanders wore Sevens jeans and Banana Republic t-shirts—and that's when they were feeling *really* stylish. Nomanlanders dressed to be ignored, and they were. Basic Rule: Um, Nomanlanders didn't need one.

"Good morning, everyone!" Glen crowed, cupping his hands to his mouth. He tucked his wiry gray bangs behind his ears and cleared his throat, waiting for them to *simmer down.* As usual, they didn't. Glen watched them with a mixture of impatience and fear, like an inexperienced chef on television.

"Welcome to the first Town Meeting of the year!" he called out, inciting a riot of hoots and hollers. "I know it's the first day and we're all excited to see each other after a long and hopefully restorative summer break. But we have a lot of very important announcements that require your undivided attention. So eyes on me. Let's do our best to focus."

At that, all 314 students assumed butterfly position on the brushed concrete floor. A hush fell over the crowd. Glen clasped his hands, pleased. But (predictably) his sense of success was short-lived. He realized their attention, though undivided, was focused on decidedly *non-Glen* subject matter. In other words, their eyes were very clearly *not* on him—but on someone else. Someone behind him.

Which is why he turned around.

Janie entered the assembly hall, mortified to find every single pair of eyes fixed on her. She tugged at the hem of her green miniskirt

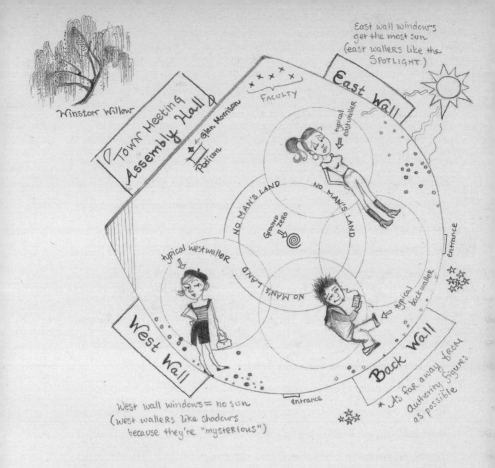

Winston Willow

Town Meeting Assembly Hall

← Glen Morrison

Podium

FACULTY

East Wall

East wall windows get the most sun (east wallers like the SPOTLIGHT)

typical eastwaller →

NO MAN'S LAND

NO MAN'S LAND

GROUND ZERO

NO MAN'S LAND

typical westwaller

← typical backwaller

West Wall

Back Wall

entrance

entrance

West wall windows = no sun (west wallers like shadows because they're "mysterious")

* As far away from Authority Figures as possible

and stared at the ground. She knew what they were thinking: *here comes Janie Farrish, Melissa Moon's new hood ornament. Make way for Janie Farrish, Melissa Moon's personal speed bump. Check out Janie Farrish, Melissa Moon's latest roadkill.* Except, of course, she was worse than roadkill.

Roadkill had the decency to die.

In order to get to her seat in No Man's Land, she would have to weave through the vast crowd of kids sitting on the floor. Under normal circumstances, walking through the crowd was no big deal. But today she was wearing the micro-mini. All someone would have to do was look *up* and then . . . oh God. She couldn't even think about it.

Janie was faced with a choice: assume her rightful place in No Man's Land and risk everyone seeing her underwear, or sit down exactly where she was. Except exactly where she was happened to be the Back Wall. The Back Wall (aka "Ganja Ghetto") belonged to kids cool enough to spend lunch break in celebrity rehab. Basic Rule: if you don't resemble the best-looking member of Sgt. Pepper's Lonely Hearts Club Band, *sit someplace else.* But for once, Janie didn't care. Especially since she was wearing her Valentine panties from Target. The pair with IN YOUR DREAMS printed over and over in a tiny, bright pink font.

She found an empty space next to Joaquin Whitman and, even though he smelled like patchouli and pickles, Janie folded her knees and sat down. To her surprise, Joaquin greeted her with a gentle smile and a singsong, "wha-a-tsu-up?"

"Whatsup," she replied, half-wondering if his cheeriness was some kind of setup.

"Chillin'." Joaquin nodded, adjusting the headphones to his nano. He smiled, bobbing his head like a dashboard ornament. Janie breathed a sigh of relief. Joaquin didn't seem to care if she sat there at all. He was even *nice.*

She craned her neck, scanning the great stretch of No Man's Land for Jake. He was nowhere to be found. With heavy heart, Janie turned west. Her instincts were right. There he was, sitting next to *her.* Janie wished she could say her brother looked out of place but he didn't. With his new tousled haircut and dewy complexion, his threadbare cowboy shirt and beat-up Converse All Stars, Jake Farrish looked like your basic West Wall poster child. Janie watched as Charlotte Beverwil removed her canary-yellow headband and pushed it through Jake's hair, laughing. Jake took the whole thing in stride. *Ugh,* Janie thought. *Who does he think he is?*

Just then, Bethany Snee, one of Janie's only friends at Winston and fellow Nomanlander, caught her eye. *Who does she think she is,* Bethany's fat fish-lips appeared to mouth to Farrah Frick, a freckly redhead with an annoying laugh. Janie blushed as Farrah turned around to give her a scandalized look. Before long the two girls were cupping hands to each other's ears, whispering their gossipy heads off. Janie tried not to think about what they were saying, but she couldn't help herself. Were they making fun of her skirt? Did they think she was full of herself? Would they still let her eat lunch with them? Did they think she was on drugs? Now that she was sitting at the back wall, did *everyone* think she was on drugs?

Janie squeezed her eyes shut. If only someone would come to school in an outfit more insane than hers. An outfit so what-was-she-thinking *out* there, her micro-mini would look mild in comparison. Janie tried to imagine what that outfit would look like, but she couldn't. And then, just when she'd given up. . . .

Petra Greene walked into Town Meeting.

Janie's miniskirt was instantly forgotten.

The Girl: Petra Greene
The Getup: See it to believe it

Only two things on Petra Greene's body escaped fervent debate: her left hand and her right hand. From the tips of her tapered fingers to the delicate bone of her wrists, they were flawless. And because there's no such thing as "finger implants" or "wrist tucks," Winston attributed her flawless hands to nature, genes, luck — whatever. Even her harshest critics agreed: Petra Greene's hands were 100 percent cosmetic surgery–free.

The rest of her features, however: definitely suspect. Beauty like hers just wasn't natural. Or so everyone assumed.

Dr. Robert Greene was the most sought-after plastic surgeon in Beverly Hills. In light of his profession, Petra's looks were universally pooh-poohed. She isn't *pretty,* her dissenters insisted. She's a *product* — the latest accomplishment of "Daddy's magic wand." It was just a rumor, of course, but a rumor even Daddy spread around. When clients gushed over a prominently displayed photograph of his daughter, Dr. Greene would wink and say, "my best work to date." It wasn't a lie, per se. Petra *was* his work — in the way all children are the "work" of their parents. If his patients thought he meant something else, well then *that was their interpretation.*

When Petra caught wind of her father's comments, she wasn't exactly surprised. As her mother uttered over brandy more than once, Petra's father was ruthless. In terms of price, his was the highest. In terms of dignity, his was the lowest. Dr. Greene had a reputation for doing anything for anyone at anytime. (There was good reason Michael, Cher, Liza, and Angeline were *all* said to be his clients.) Petra sometimes wished operating rooms were run like car dealerships, so people could see her father as he really was: the guy on TV telling you to *come on down.* "Come see the King of Collagen! The Baron of Botox!! The Lord of Lipo!!!" He'd holler and wave around a ten-gallon surgical cap. He'd juggle his scalpels and laugh like a maniac.

But no one saw her father like that.

No one, that is, except Petra.

Her therapist informed her *she didn't hate her father — she hated his behavior.* But no, Petra seriously hated her father, which is why she did everything humanly possible to wreck the perfect looks God gave her. She would not be his free advertising. She refused. She would float around in ratty smocks and moth-eaten sweatshirts. She would never wash or brush her hair and she would never, ever wear makeup again — not even ChapStick.

Seriously.

In terms of rebellious acts, Petra Greene's ranked number seven in Winston's all time top ten, knocking Billy Bresler — who torched a tennis net in 1989 — to number eight. At Winston, not caring how you look is *way* more subversive than arson. And Petra really, *really* didn't care.

Town Meeting proved no exception.

Six hundred hungry eyes watched her float across the room. She wore a pink ballet slipper on her right foot, a black ballet slipper on her left. The fallen hem of her wine-red linen skirt dragged along the floor, and a mop-gray thermal bunched under her baby-tee. A shredded scarf dangled from her neck as a string of fake pearls fought for breath. Her yellow t-shirt, which looked about ten sizes too small, read: PROPERTY OF SPONGEBOB. As a final touch, Petra topped her matted locks with a lopsided paper Burger King crown.

Still, you know how Johnny Depp insists on accepting roles that ruin his looks? And yet — despite the scissor hands in one film, the mouthful of rotting teeth in another — he manages to be mind-blowingly beautiful? Petra Greene suffered from the same sort of disease. Try as she might, she couldn't *not* be pretty. In fact, the less she cared, the more you stared.

It was really quite tragic.

"Take a seat, Petra," Glen nodded as she sat down, her skirt blooming like a wine-red mushroom cloud. "It's nice to see you."

And wasn't that the truth?

Winston Prep lifted the term "Town Meeting" from the Quakers, a centuries-old community of nonviolent Christians who — if they were anything like that guy on the oatmeal box — considered pirate hats the absolute height of fashion. Which is to say, the

similarities between Winston Town Meetings and Quaker Town Meetings began and ended with the name.

Winston Town Meetings were all the same: boring announcement after boring announcement until the ultimate reward of boring bagels, accompanied by only slightly more compelling individualized cream cheese packets. Then, while the seventh graders sat consuming their carbs (upperclassmen knew better), Glen reminded them that, in addition to announcements, Town Meeting provided a platform for *community expression*.

"Come on, guys!" He scanned the meeting for volunteers. "Town Meeting doesn't *have* to be boring!"

That was the most boring announcement of all.

No one in their right mind took advantage of community expression, which expressed one thing and one thing only: I am a big fat loser. Take Owen Meyer, for example. In commemoration of the thirteen-year anniversary of Kurt Cobain's death, Owen had performed an a cappella rendition of "Jesus Doesn't Want Me for a Sunbeam," and then—to the shock and mirth of all present—he actually *cried*. After that, everyone called him Owen Crier, which made him cry more, which only proved the point. Eventually he moved to Texas, which students dubbed the Lone Tear State, but only for about a day. By the next, Owen and his blotchy face were forgotten.

"I did a lot of thinking over the summer." Glen looked off into the distance, nostrils flaring like a conquistador. "I thought about the way Town Meeting used to be. And then I thought about the way

Town Meeting is *now*—strained of creativity like so much pulp from orange juice. *Even though the pulp is the most nutritious part!*"

He bored into them with his sternest look.

"I realized we need to make some serious changes around here," he announced. Students shifted their weight and exchanged worried glances. What, exactly, was Glen capable of? Was he allowed to ground them? Send them to boarding school? Military school? ITT Tech?

"I'd like to introduce our new director of Special Studies." Glen turned toward the right corner of the room. "Miss Paletsky."

That no one knew what a "special study" was really didn't matter; the insult was obvious. Everyone knew "special" was synonymous with "retard," even Glen. But before they could cry out in protest, Winston's newest teacher approached the microphone.

One thing you could say for the new director of Retard Studies: she knew how to dress the part.

Her clothes looked like something you'd trade for cigarettes behind the Berlin Wall. Meaning they were, like, eighties—but in a very non-cool way. She had paired high-waisted tan stretch pants with a magenta leotard and an asymmetrical white leather belt. Her boots were little white spikes. Her kitten-face earrings were clip-on. She smelled like apples and menthol and Suave. She looked about twenty-eight years old, roughly the same age as her lipstick, which was roughly the color of borscht.

The forces of fashion had united against her. And yet. She was cute.

You could tell by the way some of the male teachers straightened in their seats. For the most part, Winston faculty hulked like vultures. They slumped at laptops. They stooped over coffee. They wilted by dry-erase boards. Winston faculty earned their bad posture in college, having slowly collapsed under the weight of their brains. Most of them graduated from Stanford or Yale, which was sort of depressing when you thought about it (you know *they* thought about it, like, all the time.)

Miss Paletsky pressed her hands to her thighs and tipped into a little bow. "Ch'ello, stewdents," she murmured into the mic. Her voice was both breathy and Slavic, a strange mix of Marilyn Monroe and Dracula.

"Ch'ello," she repeated, a little louder this time.

Glen cupped his hands to his mouth. "Community Expression needs our help!"

Miss Paletsky knitted her brow, confused by his random, enthusiastic outburst.

"Ye-es," she continued with a timid smile. "This 'Community Expression' is not so popular. But as the new director of Special Studies, I'm here to fix it. *So.* What is Special Study? Special Study is class that you, the *stewdents* create. It can be anything you like, and as long as your study is approved, you have *one period each week* to meet. Which means —"

"You must have a minimum of four students!" Glen interrupted, bursting with excitement. "That's no less than *four* to qualify as an official class. Every Special Study must involve *legal* and *age-appropriate* activities. Which means absolutely no drugs, no sexual activity, and no violence of any kind! If you have an idea, please talk to Miss Paletsky. All it takes is four or more interested students and it's official: your very own Special Study is good to go!"

With a grave look of concern, Miss Paletsky observed Glen pump his fist. She returned her gaze to the students, smiling bravely.

"Okay!" Glen continued, still beaming like the Patron Saint of Dorks. "Town Meeting dismissed!"

The strange and mysterious effects of Suave hair spray...

Octagon eyewear → (can we say octa-GONE?)

optimistic "please like me" smile

hoop earrings with yellow and purple plastic star charms (possibly edible)

Miss Paletsky

teaches "Perfectly Pretty Faces and how to destroy them"

Jake had two classes lined up before lunch: Advanced Physics and French Cinema. (Guess which one Charlotte was in?) Advanced Physics took place in an unremarkable Winston classroom (mahogany desks, chalkboards, French windows with spectacular canyon views), and French Cinema didn't take place in a classroom at all.

Thanks to the generous contribution of Alan and Betty Kronenberg, the Winston campus came equipped with a 100-seat movie theater. Except for the screen, which was state-of-the-art digital, the theater was straight out of the twenties. Creamy silk curtains hung in scalloped pleats. Chairs held out arms of warm red velvet. The seashell-shaped sconces fanned the walls with golden beams. There was even a ticket booth with a window that opened and shut like a brass accordion. The more sophisticated students dismissed the theater as "cheesy," but then they'd sink into their seats, tip their heads back, and sigh. The black ceiling twinkled with a galaxy's worth of tiny white lights.

As far as cheese goes, this stuff was world-class brie.

Charlotte invited Jake to sit with her in the back row — and he accepted. The lights went down and the title came up. The first film of the year was a black-and-white French classic called *Les Quatre Cents Coups*.

"Four Hundred *Blows*?" Charlotte translated the title with a coy smirk. "*This* should be interesting."

"Dude," Jake replied. "Get your mind out of the gutter."

Charlotte threw back her long neck and laughed, breezy as a wind chime. Jake stole a quick glance at the soft shadow between her breasts. When he looked up he noticed Kate Joliet, Charlotte's best friend, staring back — disgusted. Jake looked ahead and pretended to focus on the film.

After class, Charlotte excused herself to the bathroom, her two best friends in tow. The two girls had spent the film staring at Jake in this super-critical way — and Jake thought he knew why. *Why* was why. Charlotte sat next to him? Why? Laughed at his jokes? Why? Asked to borrow his sweatshirt when the air kicked in? *Why?*

Once they asked, Jake could kiss his luck goodbye. Because once they asked, Charlotte would realize: she really didn't *know* why. Before long *why* would become *what* (had she been thinking?) and *how* (could she let this happen?) and *where* (could she blow him off?) and *when* (as soon as possible).

Jake watched the object of his affection drift toward the exit, growing smaller and smaller, like a balloon he'd let go by accident. As a kid, he would have thrown a tantrum. But he wasn't a kid anymore. He shoved his hands deep into his pockets and shrugged it off. It was just a balloon. It was just a girl.

The tide of the crowd guided him to the exit, through the corridor and into the sun. He blinked, taking a moment to adjust his eyes to the light. Jake was on Accutane, and one of the side effects — sensitivity to light — made exiting buildings somewhat of a challenge.

It was a small price to pay.

When Jake and Janie first transferred to Winston last year, their skin had gone from bad to worse. Pores gave way to pimples. Pimples gave way to pustules. Pustules gave way to pustules with pimples.

Which was to say, even their zits had zits.

"We're lepers!" they had cried to their parents, wringing their hands and running through the house.

"Good," their dad muttered, tightening a string on his twelve-string guitar. "We can send you to a colony."

But Mrs. Farrish booked them an appointment with a dermatologist.

Dr. Kinoshita spent the entire appointment connected to a swivel stool with little wheels that squeaked. Instead of walking, Dr. Kinoshita pushed his feet to the floor and launched. He rocketed across the smooth, white tiles. He swung an enormous mirror in front of their faces and stared with one unblinking, magnified eye. He was a cyclops. A cyclops on wheels.

"This is a very bad case of acne," he declared, slapping his hands to his knees. Jake and Janie looked at each other. Can you say, "duh"?

"We've tried everything," their mother sighed.

"I'm going to ask you two a question." Dr. Kinoshita laid a hand on Mrs. Farrish's shoulder. "I call it 'the paper bag test.' It's very easy, only one question long, and the question is this: when you go outside, do you feel like wearing a paper bag over your head?"

"More like an entire paper luggage set," Jake said.

Dr. Kinoshita nodded. "There's a medication called Accutane," he explained, "but I only prescribe it to people with acne so severe they feel like they can't go outside in public."

"Well, I feel like I can't go outside in public, and my skin is fine," joked their mother. Dr. Kinoshita chuckled. Her children were unamused.

"Does this stuff actually work?" Jake couldn't help but feel suspicious.

"Well, everyone is different. But let's just say all of my patients have been very happy with their results."

"Doesn't this medication have side effects?" Mrs. Farrish interjected. Jake and Janie groaned in dismay. Their mother wasn't going to let a little thing like side effects stand in the way of clear skin, was she? They could turn into twin Hulks for all they cared! As long as their green skin was blemish-free, *who the hell cared*?

"It does have some," Dr. Kinoshita confirmed, handing their mother a glossy paper insert, "but it's important to keep in mind —"

"Oh my Lord!" Mrs. Farrish gasped, her eyes darting down the list. "Hair loss? Rectal bleeding?" Jake and Janie looked at each other. Okay. No one wanted to be a balding butt bleeder, not even the Hulk.

"Keep in mind most of those reactions are extremely rare," Dr. Kinoshita replied. "I've never experienced anything like —"

"What have you experienced?" Mrs. Farrish interrupted again.

"Chapped lips. Dehydration. Sensitivity to light. . . ."

Mrs. Farrish lowered the list to her lap. "So, what's in this pill? Jack Daniels?"

Dr. Kinoshita chuckled again. "No, nothing like that. As a matter of fact, drinking should be avoided while taking this medication. It lowers tolerance significantly."

"Right," Jake responded with a thoughtful nod.

"What do you mean 'right'?" his mother interrogated. "Are you *drinking*?"

"Also," Dr. Kinoshita interrupted, "this medication causes *severe* birth defects. If you decide to take it," he advised, turning to Janie, "you *must* use some form of birth control."

Mrs. Farrish trilled with laughter. "Oh, I don't think *that's* necessary," she chortled, oblivious to her daughter's mortified glare. Janie's utter lack of sexual experience was one thing. But that it should prove the subject of her mother's hilarity!

It was a little much.

"So then we can get it?" Jake asked, his tone hopeful.

"Well, I don't know." Mrs. Farrish wiped a tear from her merry eye. She turned to take a good look at her two children. They seemed to really want this. They were practically salivating out of their zit-encrusted mouths.

"I suppose it's up to you guys," she sighed.

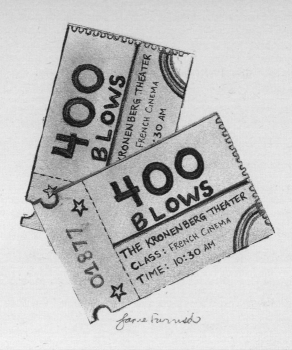

Janie Furnish

When Jake's eyes finally focused outside of the Kronenberg Theater, he spotted his sister exiting the Showroom. Juniors and seniors were allowed off-campus lunches, a privilege Janie seemed impatient to use. She punched the crosswalk button like a woodpecker as Jake broke into a trot, catching up to her just as the light turned green.

"You goin' to Baja Fresh?" he asked, following her into the street.

"Get away from me," she replied.

"What? Why?"

Janie stopped in her tracks, planting her foot like a kick-stop. "Did you see what happened in the Showroom?"

"No," Jake said, confused. "What happened?"

Janie narrowed her eyes. "Nothing," she seethed, steaming ahead.

"Wait!" He grabbed her bony elbow. "What happened?"

"I guess you were too busy flirting with the enemy to notice!"

Jake blushed. "We weren't flirting."

"Ha."

"We're just — friends!" he sputtered. "Besides — who are you? My keeper?"

Janie darkened with fury and Jake stepped back. His sister could be a little intense. "Don't you remember anything?" she asked. "She's the one! She called me 'Pompidou' for like a whole semester!"

"She did?"

"You seriously have the memory of a goldfish!"

"Yeah, well, better than the memory of an elephant."

"I am not an elephant!"

Jake folded his arms across his chest and frowned at the ground. How was it he and his sister were actual twins? They weren't even the same species!

"How did this even happen?" Janie eked out, her eyes now growing glassy. "How are you guys quote-unquote *friends?*"

Before Jake could answer, a nasal beeping distracted them both. They looked up to find Charlotte's gleaming, cream-colored Jag lumbering at the curb. She leaned toward the window, her glossy black curls tumbling across the shoulders of a slouchy gray hoody. At first Janie was confused. Charlotte Beverwil wouldn't be caught dead in a hoody. Then she noticed a small object glint next to the zipper. An Amnesiac pin. Janie blanched in horror.

She was wearing her brother's sweatshirt.

"Hey!" Charlotte called to Jake, flashing a dazzling white smile in Janie's direction. Janie pretended not to notice.

"Just gimme a sec," Jake said, sidling up to her car. The engine greeted him with a throaty purr. Music wafted through the window like cigarette smoke.

So did cigarette smoke.

"We're heading to Kate Mantellini," Charlotte announced, ashing her gold-tipped Gauloise into the street. "Wanna come?"

"Oh." Jake bobbed his eyebrows in surprise. An invite to Kate Mantellini, the expensive chopped-salad mecca on Wilshire Boulevard, could mean only one thing: he had passed the Best Friend Test. Jake's instincts were correct. After a brutal (but necessary) bathroom interrogation, Kate and Laila conceded Jake's new status as "hottie." On a scale of one to five butterflies, he earned a staggering *four and a half* (his unfortunate lack of a British accent worked against him). Using her brand-new Treo, Kate reported Jake to the student-run site: Winston's Most Wanted. Jake Farrish was instantly inducted.

He glanced into Charlotte's backseat, where Kate and Laila sat staring into identical black MAC compacts. At the moment of his attention, the compacts snapped shut. They turned, smiling their synchronized, glossimer smiles.

"Well?" the two girls asked in unison.

"Um . . . ," Jake turned to check on his sister, but she was half-way down the block. "Yeah," he said at last. "I guess I'm down to be abducted."

Jake reached for Charlotte's passenger-side door. The lock released with a luxurious click and he ducked inside, sinking into the buttery leather seat. Charlotte leaned toward him. Her leather seat crackled. Her eyes snapped with light. And she didn't smell like cigarettes at all. She smelled like orange blossoms. She smelled like summer rain.

She smelled a little like his grandmother.

"Ready?" Charlotte asked.

Jake didn't have to answer. He'd already shut the door.

With the exception of Amelia, Janie's Canson Field Sketchbook was her best friend. She'd flip through magazines and draw the things she wanted, the things she needed, the things she *had to have.* When she got bored, she drew things that didn't exist. She window-shopped her imagination and drew what she found. Gossamer baby doll dresses and mermaid-tailed cocktail dresses. Cap sleeves and poet sleeves, bell sleeves, ballet sleeves. Skirts with slits and skirts with pleats. Military jackets, puffy jackets, pea coats, and trench coats. She drew petticoats. Hip-huggers and sailor pants, cowboy hats and pillbox caps. Frills and fringe, bows and buttons, ribbons and sashes, buckles and zips and ties and clips.

She drew all the things she *would* wear, someday — as soon as she worked up the nerve.

But that day, as she sat down for lunch at the Baja Fresh in Beverly Hills, Janie drew for another reason altogether. She flipped open her sketchbook, readying her graphite pencil like a thunderbolt. She stabbed the paper with electric force. This wasn't a drawing. This was, in the tradition of Dr. Frankenstein and other mad scientists, *a creation*.

First she drew her model: a slender girl with bobbed light-brown hair and killer legs (resemblance to self — pure coincidence). She drew a t-shirt, black and slashed around the shoulders, a haphazard crosshatch of red stitching around the collar. She penciled in a pair of shorts. Short-shorts. Janie edged the contours with the tip of her eraser, creating the effect of reflecting light. Only one material reflects light like that: vinyl. And she'd cut these from the slickest, tightest, hottest vinyl available. They'd stick to her skin like Fruit Roll-Ups. They'd come in artificial cherry red.

She'd call this little number "Sweet Revenge."

High heels came next. Black, with rounded toes and platform heels, ribbons laced to the knee. Janie squinted at her work, adding an inch to each heel for good measure. More than three steps in shoes like these and she'd be timber, sprawled on the floor and down for the count. But these shoes weren't made for walking.

They were made for standing around and looking pissed.

Janie moved on to accessories. Nothing over-the-top: just a few leather bracelets, some safety pins, five earrings, eleven rings, two chain-link belts, and...a tattoo? She frowned, nibbling on her last remaining cuticle—she just couldn't decide.

"Number h'eighty-two? H'eighty-two, order ready."

Janie scooted her chair back and approached the counter.

"Thank you." She nodded, transporting her order to the salsa bar. Janie studied her options: pico de gallo, salsa fresca, chipotle, chopped cilantro, lime slices, pickled jalapeños. She unwrapped her order, adding a little bit of everything. Okay, so she tended to over-accessorize, even when it came to tacos.

"Ouch," exclaimed an unidentifiable male voice.

Janie glanced up at the guy standing directly next to her. He looked like a less grumpy version of Heath Ledger, one of Janie's absolute favorite actors. He was tall and strong, with well-wrought limbs and smooth golden skin. His longish hair, which was flecked with more gold, ended in soft flips around his ears. His hands appeared capable and calloused (Janie could only guess) from surfing, and he was dressed for the beach: olive green board shorts and rubbery flip-flops, an oversized brown sweatshirt. In short: he looked like the kind of guy who wouldn't talk to her in a million years.

And yet.

"How can you *handle* that?" He regarded her salsa-soaked taco with something close to awe.

"Oh," Janie replied, somewhat shell-shocked. "It's really not that hot."

"Well." He grinned, revealing a to-die-for set of dimples. "Maybe not for you."

Maybe not for *her*? What was *that* supposed to mean?

With all the courage she could muster, Janie allowed their eyes to lock. To her surprise, they seemed familiar. What was it about that half-moon shape? That chlorine blend of blue and green?

"Evan!" At the sound of his name, Heath Ledger Boy diverted his attention from Janie to Joaquin Whitman, who had his face pushed against the outside window. "We're outta here, dude," called Joaquin, fogging the glass with his pot breath.

"I'll *be* there." The boy whose name was Evan waved him away.

"You go to Winston?" Janie blurted in disbelief. Had he really escaped her attention all this time?

"I just transferred senior year," he replied. "It's sort of a long story."

"Oh." Janie nodded, hoping she'd come off as the sort of girl who knew all about long stories. Even though she didn't. Her own story, if you could call it that, was pretty short. Not to mention pointless.

"My name's Evan," he extended his hand.

"Jane," she replied. "Jane" sounded more sophisticated.

"Jane," he repeated, sounding solemn. Janie laughed. Was it just her or did he sound a little like Tarzan?

"What's so funny?" Evan furrowed his brow.

"Nothing." She smiled. "It's just, like, *you Evan. Me Jane.*"

He seemed confused. In a desperate attempt to ram the joke home, Janie thumped her chest and released a Tarzan-esque yell.

Ahhhh-ee-yah-ee-yaaaaah-ee-yah-ee-yaaaah!

There was a long, excruciating pause. The Baja Fresh janitor looked up from his mop. In the near distance, a burrito wrapper crinkled.

"Oh-kay . . ." Evan nodded like maybe she was crazy. He picked up his tray and lifted his chin. "Late."

Janie hurried back to her table and checked her phone: one missed call from Amelia. She looked at her untouched taco and debated what to do with her mouth. Talk or eat? If she ate, she'd obsess over her train wreck of a conversation with the boy named Evan. If she talked, however, she might starve. Okay, so maybe the choice was obvious.

She picked up her phone and punched SEND.

"Creatures of Habit booked a show at SPACELAND!" Amelia exploded in greeting. Janie's jaw dropped a little. Spaceland was, without a doubt, the coolest music venue in L.A., having launched such music legends as Elliott Smith, Death Cab for Cutie, the Foo Fighters, Jurassic 5, the Shins, the White Stripes, Jet, Supergrass, Modest Mouse, and Weezer. The list went on and on. As did the line to get inside. Not that she had ever been inside. The closest she'd come was the strip of broken sidewalk outside the main entrance. Janie had stared at the drab stucco exterior, wondering if

Sweet Revenge

Janie Parrish

she'd found the right place. If it wasn't for the compact neon SPACELAND sign on the roof, the building may have resembled an abandoned, possibly haunted motel. Of course, she was there on a Sunday at the unglamorous hour of 2:45 p.m. Bright sunlight and Sunday quiet have a way of exposing nightclubs for what they are: sad little windowless boxes. If only she could see what Spaceland was like on a *Saturday night,* when dark concealed the cracks and neon lit the sky. If only she could pass through those heavy, barn-like doors, down that black throat of a hallway, and into the pulsing, reverberating world within.

But of course she couldn't.

"How did you book a show at Spaceland?" she asked. "Don't you have to be twenty-one?" Unlike the majority of kids her age, Janie had yet to procure a fake ID.

"You have to be twenty-one to *go,* not to *play,*" Amelia explained.

"Oh," Janie replied, still feeling confused. Weren't new bands supposed to start low profile? Weren't they supposed to get some practice in first, then improve their technique, build a fan base, and slowly, *slowly* work their way up?

Amelia seemed to read her mind.

"Chris says he likes to throw new talent into the deep end. It's all about sink or swim."

"Who's Chris?"

"Chris *Zane,*" Amelia clarified, as if that made things clear. "The music producer?"

"O-oh." Janie pretended to recognize the name.

"We met him at Paul's aunt's engagement party —"

"You went to a party?" Janie interrupted, failing to conceal the hurt in her voice. Since when did Amelia go to parties and not invite her?

"J!" Amelia groaned in frustration. "We went to perform! It wasn't like a *party,* party. It was *work.*"

"Oh," Janie said. "Right."

"So," Amelia continued, "after the set, Zane comes up to us and he's, like, listen. You guys are *ready to go.* And we're, like, what? And then he takes out his phone and puts in a call to Spaceland, like, right *there.* Like, in front of us! It was so . . . awesome!"

"Wow!" Janie warbled in a small voice.

"Ew," Amelia replied. "That wow sucked butt."

"I'm sorry," Janie sighed. "It's just . . . I guess I just wish I could come."

"But you *can!*"

"You have to be twenty-one."

"Dude, don't you get it? *You're with the band!*"

Janie stared into her basket of tortilla chips. The chips pointed at her like golden arrows of destiny.

"Hello?"

"Sorry." Janie tried to recover. "I . . . I think I'm still in shock."

Amelia laughed. "Listen. Will you make me that dress? The one you drew at my house last weekend?"

"The London Vampire Milkmaid dress?" Janie flipped to the sketch in question. As she examined the drawing, her heart sank. "I can't. The materials alone would cost, like, two hundred dollars."

"We'll raise the money!"

"Yeah, right." Janie rolled her eyes. Amelia was only, like, *the* worst spendthrift on the planet.

"Well, it's our only option," Amelia declared. "I have to have that dress."

"You know what I could do?" Janie mused. "Start a Special Study."

"A what?"

"It's this new thing at Winston. We're allowed to create our own classes and, like, they can be whatever we want them to be. I could start, like, a Dress Amelia Fund!" Janie laughed at the notion. "Problem solved."

"That is . . . ," Amelia replied, "totally brilliant."

"I was kidding."

"Well, obviously you don't call it the Dress Amelia Fund. You say it's Costume Design or something. And then you collect dues. *Major* dues. It's not like those rich Winston biznatches can't afford it."

"I don't know," Janie hesitated.

"Janie, *please*?" Amelia whimpered. "I just invited you back-stage, at Spaceland, so you can spend a whole night doing nothing more than stare at Paul's ass."

"Okay, okay, okay!" Janie blushed. "I'll propose a Special Study."

"Yay!" Amelia cheered.

"I can't promise anyone'll sign up," Janie added.

But her best friend had already hung up the phone.

APPLICATION FOR SPECIAL STUDIES

Name: Janie Farrish

Class: Sophomore

I.D.#: 804-228

Proposed Course Title: Costume Design

Please use the following space to define your special study:

We all have a perfect outfit in our head. It's the outfit you can't find in a department store or a garage sale or a vintage clothing boutique, no matter how hard you try. It doesn't matter how much money you have or how hard you search — these outfits don't exist. You have to make them. The purpose of Costume Design will be to show us how.

Please use the following space to provide a tentative ten-week course schedule:

Week one: Draw our outfits.
Week two: Critique our drawings.
Week three: Final draft drawing presentation.
Week four: Buying materials. (*** This would have to involve some kind of donation or fund-raising?)
Weeks five-eight: Making the outfits. (I kind of know how to sew-but it would be helpful if someone who _really_ knew how to sew joined the class.)
Week nine: Critique.
Week ten: Fashion Show.

If you could sum up your Special Study in one line, what would it be?

Your mind: best mall ever.

APPLICATION FOR SPECIAL STUDIES

Name: Charlotte Beverwil

Class: Sophomore

I.D.#: 804-663

Proposed Course Title: Sewing Circle

Please use the following space to define your special study:

My interest in sewing started with dance. As a student of ballet, I have always been expected to repair the ribbons on my toe shoes and darn my own costumes. I decided not to stop there, but rather improve my craft. This summer, I studied pleat-making at the Issey Miyake headquarters in Paris. I also studied embroidery at Passement Werk School in Brugge, Belgium. Sadly, due to family circumstances out of my control, I left the class before its completion.

For hundreds of years, women of all ages and nationalities gathered together to sew. In addition to sharing material and tricks of the trade, they confided in each other and traded advice. Unfortunately, as sewing falls out of the mainstream, so do the sewing circles. This special study is dedicated to resuscitating a dying tradition.

1.

Please use the following space to provide a tentative ten-week course schedule:

Every week we bring our own materials, sit in a circle, and work. The class should develop naturally, without a formal structure.

If you could sum up your Special Study in one line, what would it be?

Keep your eye on the needle.

APPLICATION FOR SPECIAL STUDIES

Name: PETRA GREENE

Class: SOPHOMORE

I.D.#: 804-554

Proposed Course Title: MORAL FIBER

Please use the following space to define your special study:

THIS SCHOOL IS SO OVERLY OBSESSED WITH FASHION, IT MAKES ME SICK.
I PROPOSE A LINE OF CLOTHING THAT STANDS AGAINST FASHION, NOT FOR
IT. THE NAME OF MY ANTI-LABEL IS "MORAL FIBER." THE FIVE GOALS OF
MORAL FIBER ARE AS FOLLOWS:
1. TO BANISH FASHION'S CORRUPT AND IMMORAL CRAVING FOR FUR AND
LEATHER.
2. TO PROMOTE <u>CRUELTY-FREE</u> NATURAL FIBERS LIKE HEMP AND CORN
SILK.
3. TO CHAMPION ENVIRONMENTALLY FRIENDLY DYES LIKE POMEGRANATE
JUICE AND SQUID INK.
4. TO ADDRESS OUR CRIMINAL DEPENDENCE ON SWEATSHOP LABOR.
5. TO RAISE SOCIAL CONSCIOUSNESS.
IT'S TIME TO REFOCUS THE AMERICAN CONSUMER AWAY FROM COST, TO
<u>CAUSE</u>. FROM MORE-MORE-MORE TO MORE-MORE-<u>MORAL</u>.

1.

Please use the following space to provide a tentative ten-week course schedule:

WEEK #1: INTRODUCTIONS. TRUST EXERCISES.
WEEK #2: BUY COTTON T-SHIRTS FROM SWEATSHOP-FREE UNITED STATES OF APPAREL.
WEEK #3: DISCUSS UNITED STATES OF APPAREL'S SLEAZY ADVERTISING. DOES UNITED STATES OF APPAREL EXPLOIT THEIR FEMALE EMPLOYEES?
WEEK #4: RETURN COTTON T-SHIRTS.
WEEK #5: MAKE OUR OWN COTTON T-SHIRTS FROM SCRATCH. TIE-DYE.
WEEK #6: DESIGN THE MORAL FIBER LABEL. EACH TAG WILL READ: MADE WITH 100% MORAL FIBER.
WEEK #7: SELL T-SHIRTS TO RAISE MONEY TO DONATE TO CHARITY OF CHOICE. VEGAN BAKE SALE.
WEEK #8: ATTEND PETA RALLY.
WEEK #9: DISCUSS EVERYTHING LEARNED.
WEEK #10: SILENT MEDITATION.

If you could sum up your Special Study in one line, what would it be?

FASHION SUCKS.

APPLICATION FOR SPECIAL STUDIES

Name: Melissa Moon

Class: Sophomore

I.D.#: 804-262

Proposed Course Title: Melissa Moon: The Class

Please use the following space to define your special study:

In the grand tradition of Jennifer Lopez and Oprah, I dream to be more than just a person. I dream to be a <u>brand</u>. I see "Melissa Moon: The Class" as the first small step toward that ultimate goal. Today the classroom, tomorrow the world.

Unfortunately, a lot of people think I should just ask my dad for help. He transforms nobodies into icons with a snap of his fingers. If you want proof, look at his girlfriend, Vivien Ho. She went from "random video chick" to "reigning princess of purse design" in like an hour. Sure, "Ho Bag" can be found in luxury department stores from Tokyo to Timbuktu. But seriously, <u>so what</u>? That is all my dad's achievement, not hers!

I never want people to say, "oh, that girl accomplished that because of her family." Paris Hilton has to deal with that. Maybe it's fair. But <u>maybe it's not</u>. It's really impossible to know, right? Well, when the time comes, I want people to 100% without a doubt KNOW: Melissa Moon's success is ALL HERS. And Special Studies is exactly the kind of small-time, grassroots beginning I'll use as proof. Because <u>my</u> destiny sprung from HARD WORK, NOT HANDOUTS!

1.

Please use the following space to provide a tentative ten-week course schedule:

MM1: As a brand, what does Melissa Moon represent? What dream do we sell? Who buys Melissa Moon? Open discussion.

MM2: Finding our "Look." Designing a Label.

MM3: What is the Melissa Moon Launch Product? Makeup? Perfume? Jewelry? Clothes Line? Calendar? Album? ANSWER: ALL OF THE ABOVE. Melissa Moon makeup: natural or glam? Perfume: floral or spicy? Jewelry: gold or platinum? Clothes: accessible or designer? Calendar: tasteful or sexy? Album: pop or critically acclaimed?
ANSWER: ALL OF THE ABOVE.

MM4: Educational Field Trip to Rodeo Dr.

MM5 - MM12: I think the rest of the course should be planned according to committee. I firmly believe every member of my team should have an opportunity to offer personal creative input. Every member has <u>value</u>. I never want to give the impression that "Melissa Moon: The Class" is all about me.

If you could sum up your Special Study in one line, what would it be?

Make Moon a Star.

The Girl: Miss Paletsky
The Getup: Plum-colored oversized I.N.C. blazer with shoulder pads, brown stretch pants with side zip, gray pleather slouch boots, gold starfish earrings

Miss Paletsky stuck Melissa Moon's application in the middle of the thick pile of paper on her old oak desk, pushing the other hand under her octagon-shaped reading glasses. She pressed a finger and thumb to each of her closed lids. She kept pressing until she saw fireworks, which exploded around one question: were all of these students completely crazy?

In addition to Melissa's campaign for world domination, Miss Paletsky read a proposal for a Naptime Alliance (why should five-year-olds have all the fun?), a Pedicure Group (pedicure, from the Latin "ped" meaning "foot," is an ancient art), and an S&M&M Society (do you like to hit others and/or be hit by hard chocolate candies?). *What about a book club?* she wondered. *A new political party? A language society? A cooking class?*

The young new teacher sighed, preparing herself for the mind-numbing task of compiling multiple proposals into a few solid classes. For example, by combining the Naptime Alliance and the Dream Interpretation Club, she not only created a stronger proposal, but also ensured the interest of at least two students. Unfortunately, she'd have to put the Pedicure Group and the S&M&M Society in the REJECT pile.

Steadily she worked, listening to Johann Sebastian Bach's Goldberg Variations at a rebelliously loud volume. Every time she reached Melissa Moon's application, she'd stick it back into the middle of the pile. The girl's ambition was compelling—if a little scary—and Miss Paletsky could not decide where it belonged. She'd just about dropped Melissa Moon: The Class in the "RE-JECT" pile when, during the very first notes of Variation 20, she read an application that created a mental spark. A very interesting proposal for a "Costume Design" class, complete with an array of imaginative sketches executed with surprising skill. It was easy to see that the girl who drew them had talent.

She decided to combine "Melissa Moon," "Costume Design," "Sewing Circle" and an outlandish but nevertheless noble-minded class called "Moral Fiber." She fanned the four applications in the center of her desk and nodded. Together, these four girls might have real potential. Yes, their ideas were vastly different, but each sprouted from the same seed: fashion. Miss Paletsky entered their names into her Excel spreadsheet.

Melissa Moon. Janie Farrish. Charlotte Beverwil. Petra Greene.

Miss Paletsky smiled, revealing her overlapping eyetooth. She liked the sound of the names together. There was a ring to it. A harmony.

Yeah. You'd think a "music scholar" would know better.

The Girl: Janie Farrish
The Getup: Used Seven jeans, extra-long light blue
cotton tank, red Pumas, black gummy bracelets

By the time the bell rang on the fifth day of class, that crazy, back-to-school buzz, that fantastic feeling of newness, had completely disappeared. The shock of radical haircuts and drastic weight loss had dissipated. Flashy new cars were already old, pens and protractors already lost, three-ring binders already busted. The freshest gossip had been passed around. Twice. And there was already too much homework, too much pressure, too little sleep, too little time.

But perhaps the most obvious sign of hangover was the sudden irrelevance of summer. As a conversation piece, "what I did for vacation" was way, way over. The only kids behind the curve were Jake Farrish and Charlotte Beverwil, both of whom found the subject endlessly fresh and topical. Of course, "summer" was but a thinly veiled disguise for the *true* subject at hand.

Each other.

"We gotta stop at Charlotte's on the way back," Jake informed his sister as they prepared for their end-of-day drive home.

"Why?"

"I dunno." Jake smiled at his black Nokia. "She just texted me."

"She *texted* you?" Janie grimaced. "You guys were just *talking*, like, two seconds ago!"

"So?"

Janie pulled out of her spot so fast, Jake lost his next sentence in a cloud of dust. As she turned into the street, the car wheels squealed—quite a feat for a Volvo.

"What is wrong with you?" Jake asked, leaning into the corner of his seat.

"Nothing! *You're* the one obsessed with the Bever-bitch."

"I haven't put on my seat belt," he pointed out.

His sister stared straight ahead. "Who am I, your keeper?"

When she was little, Janie had recurring nightmares. In one Jake fell into an ivy-covered well. In another, an escalator ate him alive. But the one that really got her, the one that haunted her for hours after she woke up, was the dream where Jake got into a strange car and drove away. Right when the car turned down the street, Janie would get this feeling, like something horrible was about to happen.

She never let him not wear his seat belt. Ever.

"Fine," Jake said, letting go of his shoulder strap. Janie listened to the nylon whirr and snap against the window. After a few seconds, she jerked the car to a stop.

"Okay," she surrendered. "Put it on."

Jake did as he was told, shaking his head in exasperation. In fact, he was relieved. It was one thing to deal with his sister's wrath, quite another to deal with her apathy. That she still cared whether he lived or died—it meant a lot to him. It meant so much he wanted to hug her. Jake stole a glance at her. No, he decided. Way too pissed off for hugs. He sighed, resigning himself; he'd have to express himself in some other, more stealthy way.

And so he farted.

"You are disgusting!" Janie exploded, rolling down the window while Jake cackled in triumph. She leaned her face into the wind. "Seriously, what is wrong with you?!"

"I'm sorry." He arranged his features into a "sad clown" face. In retaliation, Janie flipped him off. Jake widened his eyes, touching the tip of her middle finger with the tip of his.

"Friend," he croaked in his best E.T. voice.

Janie withdrew her hand. The corners of her mouth twitched, but she stopped herself. If she cracked a smile, Jake won. She gritted her teeth. "How is it everyone in school knew about your big Summer of Love before I did?"

"Would you stop calling it that?" Jake groaned. "All we did was *chill*."

A rueful laugh escaped her lips.

"Look. Charlotte and I spent twenty-four hours a day for three weeks on a movie set in the middle of nowhere. It's weird. You're, like, cut off from the world, in this artificial yet real place. It's pretty intense. Charlotte's like . . . she's like my *army* buddy."

Janie looked at him as if he'd confessed to public urination.

"I'll do it." She nodded after a long pause. "I'll drive you to her place."

"Thank you."

"Where did you say she lived?"

"On Mulholland," Jake sat up in his seat. "Just east of Beverly Glen."

"Okay, but just so you know" — she flipped the blinker — "I'm gonna tell her you fart in the car."

Jake looked stricken. "No, you are not."

Instead of answering, his sister turned the radio up and bopped her head like a demented metronome. Jake stared. The grin on her face was seriously unsettling.

"You're not," he repeated with feigned confidence. Nevertheless, he — and his butt — stayed quiet the rest of the ride.

The Girl (sort of): Don John
The Getup: Vince plaid Bermuda shorts, yellow Lacoste
polo, blue Burberry frill scarf, Gucci sandals, blue
plastic headband from Target

Ask Charlotte Beverwil to describe her bedroom in one word and she would answer *parfait,* the French word for "perfect," and the American word for "pastry." She fit her four-poster mahogany bed, imported from a luxury store in Martinique, with a silk coverlet of meringue white and lemon yellow brocade. Her pillowcases, made from the finest Egyptian cotton, were the color of mint. A centuries-old shoji screen from Kyoto was placed, half-unfolded, beside her tiny fireplace. When the fire was lit (she made sure it almost always was), the delicate pattern of cherry blossoms lit up and flickered like stars. As a final touch, she hung a line of vintage slips all along her floor-to-ceiling bay windows. The sheer lingerie floated and filled with sunlight, an effect, Charlotte decided, that was quintessential *parfait:* pastry-sweet, picture-perfect, and undeniably *Français.*

But that afternoon, as she clung for dear life to her mahogany bedpost, the word of the day was *pain.* Behind her, his foot against the bed frame, Charlotte's friend Don John strained with the laces of her jade-green corset, cinching her already tiny waist to an excruciating degree.

In addition to being the Beverwils' next-door neighbor, eighteen-year-old Don John was also Charlotte's true confidant. His round face, with its eternally flared nostrils and bulging "Bette Davis" eyes, was unremarkable, and his endless devotion to Tweezerman, salon hair products, and Guerlain self-tanner made the situation ten times worse. Nevertheless, Don John was convinced: his was a face that would take Hollywood by storm.

Six months ago, Don John ran away from Corpus Christi, Texas, changed his name (from the spirit crushing Dee Jay), and moved into the adobe guesthouse next door, a poolside affair belonging to the Beverwils' ancient wheelchair-bound neighbor, an ex-Hollywood producer who went by the name "Mort." In exchange for "light housework, meal preparation, and stimulating conversation," Don John got to live at Mort's rent-free. Charlotte had no idea how he managed to fulfill his duties to Mort *and* spend nearly twenty-four hours a day with her, but he did. If she so much as mentioned his real job, Don John clucked his tongue and said, "Oh, the old bean can wait." Who was Charlotte to argue? She *needed* Don John. Don John was the best personal stylist a girl could ask for.

Or so she thought until this afternoon.

"I can't possibly wear this!" Charlotte cried once the corset was in place. She turned toward one of her many gilded mirrors. "I look like a *Moulin Rouge* background dancer!"

"And?" Don John cocked his head, perplexed. What kind of girl didn't want to look like a *Moulin Rouge* background dancer?

"Just, get it off! Get it off!"

"Yes, Miss Charlotte," Don John grumbled like Mammy in *Gone with the Wind*. *Gone with the Wind* was Don John's favorite movie. *Moulin Rouge* was a close second.

"Why does everything make me look like I'm trying *so* hard?" Charlotte complained.

"Because you are," Don John replied, sitting on the edge of her bed. "You need to *relax*. It's not like you're getting married."

"I know," she sighed with a dreamy smile. What if she and Jake *did* get married? Stranger things were possible.

"Okay, okay, okay!" Don John snapped his freshly buffed fingers in front of her face. "What's your mantra?"

"Clothes before bros," she replied. But she'd never believed it less. Charlotte peeled the loosened corset from her waist and, like a true *chipie,* threw it against wall. Don John was not pleased.

"Just look what you did to Dylan Leão!" he scolded.

Technically the corset was by the British designer Vivienne Westwood—but Don John never called clothes by their maker. He had a whole other method, one he imposed on Charlotte like a military commando. Per his instruction, she must a) keep a journal with a strict record of every outfit she ever wore for every boy she ever kissed, and b) if the guy got so far as to actually *remove* something, name that garment in his honor. In addition to "Dylan Leão," Charlotte christened her lavender Chloé halter "Henry Fitzgibbon," her Nanette Lepore bolero "Max Bearman," and her fringed Missoni mini-dress "Gopal Golshan." And then, of course, there was Daniel Todd, the gorgeous nineteen-year-old photographer she met on the Côte d'Azur last spring. For their final night together, Charlotte paired a shrunken cashmere cardigan with a Dolce & Gabbana skirt, the back of which came together in a thrilling row of hook-and-eye clasps. Most guys would be daunted (isn't undoing a bra enough of a challenge?), but Daniel Todd managed—hook by hook, eye by eye—until, finally, the skirt lay on the floor of his room, empty as a book jacket (and just as easy to read). Moments later, Charlotte rewarded his efforts with her virginity. Which made "Daniel Todd" the most important outfit in her closet.

"Most important outfit does *not* mean most important guy!" Don John reminded her when, three weeks after the event, Charlotte lay crumpled in a sobbing heap at his feet. She'd been back in L.A. for three weeks and Daniel had not called. Even though she gave him her flower.

Even though she gave him the *entire bouquet*.

"You know what this man is?" Don John had snipped. "A cheap trend! Something you try on, take off—then *pfoo*! You throw him away!"

"But *why*?" Charlotte moaned in despair.

"Because he is *out of style*!"

"Are you sure?" she whimpered. "I mean, how can you know?"

"How can you know?" he repeated for his invisible audience. Returning his focus on Charlotte, he posed the ultimate question: "Charlotte. Who decides what's in style?"

"*Vogue?*"

"No, not *Vogue*! You! *You* decide what's in style!"

From that day forth, Charlotte Beverwil reformed. Never again would she let a guy mean more to her than the latest accessory — the stupid trinket you pick up as an afterthought only to forget about in the car ride home from Neiman's. Guys were no more than that *thing* you wear on impulse, only to later re-examine in photographs and ponder, *What the hell was I thinking*? Once you see guys that way, it's so much easier to get involved. Which is to say not involved. For months Charlotte went on this way. For months, she had it all figured out.

And then she met Jake Farrish.

Just the thought of him made her feel soft and sweet and gooey, like a Cadbury egg left in the sun. To think she'd once ignored him. To think she'd been so clueless! It seemed impossible now, and yet — who could have known that underneath the pimple lived a prince?

As Don John disappeared into her closet, Charlotte returned to the idea of marriage. The more she thought about it, the more inevitable it seemed. She and Jake would fall in love, date through high school, and, because of outside pressure, break up before college. Charlotte would attend *La Sorbonne* in Paris, consume nothing but coffee and cuticles, and begin a destructive affair with a handsome but cruel professor of . . . botany. Meanwhile, Jake would inherit the craft service business, take up fishing, start drinking, and date a simpleminded wardrobe assistant named Charlene. Five years later, Jake and Charlotte would run into each other (perhaps at a gas station in Cherbourg, France?), look deeply into each other's eyes, and . . .

"This is *it*!" Don John pranced from her closet, pinched the corners of a red DVF skirt, and snapped it out like a bullfighter. "Am I *right*?"

July 14

Event - Kate Joliet's annual Bastille Day Crêpe Party at the Château Marmont Hotel.

Outfit - fringed Missoni red, green, and gold minidress, gold Lanvin platform sandals, mother's topaz bangles.

Boy - Gopal Golshan, 5'11, poli-sci major at Brown, perfect skin, thick black hair, Marc Jacobs Aviator sunglasses, a lot of anger. Unzipped my dress in the elevator at approximately 2:15 a.m. Vive la libération!

Charlotte sighed. "I don't think so."

"Okay, who is this guy?" He threw the skirt to the walnut and maple chequerboard floor. "Orlando Bloom?"

She collapsed across her bed. "Imagine the one guy in the world who never goes out of style."

"Oh, sweetie. Everything goes out of style."

"Not everything."

"Name one thing," Don John challenged. "Besides this boy, I mean. And Orlando Bloom."

She furrowed her brow in thought. There had to be *something*. And then in a flash it came to her. "That's *it*!" She bolted upright.

"What? What's it?"

Charlotte faced her dear confidant with an expression so bright, he actually winced. She clapped her hands like a baby seal.

"I figured out what to wear!"

The Girl: Blanca (last name unknown)
The Getup: Gray wool fishbone knee-length skirt, gray
button-down collared cotton shirt, white apron,
Naturalizer black loafer pumps, rattlesnake tattoo
on lower back (top secret)

Blanca, the Beverwil's *dame de la maison* (French for "lady butler"),
let the twins in with a small nod. As far as nods go, Blanca's was top-
notch: inviting yet scornful, deferential yet superior, polite yet
withering. She was tall and severe and dour. Her hair, black and
streaked with gray, was pulled into a bun the size of a bullet. Her
skin — the color of leather, but thin as paper — revealed a spastic
blue vein at her temple. Her heavily lidded eyes gleamed with
what looked like slicks of Vaseline. Her mouth was thin and wide
like a frog's, and so firmly clamped as to render it airtight and im-
penetrable. Could a mouth like that speak? Eat? Could it laugh?

Could it even breathe?

Jake and Janie didn't dare ask. They followed the lady butler
through the black wrought-iron Beverwil gates with the quiet rev-
erence of fairy-tale orphans.

Chateau Beverwil looked like your basic Hollywood manor
on growth hormones. The main house was an 8,000-square-foot
Spanish Colonial with classic Honduran mahogany windows and
exterior doors. Upon entry, however, old-fashioned gave way
to ultra-modern. Everything, from the bold abstract art to the

high-concept furniture, ran in straight, neat lines. Even the beams of sunlight, which streamed in from pristine windows and skylights, seemed thought-out, controlled, *designed*. Jake and Janie had never seen anything like it. It was like entering the Apple Store of the Gods.

Blanca shut the door with a solid thud. Janie held her breath as two doves lifted into the air. A moment later, the doves returned to the exposed ceiling rafters, turned to one another, and softly cooed.

Then they crapped all over the floor.

Without missing a beat, Blanca yanked a cloth from within the folds of her light gray skirt and kneeled to the floor. Janie made a motion to help, but Blanca blocked her with a small, waxen hand. Janie stepped aside, allowing Blanca to wipe the mess with one of her patented mixed-expressions (this time: repugnance and pleasure.)

"Hey!" a voice fluttered from above. The twins turned from the spectacle of Blanca vs. Birds to the crest of a wide, sweeping staircase. Charlotte stood — one hand on the wrought-iron banister, the other on her angular hip — and smiled. She was wearing the most perfect little black dress Janie had ever seen. It was the kind of little black dress Audrey Hepburn might wear. The kind of little black dress every girl was *supposed* to own, but no girl ever did. It was the little black dress of myth. The little black dress of dreams. The little black dress that stays in style. Forever.

"Thanks for stopping by." Charlotte stepped lightly downstairs. "If I don't take care of these things right away, I *never* take care of them. Know what I mean?"

They didn't.

"You mean I didn't tell you?" Charlotte touched her hand to her forehead. (Why was she acting like a bad actress?) "Jake, um, you left something in my car."

"I did?" He continued to look perplexed.

Charlotte turned to Janie with a trembling smile. If Janie didn't know better, she could have sworn she was nervous. But girls like Charlotte didn't get nervous.

Did they?

"Can you hold on for just a sec?" Charlotte asked. And then she went upstairs — more swiftly than she came down — hips swaying, butt bouncing, feet slipping from their black kitten-mule heels. Jake couldn't help but stare.

Janie couldn't help but stare at him staring.

Once she was out of sight, Charlotte bolted down the hall and knocked on her older brother's bedroom door with all her might. She loved an excuse to knock with all her might. Her bony little knuckles were harder than brass.

"*What?*" He appeared at last, his face a plaster of annoyance. She'd interrupted a crucial set of sit-ups, but Charlotte didn't care. She yanked the iPod wire from his ear like a weed.

"You need to help me. Now."

"Um . . . no," he replied, attempting to close the door.

"It's important!" Charlotte stopped the door with her lightning-quick size-six foot. Her brother groaned.

"Don't you have *Bonbon* for this sort of thing?"

"*Don John,*" she corrected, "is walking Mort." She pushed her way into his room, shutting the door behind her. She leaned up against it and her breast heaved with urgency. "There's a girl downstairs," she informed him in a harsh whisper.

"What?"

"You need to distract her."

"Why? Who is she?" he asked, growing suspicious. Charlotte took a deep breath, readying herself for a lengthy explanation. Her brother stopped her like a crossing guard. "Wait! Wait! Never mind!" he ordered. She closed her mouth. "Okay," he continued once he was safe. "All I wanna know is, is she hot?"

Charlotte squinched her nose at the word "hot." She knew it was in her best interest to say yes, but she was feeling a little stingy. She had made a real effort to be nice to Janie — she'd even said *hello* — and Janie had narrowed her eyes like a viper. True, Charlotte teased her in the ninth grade, but that was, like, a *year* ago. Janie Farrish should know better. Grudges are the pastime of old ladies and gang members, not attractive young girls. Attractive young girls obsess over *themselves,* not *other* people.

Could it be Janie didn't quite know she was attractive?

After all, her transition from Ignorable to Adorable came at mind-bending warp speed, and identity-switches that quick *can* screw with the system. But while Jake handled his with unparalleled cool, Janie was completely freaking out. Charlotte guessed she suffered from an acute Ugly Duckling Complex, or "UDC." Charlotte was concerned—not because she cared about Janie, but because she cared about her future with Jake. As long as his sister's UDC went untreated, Janie would continue her grudge, which meant she might do or say anything to turn Jake against her.

Charlotte wasn't about to let that happen.

"Well?" Evan prompted. "Is she hot or not?"

"She's . . . okay," Charlotte managed to admit. Her brother raised his eyebrows with interest. He knew his sister too well. Charlotte insisted her friends—who looked like hairless dogs in makeup—were "cute." Only the very hottest girls earned the resentful "she's . . . okay."

"*She's okay,* huh?"

Charlotte smiled. She knew her brother too well. Nothing excited him more than a "she's . . . okay." Now Evan would flirt his head off, Janie's UDC would be gone in half a heartbeat, and Jake would finally belong, truly and completely, to Charlotte.

"So?" Charlotte repressed a smug smile of triumph. "Will you do it or what?"

He pulled a fresh t-shirt over his cherished abs and grinned. "Do it."

Evan could not believe his truly excellent luck. Not only was the girl downstairs hot, she was *that* hot girl. The hot girl with the *dress*. Or was that green thing a skirt? Like any self-respecting guy, he could never remember the difference.

Since their salsa bar encounter, he'd decided to ask around about a girl named "Jane"; no one seemed to know who on earth he was talking about. There wasn't a chance of their crossing paths in class (Evan was a senior and Jane, he guessed, was a junior or a sophomore), and the next Town Meeting wasn't for another two days. He loitered around Baja Fresh, but she never showed again. Weird. Winston was a fairly small school. Could a girl like that just disappear?

And then, just as mysteriously, reappear in his parents' foyer?

Evan tramped downstairs in his bare feet and greeted her with his best hot guy grin. "Whattup."

"What," Janie stammered. "Um, hi." Her foot turned toward her ankle, like it always did when she was discombobulated. *Heath Ledger Boy was Charlotte's brother?* She couldn't believe it. If her foot turned a fraction of a degree more, her ankle might snap.

"I was beginning to think you were abducted," he joked.

"What?" Janie felt her cheeks grow hot. "Why would you . . . ? Ha. Abducted. No."

Jake watched the interaction between Evan and Janie with a puzzled frown. "You guys know each other?"

His sister simultaneously nodded and shook her head. She couldn't say she knew Evan. At the same time she couldn't say she didn't. All she could say for sure was, in a misguided effort to make him laugh, she'd imitated Tarzan in the middle of a Mexican restaurant, reaching levels of dorkyness not meant to be explored. When she thought about it (*Ahhhh-ee-yah-ee-yaaaaah-ee-yah-ee-yaaaah!*) she became too mortified to breathe. Which is why, the four times she'd glimpsed Evan on campus in the past two days, she'd darted for cover.

"Evan darling, give Janie the tour!" Charlotte ordered from down the hall. She tugged Jake by the elbow.

"So," Evan said once their siblings were gone.

"So," Janie said back. Of course, she'd heard Charlotte's brother had returned to Winston for his senior year, just as the guy in Baja Fresh claimed *he* had. Why hadn't she put two and two together? Why hadn't she realized Charlotte's brother and Heath Ledger Boy were one and the same?

"Can I, um . . . get you something to drink?" he asked, desperate to fill the silence. "A spritzer?"

"Sure," Janie replied, following him into the sleek, monochromatic kitchen. Evan pulled the heavy door of a silver Sub-Zero refrigerator, and it released a sound like a loud sucking kiss. He found an Orangina and handed it to her, unscrewing the cap.

"Thanks." She took a birdlike sip before returning the bottle to the counter. They'd stationed themselves on either side of the massive granite-topped kitchen island. Evan planted his hands on both corners, facing Janie like an air hockey opponent. He could really go for a game of air hockey, he realized with a pang.

"I like the bottle," Janie observed, turning her Orangina so the label faced her.

"You're exactly like my sister," came Evan's amicable reply. Charlotte liked the bottles so much, she refused to throw them out. She lined them on her windowsills like little glass soldiers.

"I'm nothing like your sister," Janie countered with a small laugh.

"Yeah." He smiled. "I guess not."

"Really?" Janie paused. "You really think we're *nothing* alike?"

Evan took a deep breath. He'd only meant the sister remark as a throwaway comment. How had it turned into this, like, *big deal*? But Janie was waiting on his answer, so he'd better come up with something. He scratched the back of his ankle with his flip-flop and thought it over. His sister was short. Janie was tall. His sister had curly hair. Janie had straight hair. His sister was his sister. Janie was *not* his sister. "I guess you guys seem pretty different," he concluded.

She nodded. Of *course* he'd say they were different. Charlotte was pretty and confident and rich and fashionable and popular. Janie was not. She crossed her arms in front of her chest and stared at the floor.

It took Evan all of .5 seconds to realize he'd said the wrong thing (*why* it was wrong remained a mystery.) But before he could retract his answer, her brother walked into the kitchen.

"Jake!" Janie exclaimed with relief.

Jake just stood there, his smile enormous to the point of distorting his face.

"What's wrong with you?" she asked.

"Nothing," he responded in a vague sort of way. "Hey, man." He nodded to Evan.

"Whattup." Evan nodded back.

Janie turned back to Evan with a half-wave. "It was nice meeting you. Again."

"Yeah," Evan murmured, watching her exit. Her narrow hips tick-tocked like a clock. *Sorry, buddy,* they seemed to say. *Your time is up.*

Evan made a slow lap around the kitchen island and tried to make sense of what happened. He stared at Janie's virtually untouched Orangina, his words echoing in his ears. *Can I offer you a spritzer?* He cringed at the memory. What kind of self-respecting dude says *spritzer*?

Evan grabbed the Orangina bottle by its neck, carried it to the sink, and tipped it on its head. The orange liquid gurgled and fizzed. He watched it for a second, then turned on the faucet, letting the water run. Just like that, the drink was gone—out of his sink forever.

If only he could get her out of his mind.

If only he could get her out of his mind.

As of only twenty-three minutes ago, Charlotte Beverwil had pulled Jake into her laundry room, where — amid the steamy hum of a polished steel washer and dryer — she'd given him, at long last, "that thing he left in her car." Jake had been expecting his gray sweatshirt. Or maybe his Arcade Fire CD. Instead, he got a very urgent, extremely passionate, push-against-the-wall-style kiss. It wasn't what he'd been expecting.

It was exactly what he'd been looking for.

Only now, as he sat in the Volvo with his brooding sister at the wheel, did panic begin to seep in. Because this was the thing: Charlotte Beverwil had experience. In fact, according to his buddy Tyler, she hadn't even *gone* to embroidery school in Belgium. According to his buddy Tyler "embroidery school" was just an elaborate metaphor for, well, *you know.* "Yeah, even I do *that* kind of embroidery," he snickered, tying his shoe by Jake's locker. "The needle goes in, the needle goes out. The needle goes in, the needle goes out. Dude, you *know* what she was up to in jolly ol' *Belgium.*"

Jake slammed his locker shut, grimacing at his friend. "Man, are you as dumb as you sound?"

But Tyler had a point. Girls like Charlotte didn't just *not have sex.* They exuded sex. They *were* sex. And they *definitely* did not jaunt all the way to Europe to *sew*. No doubt about it, Charlotte Beverwil had experience. And experience led to another dreaded ex: *expectations*. A girl like Charlotte expected a lot—and Jake wasn't sure he could deliver. After all, he was still a virgin. What if she were to find out? What if she could somehow *tell*? Jake paled at the thought. If Charlotte knew he was a V-boy, she'd realize how uncool he was and Jake would turn into the worst form of ex there was:

The ex-pseudo-boyfriend.

Jake could narrow down his entire sex life to one girl: Melody Chung. He met Melody last spring in Advanced Kuman, a math class taught according to a strict Japanese method. Melody Chung had tan skin, straight black hair, and long, wispy bangs. She wore platform flip-flops and rolled the cuffs of her jeans. She had a pretty, tiny mouth—the same shape and size as the drugstore butterfly clips she attached to her hair—and a freckle on her right ear.

At first sight, Melody looked timid and sweet. She wasn't. She barked equations like a dictator. She clicked her Hello Kitty pen as if it connected to an explosive device. She was fond of the expression "What are you, stupid?" But she was nice to Jake. And she smelled like strawberry Runts. So when she sat next to him during class, Jake liked it. And when she continued to sit there, even *after* class, Jake liked it even more. And then, out of nowhere, Melody Chung asked if he'd like to "sit outside."

They commenced a frantic make-out session in the alley behind the Unitarian church where Evergreen Kuman rented class space. They could hear the beginners' class, which met directly after theirs, chanting through the open windows: *five times two is ten! Five times three is fifteen! Five times four is twenty!* Jake and Melody sucked nonstop face 'til *nine times eleven,* at which point he made the mistake of touching Melody's nipple, and she stabbed her Hello Kitty pen into his ribs. This brought things to a grinding halt.

The next day, Melody avoided him. She refused to make eye contact or speak—unless you count the time Jake blanked on a prime number, at which point he heard (softly, from the back of the room), "What are you, stupid?"

So, that was it. Jake's experience in a nutshell. The whole shabang (minus the bang). He was no match for Charlotte. He wasn't even a contender. Seriously, what had he been *thinking*?

At the most heated point of their laundry room make-out session, Jake had broken away from Charlotte and stared hard at the floor. "What's wrong?" she asked.

"Nothing. It's just . . ." He tried to think up something to say, anything—as long as it wasn't the truth. Charlotte folded her arms across her chest as Jake looked up and gazed into her eyes, those twin pools of chlorine-green, and drew a blank.

She cleared her throat. "Does this have something to do with your sister?"

"Ye-es," Jake agreed before he could think it through.

He felt bad pinning it on Janie, but what was he supposed to do? Pin it on his pathetic lack of *balls*? To *Charlotte*? Jake ground his palms into his eye sockets. If only he didn't *like* her so much. Things would be so much easier!

But he did like her and so they weren't.

"You wanna put on a CD?" Janie asked, interrupting his thoughts. With a little effort, Jake managed to return to the reality of the Volvo. Down the street, the Beverwils' automatic gates closed, locking into place. The wrought-iron shuddered.

Jake flipped through their CD case. "Here," he handed her an Elliott Smith album.

"Uh-oh," she said, examining his choice. "Is someone feeling saddy-poo?"

"Shut up," he replied. But his heart wasn't in it.

"Hey." Janie smiled. "It's alright. I'm saddy-poo too."

After that, they let Elliott Smith do the talking. Jake leaned his head to the window, watching the sun disappear behind a rust-tinged veil of smog. No doubt the Beverwil laundry was done by now: folded into tidy creased squares, stacked into those tall cedar chests from Sweden, resting in the cedar-scented dark. The image filled Jake with a strange, hollow ache. His thoughts tumbled in his brain, like sheets that refused to dry.

The Universe Revolves Around ...

Long Lost
Coffee Stain
Island →

Melissa
Moon ☆

Should she wear
her Armani's?

OR her CHRISTIAN
LOUBOUTINS?

Janie Smith

The COFFEE STAIN
ISLANDS

The Girl: Melissa Moon
The Getup: A&G denim miniskirt, pink Rebecca Beeson cotton t-shirt, silver Baby Phat puffy vest, silver stiletto mules with rhinestone detail, saucer-sized platinum hoops, manicure (in Chanel's "Paparazzi")

Melissa Moon was not happy.

Her Special Studies proposal—which she'd spent a whole three hours on, skipping a much needed crystal therapy appointment—had been rejected.

Not only rejected, but dragged off and held hostage by another Special Studies proposal. By something called . . . wait for it . . .

The Trend Set.

As if she would sign up for something with so bland and inferior a title.

Fortunately, Melissa was not the type to just sit back and take it. She was the type to *take it out*. She turned from the library bulletin and started walking. Her stilettos popped like cap guns. Her bangles clanged like bells of alarm. Her Cinnamon Inferno gum cracked like a whip.

"OmiGAWD-uh!" Deena shrieked from her left. Melissa stopped her with the clichéd, but always reliable, hand. Deena's face fell, but she'd just have to deal.

Now was not the time.

Melissa flung open Miss Paletsky's dark-green office door.

The director of Special Studies looked up from her computer, smiling from behind her no-name octagonal eyewear. At the mere sight of those glasses, Melissa wanted to scream, "I have four words for you! *Gucci rectangular tortoiseshell frames.* Buy them before I *slap* those damn stop signs off your face!"

But she didn't.

Instead, in her very sweetest voice, she asked: "Do you mind if I shut the door?" Miss Paletsky invited her to take a seat. Melissa stared at the green velveteen couch, where Miss Paletsky had propped a row of small, forest creature cushions. An embroidered quail sat next to an embroidered rabbit. An embroidered squirrel ate an embroidered nut. The pillows gave Melissa the embroidered creeps. Especially the squirrel, who seemed to be looking right at her.

"Is everything alright?" Miss Paletsky asked in her Slavic purr. She wondered why Melissa continued to stand, frowning at her couch as if it had insulted her family's good name.

"Not exactly," Melissa sighed, perching on the very edge of the couch's saggy arm. She clutched the squirrel pillow and pressed it to her lap. "My Special Study . . . ," she began, pausing for effect, "was rejected." She sighed a heavy sigh, waiting for her teacher's gushing apology. It didn't come. Miss Paletsky just smiled and looked generally pleasant.

It was infuriating.

"I was wondering," she continued, hardening her tone, "if there was some kind of mistake?"

Miss Paletsky clasped her soft hands until they sat like a potato in her lap. "Dah . . ." She cleared her throat. "The main mistake, I think, is choice of word 'rejected.' Your proposal was not rejected. It was *accepted* and *combined* with some other proposals to make it stronger."

"So you're saying my proposal was *weak*."

"I am not saying that," Miss Paletsky replied with a sweet smile. "All four proposals were very strong. But because they had so much in common . . ."

"I don't have anything in common with people who think 'The Trend Set' is a cool name for a class."

"Well, I came up with that, not them," Miss Paletsky admitted, a little embarrassed. She thought "The Trend Set" was pretty clever, actually: a *set* of girls who *set* the trends. *Get it?* Miss Paletsky tugged self-consciously at her flower-print scrunchie.

"I'm sure you and the girls can come up with something more . . . how do you say it . . . catchy."

"More catchy than 'Melissa Moon'?" Melissa asked, incredulous. "If 'Melissa Moon' is not catchy, I don't know what is."

"Why not suggest it to the other girls and see what they think?" suggested Miss Paletsky.

"I can't. They'll think I'm an egomaniac."

The teacher laughed lightly. "You're not egomaniac." (F.Y.I., Miss Paletsky's job required her to *discourage* students from regarding themselves as egomaniacs. Even when they kinda were.)

"Well, *I* know that." Melissa collapsed backward on the

velveteen couch. "And my *friends* know that. But everyone else is, like, 'Oh, Melissa! She's so full of herself!' Even though I'm not."

"Of course you're not."

"I just have a strong personality!"

"Exactly."

"I feel my Special Study should consist of me and my *friends*," Melissa concluded. "My friends get the way I tick."

"Yes," Miss Paletsky nodded. "Your friends are passionate about fashion like you?"

"Oh yeah. They shop, like, all the time."

Miss Paletsky raised her eyebrows and removed her glasses. "Is that how you define passion? By shopping?"

Melissa had a sinking feeling it wasn't.

"Just so you know," Miss Paletsky said, "Charlotte Beverwil studied embroidery and lace-making with Belgian nuns." She lowered her glasses to her lap, rubbing the left lens with the corner of her cardigan. "And Janie Farrish draws and designs her own clothes." She shifted the corner of her cardigan from her left lens to her right. "And Petra Greene wants to start her own label, just like you."

"*Petra* wants to start her own label?" Melissa snorted. "What's she gonna call it—Baglady Mischka?"

"My point is," Miss Paletsky continued, replacing her glasses, "is possible you will have more success with *them* than with shop-'til-you-drop friends."

Melissa laughed. "No way."

"Okay," Miss Paletsky conceded. "Maybe I am missing something. Explain to me why going into business with *friends* is better option."

"Friends are loyal."

"Good!" Miss Paletsky nodded. "What else?"

Melissa thought it over, but the only trait she came up with was "fun," and—in terms of her argument—"fun" wasn't the most persuasive. She'd watched her father. Starting a business was about focus and hard work, not fun.

She would have to play this another way.

"Nothing's more important than loyalty," she declared.

"Maybe so. But . . . loyalty without independence"—Miss Paletsky shrugged—"is like a dog, no?"

With great chagrin, she conceded her teacher's point. As much as Melissa loved them, she had to admit her friends weren't exactly career-driven or brainy. In fact, they *did* have things in common with dogs (albeit well-groomed, adorable dogs), more than she'd ever realized. Melissa pressed her lips together, tracing the edge of the pillow with her finger. As much as she'd *love* to go into business with a bunch of Pomeranians, it just wasn't practical.

"I hear you," she admitted after a pause. "I hear what you're saying, yeah."

She looked up, pleased to discover an expression of pure shock on Miss Paletsky's overly powdered face. Melissa always knew she'd said the right thing when people looked shocked. She stood up, returning the collectible pillow to its proper place on the couch. Strange. The squirrel looked cuter somehow. His cheeks looked cheekier. Even his nut looked . . . nuttier.

"Alright," she agreed. "I'll try it out."

"Wonderful!" Miss Paletsky beamed, clasping her hands and pressing them to her heart.

Melissa headed for the door, then stepped down the corridor and into the sun. "Loving these pillo-o-ows!" she sang. And then she was out.

Miss Paletsky stared at the open door. As much as she would like to congratulate herself for the success with Melissa Moon, she couldn't help but think of the other three girls. Each one had come into her office convinced that The Trend Set was the worst idea ever. And—unlike Melissa—nothing Miss Paletsky could say would persuade them otherwise.

She glanced to the willow branches outside her office window. If The Trend Set fell apart, then so would a substantial part of her job. And she needed this job. It was the only thing that got her out of the house, away from Yuri, the overweight, sweat-stained owner of the Copy & Print store on Fairfax. But Yuri was an American citizen. Unless Miss Paletsky found another alternative—and found it fast—she would marry Yuri in order to obtain her Visa. She and Yuri . . . *married*! She tilted her head back, so as not to spill her tears. She hoped these girls gave their class a chance.

Maybe they could make her wedding dress.

The Girl: Petra Greene
The Getup: Floor-length almond-brown hemp skirt,
rainbow-striped Danskin leotard, yellow chiffon apron,
leopard print boho bag, four-leaf clover wrapping
paper ribbons

"Don't you care about me at all?" Petra's mother asked. She raised her carving knife, halving an apple in one resounding chop. Mounds of sliced fruit rose on either side of her like sands in the scales of justice.

"You're making *another* pie?" Petra asked, dropping her trusty boho bag to the Italian tiled floor. She leaned against the terracotta-pink refrigerator and crossed her arms.

"Daughters who *like* their mothers," Heather Greene continued, raising her knife a second time, "don't go around dressed like that. Daughters who like their mothers (*chop-chop-chop!*) *care* how they look. Because how they *look* (*chop-chop-chop!*) reflects how they were raised!"

"Why is Mommy mad?" Sofia tugged on the back of Petra's skirt.

"Mommy is unhappy with Petra's choice of attire, darling," Heather explained.

"What's *attire*?!" yelled Isabel from the other room.

"Isabel, VOLUME!" Heather bellowed from the kitchen sink, squeezing her eyes shut. After a tense pause, Isabel appeared in the doorway, struggling with the twisted strap of her navy blue pinafore. "What's *attire?*" she silently mouthed to Petra.

"She doesn't like what I'm wearing," Petra replied, kneeling to untangle her sister's strap.

"But me and Sofie picked it!"

"*Yeah,*" Sofia echoed softly. At four and a half, Sofia's sole duty involved saying "yeah" after everything her six-and-one-quarter-year-old sister said. She took her job very seriously.

"Sofie and *I,*" their mother corrected, turning to Petra. "Is this true?"

"Isabel's upset about having to wear a uniform now, so I told her, if she wanted, she could choose my clothes for me. It's not like I care."

"I can be as imaginative as I want!" Isabel declared with a sassy purse of her lips.

"I see," Heather forced a smile, flicking her eyes up and down Isabel's latest selection. Petra was dragging around a long hemp skirt in a dusty shade of brown. She paired it with a rainbow-striped strapless leotard and a 1950s apron in yellow chiffon. *Ripped* yellow chiffon. Her hair hung in two tangled braids — one slightly thicker than the other — tied with wrapping-paper ribbons.

Heather looked away from her eldest daughter and ripped open a bag of Sugar in the Raw. "Don't you have that first meeting of your fashion class today?"

"Yes." Petra grimaced. She still couldn't believe she'd been roped into such a stupid waste of time.

Her mother, however, had been thrilled.

"Don't you think you should wear something that expresses *your* sense of style, not your six-year-old sister's?" She emptied the sugar into a large metal bowl, releasing a sound like faraway school bells. "I know! What about that darling Miu Miu sundress we bought in Florence?"

"You mean the darling Miu Miu sundress *you* bought," Petra reminded her mother. "Expressing *your* sense of style, not mine?"

Heather sighed over her rolling pin, sinking all ninety-one pounds of her body weight into a pale glob of dough. "What happened to you?" she asked. She directed her gaze toward Isabel and Sofia, widening her eyes for dramatic effect. "Who stole my daughter, my *beautiful* daughter, and replaced her with this *derelict*?" The two little girls—who found grown-up vocabulary hysterical—erupted into giggles. Heather smiled, delighted. Petra barely noticed the whole exchange. She was too busy staring at the rose-pink marble counters, at the lopsided piles of flour and apples and sugar, the cracked eggshells, empty and oozing. The sight filled her with dread. Petra's mother only baked when she wasn't eating. And she only wasn't eating when she wasn't taking her medication.

"Mom. Didn't you make four pies last week?"

"I like to bake!" Heather trilled, brushing her hands. "And Sheryl's dinner party is coming up."

"Yeah, in three weeks."

"I'm perfecting a new recipe, alright? Try not to be so *critical*."

But Petra couldn't help herself. The first time her mother buckled down to "perfect a new recipe" she'd baked twenty-eight pies in one weekend. Soon after, she left for what Petra's father, Robert, referred to as a "restorative, relaxation retreat," and everyone else called "the psych ward." Three weeks later, when Petra's mother returned, Robert announced their mutual decision to adopt. According to him, his wife's depression was due to a "lack of responsibility." When it occurred to Petra it might have to do with Rebecca, her father's still-in-college bombshell receptionist, her father just laughed and laughed. "Don't be ridiculous!"

Two months later they brought home Isabel and Sofia. And Rebecca was "let go."

Petra's mother ripped a sheet of tin foil from its long, rectangular box, wielding it like a shield. "Now, which side goes up?" Petra heard her say absently. "Shiny or dull?"

"Shiny!" Sofia and Isabel clapped, jumping up and down. As a general rule, her younger daughters preferred the bright side.

"I'll be right back," Petra announced to her mother. She slipped out of the kitchen and punched 3 on her cell. "Dr. Greene's office," dripped a syrupy voice on the other line. "Please hold . . ." Before she could say *okay,* Petra was connected to a blast of vibrant, call-waiting violins: Vivaldi's Four Seasons. (As an inside joke to his patients, Dr. Greene only played one season — spring — on repeat.)

Click.

"Dr. Greene's office," the voice repeated like a machine.

"Vicki?" Petra asked.

"This is Amanda."

"Can I talk to Vicki, please?" Vicki, a cheerful, brassy blonde in her fifties, had been her father's receptionist for the past three years. She wore glitter eye shadow and punctuated her laughs with a hacking cough. The chances of Petra's father making a pass for Vicki were zero to none (not that Vicki would have him).

"Vicki left a couple of months ago," Amanda sighed. "May I help you?" Petra cupped her hand to the receiver and turned to the wall.

"Hello?" Amanda sighed.

"I'm sorry, but . . . what do you look like?" Petra blurted.

"Excuse me?"

"Pet, darling?" Heather called. At the sound of her voice, Petra almost dropped her phone. She found the END button with her thumb and slowly exhaled, then returned to the kitchen.

"You're going to be late," her mother observed.

"Sorry." Petra watched her mother pinch foil around the edges of a baking tray.

The dull side was up.

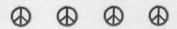

At sixteen, Petra still didn't have her license. Not because she'd failed the permit test (she'd missed only one question). And not, as everyone assumed, because of the environment (her parents promised her the brand-new hybrid of her choice). She didn't drive because she was scared. And the longer she went without a license, the more scared she got. And the more scared she got, the more she was *just like her mother*.

Which scared her the most.

"Good morning," Lola, the girls' nanny, chirped as Petra slipped into the front seat of the Greenes' gargantuan black Hummer. "Everybody ready?"

"YES!" Sofia and Isabel called from the backseat, squirming behind their seat belts.

"Almost," Petra said. "Iz? Hand me a soda, please?"

"'Kay." Isabel used both hands to pull open the built-in mini-fridge. Petra stretched her hand behind her.

"Thank you." She smiled, resting an icy Hansen's Grapefruit soda in the lap of her textured hemp skirt. She looked out the window as Lola reversed down the drive. Petra's home could best be described as the mutant love child of the Capitol Building and a New Orleans whorehouse — an overstuffed monstrosity of white columns and wrought iron, French windows and balconies and glacial staircases. The exterior walls were the creamy pink-orange color of sherbet. The hedges were stiff, symmetrical cubes. And then, in the center of it all — surrounded by sparkling white gravel and half-moon plots of petunias — her father's pride and joy: a two-ton marble sculpture of Aphrodite. Dr. Greene loved to show her off to his guests, pointing out her "many" physical flaws. "You see?" he'd chuckle, patting the statue's bulbous bottom. "Even the Goddess of Beauty could use some improvement."

Petra pressed her forehead to the window, allowing the bumps in the road to rattle her brain. She imagined one day they'd rattle her sanity right out.

Maybe they already had.

As soon as Lola dropped her off at Winston Prep's shaded south side entrance, Petra beelined for the gymnasium. The back of the gym bordered the base of a steep muddy hill; after climbing just a little ways, she could disappear from sight. She hung on to a tree branch and pulled her way up, crouching among the decomposing leaves, then cracked open her soda and emptied it on the ground. The clear liquid fizzed, scurrying downhill in rivulets. Petra pulled a bobby pin from a tangle of hair, poked it into the top of the can and made a small puncture. She could make a pipe out of anything: cans, apples, shampoo bottles, corncobs, dictionaries. At age sixteen, Petra was to pipes what Martha Stewart was to centerpieces.

She sprinkled a small amount of weed over the puncture and, using the glassy blue lighter Theo gave her during their class trip to Joshua Tree, lit up. She pulled the smoke into her lungs until her throat itched, closed her eyes, and listened to Coach Bennett yell over the steady drum of basketballs, the squeak of tennis shoes, the *sproinggg* of missed baskets.

"Lemme see some hustle, now! Lemme see some hustle! Remember, you're a winner! You're a winner! You're a winner! You're a winner!"

Petra exhaled: *winner . . . dinner . . . thinner . . . sinner . . . spinner . . . grinner . . .*

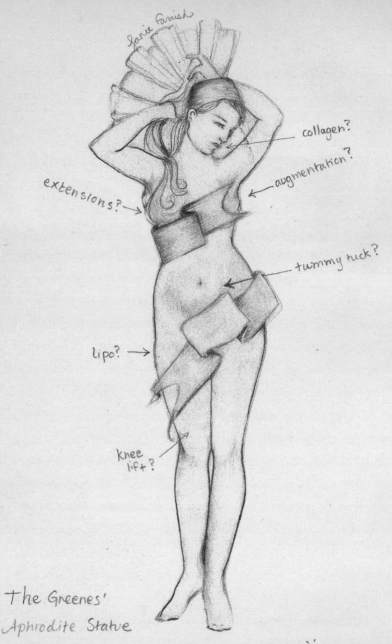

The Girl: Charlotte Beverwil
The Getup: Anna Sui silk dress with yellow rose print,
ivory slip with antique lace trim, moss green
cashmere ballet shrug, green Charlotte Ronson
platforms, gold teardrop earrings

When it came to the subject of Janie Farrish, Evan was oddly mute. In fact, the more questions Charlotte asked, the more he seemed to clam up. By the time she got down to the final three, his answers had devolved into something close to caveman grunts.

Charlotte: Did you flirt with her?

Evan: Ayanug.

Charlotte: Do you think she's pretty?

Evan: Ayanug.

Charlotte: You didn't *kiss* her, did you?

Evan: Gog! Wudjujusleemeyuhlone?

Fortunately, in addition to French, Charlotte was fluent in caveman. She understood Evan perfectly. Her brother not only found Janie attractive, he *liked* her. Which meant Janie Farrish singlehandedly achieved the dream of every girl at Winston Prep. (Every girl except Charlotte, of course.) Kate had been after Evan since she was old enough to walk. Laila amassed a not-so-secret collection of his old boxer shorts. And, three years ago, when Evan first left Winston to attend boarding school in New Hampshire, Aiden Reese cried until she lost her voice.

Charlotte felt optimistic. Janie must have gleaned Evan's feelings by now, which meant, most likely, her Ugly Duckling Complex was slowly, surely on its way out. All Charlotte had to do now was swoop in and seal the deal. She would laugh at Janie's jokes. She would compliment her shoes. She would ask her what shampoo she used. The goal was to boost confidence levels to an all-time high. If she played her cards right, Janie's grudge would be ancient history by lunch.

Charlotte arrived at school in a tight, high-waisted Anna Sui dress with a handmade print of bright yellow roses. She had cut the roses from the border of an antique tablecloth, then—with painstaking patience—embroidered them into the dress. The occasional flower she adorned with a silver sequin, creating the effect of morning dew. Charlotte liked to redefine her clothes with a personal touch. That way everything she wore was one of a kind.

According to her research, yellow roses symbolize new beginnings, forgiveness, and friendship. Charlotte got out of her cream-colored Jaguar, her cheeks flushed with anticipation. If Janie forgave her by lunch, she and Jake could take their relationship to the next level as early as fourth period. The mere thought filled Charlotte to the brim. She twirled into a little pirouette, right there in the middle of the Showroom.

But then something happened.

Charlotte spotted Jake by the Winston Willows and threw him a wave—a wave so great and sweeping and joyous that, for a moment, her hand became her heart. When her hand opened up, so did her heart. When her hand flew around, so did her heart. And together they were bursting: hello, hello, a million times hello!

But Jake didn't wave back. He took one look, sidestepped into the locker jungle, and disappeared from view.

If he was trying to be funny, Charlotte forgot to laugh.

She lowered her hand to her side. Her friends bit their lips in that *sucks-to-be-you* way.

"*What?*" Charlotte snapped.

"Nothing," they chirped together.

"Maybe he just didn't see you," Kate offered, her lips twitching into a smile. She quickly hid her mouth behind her hand.

"Of *course* he didn't see me." Charlotte frowned, smoothing the skirt of her silk dress. "The sun was totally in his eyes."

Two hours later, they crossed paths in the Breezeway, but while Charlotte smiled and slowed down, Jake just *kept on going.* "Hey." He cleared his throat, turning to face her. But still he kept on walking, one foot behind the other, stumbling backward — as if sucked into a vacuum. "I'm ... I have to ..." He pointed his thumb behind his shoulder. Charlotte stared. Last night, after they kissed (that first heart-stopping, laundry room kiss!), Jake had put his hand to the side of her face. He'd slid his thumb along the arc of her eyebrow, down the slope of her cheek until, finally, achingly, he'd found her mouth. Charlotte could still taste his thumb on her lips.

And now he was pointing it toward the door?

"I've got to . . . I'll see you . . . ," Jake sputtered, affecting utter helplessness. And just like that, he was gone.

Okay, Charlotte calmed herself. *Maybe he's late for class. Maybe he feels sick. Or maybe*—even though it would have to change course, shine through a window, and refract off a mirror—*the sun got in his eyes.*

It wasn't until he arrived to AP Physics and sat on *the opposite side of the room* that Charlotte forced herself to accept the obvious. Jake Farrish was stonewalling her. While Mrs. Bhattacharia droned on about the law of inertia, Charlotte ripped off a tiny square of paper and smoothed it on her desk. Winston banned the use of cell phones in class, so everyone resorted to the old-school tradition of passing notes. Passing notes was annoying. Not only was the act time-consuming and high-risk, it was also a huge waste of paper. Last April, the entire student body rallied to overturn the "no cell phones" rule. Their "Save a Treo, Save a Tree" campaign proved ineffective.

Charlotte shielded her tiny square of paper with a cupped hand. In the most microscopic letters she could manage, she wrote:

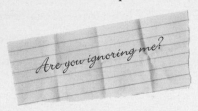

Are you ignoring me?

She prodded Kate with her pen and handed her the note. Charlotte watched her note bob from desk to desk. By the time it got to Jake she felt a little seasick. But she kept her eyes fixed, waiting for Jake's reaction. When after a few minutes he didn't look up, Charlotte surrendered and stared at the cover of her AP Physics textbook. She had nothing to do now but wait. He had to be writing some kind of lengthy, detailed explanation. Why else would he take such a long time?

At long last, she felt the point of Kate's pencil on her elbow and turned around. She snatched the note and pressed it to her lap, unwrapping with the care she would show a box from Tiffany.

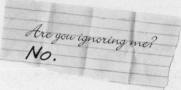

Are you ignoring me?
No.

Charlotte turned around for eye contact. Jake continued to stare at the board.

"Okay . . . it just seems like you are," she wrote back, prodding Kate a second time. And then Charlotte stared at the chalkboard. Because Jake wasn't the only one who could stare at a chalkboard as if it held the key to the universe, okay?

When the note came back, Charlotte left it on the corner of her desk, refusing to read it until — as Mrs. Bhattacharia requested of her class — she opened her textbook to page thirty-eight. She unfolded the note, doing her best to look calm.

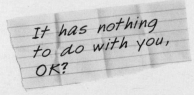

It has nothing
to do with you,
OK?

When class was over, Jake passed her desk and yanked one of her curls. His touch. She melted with relief, looked up and smiled.

But he was already out the door.

Charlotte showed up to the first meeting of The Trend Set ten minutes early. Showing up anywhere ten minutes early — let alone to something as lame as The Trend Set — could only mean one thing: she was depressed. Charlotte wanted nothing more than to sit on the windowsill and contemplate her sad, pathetic fate. The sky was blue. The courtyard was empty. The weeping willows drooped with a weight as heavy as her heart.

And then, out of nowhere, there he was. She watched him walk toward the center of the courtyard. His eyes were on the ground, his hand to the strap of his backpack. He kicked at something she couldn't see. Then he stopped and looked around. A shadow pointed from the toes of his Converse like the hand of a clock. He was alone.

Who was he looking for? Was he looking for her?

Before she could get her hopes up, Janie entered stage left, ruining the whole picture. She ran to his side and stopped, one hand on her hip, the other gesticulating. While she steamed like a teapot, Jake nodded, looking solemn. He appeared to be agreeing to something. But to what?

Charlotte unfolded Jake's note for maybe the eighty-eighth time that day.

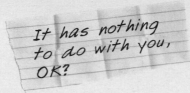

It has nothing to do with you, OK?

Her gift for analysis clicked into gear. If "it" (meaning the weirdness) had nothing to do with "her" (meaning Charlotte), then "it" (meaning the weirdness) had to do with *someone else*. Someone close. Someone with influence. Someone with an opinion that mattered.

Someone like Janie.

As recently as yesterday, Jake was torn between two allegiances: love and family. As recently as yesterday, *he'd been leaning toward love*. But now, without warning, the tables had turned. With total disregard for her pores, Charlotte pressed her forehead to the glass. Janie was still out there, ordering him around.

What was she *saying*?

Unfortunately, Charlotte could only imagine. And what she imagined stung her with rage. Of course, after so much pain and confusion, wrath was a welcome relief. Wrath sucked the blue sadness from her veins and filled them with new hot poison. She felt alive. She felt powerful.

By the time Janie stepped into the classroom, the roses on Charlotte's silk dress glowed like yellow lights. And as anyone who passed a California driver's test can tell you: yellow lights mean *Slow Down, Proceed with Caution*.

Janie had no idea what she was in for.

Janie sat at her desk and sketched a pointy high heel. When she wasn't sure what to draw, she drew pointy high heels. She left them on Post-its by the phone, paper menus in coffee shops, the corners of homework assignments. She dropped them like a trail of pointy crumbs. She could draw them with her eyes closed. Not that she dared to close her eyes. Not when *they* were there, waiting like lions before the kill. At this point, Janie felt too nervous to blink.

In the front of the classroom, Melissa Moon perched sidesaddle on the teacher's desk and perused the latest *Vanity Fair*. Her low-rise jeans and melony terry-cloth tube top framed a narrow stretch of rock-hard midriff, made terrifyingly toned by a summer of Krav Maga. Stars of light refracted from her chandelier earrings, her silver spiked heels, the "accidentally" exposed strap of her jeweled thong. All, however, was muted by the shine of her MAC Lipglass. Janie imagined the La Brea Tar Pits a thousand years from now, when paleontologists found Melissa's two lips, perfectly preserved, like mosquitoes in a glob of amber.

Charlotte chose the edge of the windowsill as her perch, staring outside like a Burmese cat. Her tight satin dress showed off a spray of yellow roses. She'd cinched the waist with a slim black belt. As usual, she looked petite, precious, and pastry-sweet. Just looking at her made Janie a bit sick to her stomach.

Janie was wearing an extra-long turquoise tank, a pair of boot-cut Levi's, and her beat-up yellow Pumas. She realized it was boring, but—after the whole miniskirt debacle—she'd developed a new appreciation for boring.

"Okay," Melissa sighed, checking the clock. She closed the magazine in her lap with a decisive slap. "I guess I'll take roll."

Janie released an airy laugh. She wasn't serious—was she?

"Charlotte Beverwil?" Melissa propped a glittery white note-book against her hip and positioned her purple pen.

"Here," Charlotte answered.

"Janie Far-eesh?"

"Fair-ish," Janie corrected her.

"Yeah—is Janie Farrish *here?*"

"Here," Janie replied to her sketchbook. Hundreds of high heels swarmed the page like bees.

"Petra Greene?"

"Oh, come on, Melissa," Charlotte grumbled from the window-sill. "*Not here.* Obvie."

"Excuse me, but if we're gonna take this class seriously, we need structure."

Charlotte spat up a small, rueful laugh. "This class is a joke."

Melissa glared with the intensity of a hair-removing laser. "Melissa Moon," she continued through clenched teeth. "*Present.*"

"Heya!" Petra leaned her somewhat bleary face into the room. "Is this . . . ?" The three girls waited as Petra took sudden interest in a beam of sunlight.

"The Trend Set," Janie finished the sentence for her.

"That is a *tentative* title," Melissa snipped, while Charlotte scoffed into the window. Melissa ignored her. "You are late," she informed Winston's favorite stoner princess.

"Whoops!" Petra smiled, dropping a dented soda can into the blue recycling bin. "Sorry." As she found her seat on the floor, Melissa jotted something into her binder.

"Did you just mark me late?" Petra looked up from the lap of her bedraggled skirt.

"Are you or are you *not* late?" Melissa slammed the binder shut. She proceeded to distribute a series of photocopied packets to the three girls. "Now that we are all *here,* we have to decide what we're all here *for.*"

Charlotte held her packet like a dripping trash bag. "What is this?"

"Copies of our Special Studies applications. Miss Paletsky thought it would be a good idea if we got acquainted with . . . *excuse me?*"

Janie followed Melissa's indignant stare to the corner of the room, where Petra had curled into a tiny ball. At the sound of her voice, the tiny ball twitched with laughter.

"What the hell is so funny?" Melissa demanded.

Petra shook her head and looked up, eyes dancing. "It's just . . . I can't believe you actually marked me late!"

"It *is* pretty lame," Charlotte agreed.

"It is not lame!" Melissa retorted.

"Ch'ello Trend Set!" Miss Paletsky leaned her face into the room. She was wearing an apple-and-worm earring set and purple eye shadow. Her hair was pulled back into a banana clip. (A banana clip!) "How's the first meeting going?"

"Good!" the girls replied in chorus, forcing their smiles.

"Wonderful," Miss Paletsky smiled, turning from the door. They waited for her footsteps to disappear down the hall.

"I don't know about y'all," Melissa broke the silence, "but I'm here to start a label. *Today*. Which means we need to create some buzz. *Today*."

The other girls looked at each other as Melissa turned toward the board with a fresh piece of chalk. In huge bubble letters she scrawled out the phrase *LAUNCH PARTY*.

"I'm sorry"—Petra knit her delicate eyebrows—"but isn't that getting a little ahead of ourselves?"

"Yeah," Janie agreed. "Shouldn't we at least have, like, a product?"

"Okay, by *buzz*"—Melissa squeezed her eyes shut—"I do *not* mean irritating, buglike noises in my *ear*."

Petra and Janie were quiet.

"At this stage of the game," Melissa continued, "our sole duty is to create an aura of suspense. We can always figure out what we do *later*."

"But . . ." Petra frowned. "If we create suspense and have nothing to show for it, aren't people gonna be —"

"Annoyed," Charlotte said.

"Okay, y'all seen that show *LOST*?" Melissa asked. The girls nodded. "You think the writers of that show have a *clue* what they're doing? You think they have *any idea* how it's all gonna end or what it all means? Hell *no*. But it doesn't matter. As long as you got *suspense,* the people are watching, and then . . . bam!" She smacked a fist into her palm. "You gotta a hit."

"Yes, but that's *television,*" Charlotte pointed out. "Who's to say the same works for fashion?"

"Can you think of a reason why it wouldn't?" Melissa asked.

Charlotte shrugged.

"Eggs-zackly." Melissa smiled.

"Ch'ello Trend Set!" Miss Paletsky called as she passed the door a second time.

"Hi!" They all waved. There was another strained pause.

"Okay," Charlotte exhaled. "We at *least* need to come up with a new name. 'The Trend Set' is killing me."

"I'm two steps ahead of you," Melissa declared. "The first part of suspense is coming up with a truly buzz-worthy name. Something smooth. Something foxy. Something *irresistible.* Any suggestions?"

Without skipping a beat, Melissa shot her hand to the ceiling. "Oh look." She observed her fluttering fingers. "I call on myself! Okay . . ." She took a breath. "What do you think of naming our label . . . now I'm just throwin' this out there, ladies!" She paused for effect. *"Melissa Moon."*

Petra and Charlotte crowed with laughter.

"Melissa Moon?" Charlotte gagged, wobbling from her precarious perch. She planted a foot on the floor for balance. "Omi-god, you *have* to be joking."

"Okay, fine." Melissa ruffled. "If you think you can do better."

"What about *Moral Fiber?*" Petra asked. Charlotte and Melissa looked at her, then at each other.

"No," they recited in unison.

Everyone sat in silence.

Janie drummed up the courage to speak. "Okay. What about something like Gwen Stefani's label? You know how the first letters of *Love Angel Music Baby* spells out *L.A.M.B.?* We could do something like that."

"Maybe we could be assigned one word each," Petra suggested.

"Okay," Melissa replied, slowly warming up to the idea.

"Each word could, like, represent who we are," Janie added.

"What would yours be?" Charlotte pinned her with a preda-tory stare. *"P* for *Pompidou?"*

At the sound of that word, Janie's ears filled with an all-eclipsing white noise. She gripped the sides of her chair. Her eyes prickled with heat. "And yours would be *H* for *Harlotte,"* she squeezed out in a gasp.

As soon as she said it, she regretted it. Rule number one with girls more popular than you: swallow their insults and move on. Never, under any circumstances, engage them in combat.

All Janie could do was hope Charlotte hadn't heard. She was too terrified to look up and find out.

"Okay!" Melissa called as the bell rang. "While you guys

brainstorm your words, I'll put the gears in motion for the launch party. I may need to contact y'all for whatever reason, so please be available on your cell or I swear on my grandmother's unmarked grave I will come to your *house* and I will *find* you. Don't think I won't!"

"Melissa," Petra muttered, "we're three feet in front of you. Do you have to raise the roof *quite* so high?"

"Just trying to make room for your big-ass head," she explained with a sarcastic smile. And then, following Petra, she was out the door.

Which left the two others alone.

"So," Charlotte began in icy containment. "*Harlotte,* hmm? That's really very clever."

Janie headed for the door. "Leave me alone," she managed in a hoarse whisper.

"Leave *you* alone?" Charlotte laughed at the irony. "What about *me?*"

Janie turned around. "What have I ever done to you?"

"I don't know, Janie," Charlotte oozed with sarcasm, "why don't you ask *Jake?*"

Janie blinked back in confusion.

"Oh, don't pull that innocent crap!" Charlotte spat.

"But I don't know what you're talking about," Janie insisted.

"Jake's ignoring me," Charlotte began. Saying it out loud was too much for her. The hot poison of wrath coursed through her in a single pulse. Her temples throbbed. *"Tell me what you said!"*

Janie shook her head in terror. "Nothing!"

"You're lying. It doesn't make sense."

"You, you really think Jake would ignore you because I *told* him to?" Janie stuttered in despair. "He's his own person!"

"What does *that* have to do with it?" Charlotte glared. "*My* brother's his own person. *He* does what I ask. In fact," she scoffed in recollection, "the only reason he deigned to talk to you was 'cause I told him to!"

"That's not true," Janie squeaked. The two girls faced each other from opposite sides of the doorway: one short, the other tall, one angry, the other terrified — like reflections in a fun-house mirror.

"Oh come *on,* Janie. You really think Evan would talk to you unless absolutely forced?"

As Charlotte whisked into the corridor, Janie sank quietly into a chair. She stared ahead, too sick to stand.

At the end of the hall, Charlotte locked herself into a bathroom stall, leaned against the cold metal door, and burst into tears. The look on Janie Farrish's face haunted her. She just looked *confused,* not to mention wounded. Charlotte's anger subsided, freeing her to entertain a new, more terrifying truth. Janie was innocent. And she, Charlotte Sidonie Beverwil, was just a bitch. As the revelation took hold, she spluttered with sorrow.

She felt farther away from Jake than ever.

The Girl: Nikki Pellegrini
The Getup: Track uniform: red nylon shorts with white
piping detail, red nylon jersey tank over white
Champion sports bra, white Adidas knee socks.
Team number: 2

"Click it or ticket, mofos!" Jake called to the jumble of knee-socked eighth-grade girls in his backseat. Nikki, Carly, and Juliet giggled, digging their seat belts from under their poly-blend team-shorted butts. Earlier that afternoon, Janie had cornered Jake in the courtyard and begged him take over her volunteer carpool — just this once. Jake was reluctant — but then she put her hand on his shoulder, looked him in the eye, and promised him he could have the Volvo all weekend.

Deal.

He put the car in reverse and looked behind him, stretching his long, lanky arm across the back of the tan vinyl passenger seat. Nikki Pellegrini, who happened to be sitting in that passenger seat, had never been so excited in her life. She closed her eyes, breathing deep the intoxicating scent of Jake Farrish's Speed Stick. The muscles across her back twitched like rubber bands. His arm was right behind her! If you thought about it (which Nikki most definitely did) his arm was practically *around* her. For the first time in her life, she was too happy to speak.

Nikki had been in love with Jake Farrish since the first moment she saw him, the second day of seventh grade, one whole year ago. At first, none of her many friends could understand. Sure, Jake was an "older boy." But could she *not* see the rancid crust of zits? The weird, pointy elbows? The disgusting rat ponytail? Well, Nikki did see. But she also didn't. There was something about Jake Farrish that — try as she might — she couldn't explain.

And then, one day, she didn't have to. His skin cleared up. His elbows smoothed out. His hair de-puffed into cutely mussed, brunette tufts. Suddenly, everyone could see what Nikki saw from the very beginning: Jake Farrish was absolutely, without-a-doubt adorable. But, as much as she enjoyed the vindication, Nikki also felt possessive. After all, she liked Jake *first,* and that gave her certain rights. Property rights.

Jake Farrish belonged to *her*.

"Hey, what's your name?" he asked, looking right at her. Nikki's heart somersaulted like a circus poodle.

"Nikki Pellegrini?"

"I got some CDs in there." Jake nodded to the glove compartment. "You wanna pick one?"

"Sure," she warbled, leaning to turn the latch. As she pulled out his square black nylon CD case, a tiny oval of cardboard fluttered into her lap. She picked it up and stared. In the middle of the tiny oval was a picture of a pregnant woman. She stood in profile, right smack in the middle of bright-red circle and line. When Jake saw what Nikki had in her hand, he laughed.

"Don't worry," he assured her. "It's from my Accutane."

"What's Accutane?" Nikki's friend Carly Thorne interrupted from the backseat.

"It's, um . . . this medication I'm taking. You have to, like, punch out the pills, and one of those cardboard things pops out. It's supposed to remind me to not get pregnant," Jake added, raising an eyebrow.

"Um . . . aren't you a *guy?*" Carly laughed while Nikki grew dark and seethed. Carly was talking about pregnancy with Jake. Which meant, ever so indirectly, she was talking about sex with Jake. Which meant, ever so indirectly, Nikki would have to kill her.

"Oh, I get it." Jake nodded with a wry smile. "Just 'cause I'm a guy, I'm not *allowed* to get pregnant. Well, let me tell you something. Just because *traditionally* pregnancy is a female role . . ."

"GUYS CAN'T GET PREGNANT!" The backseat brigade screamed in unison.

"You guys are so sexist," Jake said, shaking his head in mock disappointment. Meanwhile, Nikki could have cried. Her friends had completely taken over! Worse, Eastwood Field was at the end of this street. Which meant she had less than one minute to distinguish herself from the giggling idiots in the backseat.

"Okay, guys," Jake announced, pulling to the curb, "get the hell out of my car."

While the rest of the girls spilled out of the backseat, Nikki remained where she was. She turned toward Jake, willing their eyes to meet. Her heart beat like a sacrificial drum.

"Play this one," she said, gazing at him as she handed him a CD.

"Oh-kay." Jake covered up his dismay with a bright smile.

"Haven't listened to Jewel in while. It's actually my sister's CD," he explained. *Which she bought me as a joke,* he thought.

Nikki pushed open the heavy black door, swinging her legs into the sun. She got to her feet and turned, bending down to face Jake. Was it her imagination, or had his eyes just flicked up from her legs to her face?

"Play track number six," she blurted before she lost her nerve. Then she shut the door and ran.

Like any self-respecting dude, Jake would rather die in a snake pit than listen to Jewel. And yet, he was curious. Jake sank into his seat, rolled up the windows, pressed PLAY, and turned up the volume.

Inside my heart
There's an empty room
It's waiting for lightning
It's waiting for you

Nikki's message was pretty clear: she had a crush. And not just any crush. A *waiting for lightning* crush. Jake smiled to himself. He'd never thought of himself as lightning before. He had to admit, he liked the comparison. Sort of like Zeus.

Jake stared out the window and attempted to relocate Nikki in the crowd. The stampede of eighth-grade girls circled the running track, kicking dust into the air. As the girls neared the car, he rolled down the passenger-side window. They rumbled by him like thunder.

The Girl: Charlotte Beverwil
The Getup: Strapless pearlescent Eres bikini,
Marc Jacobs red-frame aviators, peach vintage
silk kimono with blossom detail

The Girl (sort of): Don John
The Getup: D&G metallic gold thong bikini with
matching stretch headband. Royal purple velvet cape
imported from Denmark (costume piece for *Hamlet*)

Don John needed to practice *Hamlet* for his second week of Film Actors' Boot Camp and — so long as he agreed to soliloquize by the pool — Charlotte was happy to listen. The Beverwils' pool was enormous; unless you stood on the roof, it was impossible to see the whole thing at once. Swimmers were treated to hidden grottos and secret caves, pristine waterfalls and — for parties — an underwater bar. The water was tempered with oil of eucalyptus, dead sea salts, and heated to a perfect 78 degrees all year round.

Don John, who liked to incorporate his surroundings into his performance, found Charlotte's choice of setting a little annoying. He was Hamlet, Prince of Denmark. Not Hamlet, Prince of Cabo.

Good thing he was such a great actor.

He held his compact body perfectly still — feet planted wide, small belly distended — like a toddler learning to stand. A gentle breeze coaxed a trio of blossoms from the branch of a nearby Jacaranda. They twirled through the air like light purple snow. Birds twittered and hopped. The great lawn stretched out and grew hazy in the sun. The pristine pool sparkled.

Don John clenched his Guerlain moisturized fist.

"'T'ew be or *not* t'ew be,'" he began in a moaning whisper. "'*Thaht* is the question. . . .'"

Charlotte drained the last of her calcium-fortified mimosa and reached for another. The sun blazed her Clarins sunscreen into an oily slick, and perspiration puddled in her belly button. Her sunglasses slid down the bridge of her tiny, pert nose. Fortunately, her parents' bright white art nouveau deck chairs were fitted with Canvex, a state of the art fabric specially calibrated to wick away sweat.

"'T'ew sleep! Perchahnce to dream! *Thaht* is the rub!'"

Charlotte closed her eyes and let the words seep in like toxic UV rays. Anything to block out her thoughts. Nothing — not even Don John's pathetic attempt at a British accent in 666-degree heat — compared to the misery of thinking about Jake Farrish.

If only she had a lounge chair to wick away the pain.

When he was done, Don John threw his arms back like an Olympic gymnast. "YES!" he cried out to the sky. Charlotte took a long sip from her mimosa and sighed. "Did I nail that or what?" he asked, flopping to the foot of her chair. Charlotte winced with annoyance. She hated to be jostled.

"You're amazing." Charlotte rattled the ice in her champagne flute. "The next Ethan Hawke."

"Except *tan*," Don John pointed out, pulling down the elastic waistband of his metallic gold banana-hammock. "I think I'm tanner now than when I started. You?"

"Ew!" Charlotte said, waving him away.

"What?"

"I can see your slings and arrows." She gagged, squeezing her eyes shut.

"Whoops!" Don John grinned, snapping his bathing suit back into place. He got to his feet and padded around the pool, lolling his head around his shoulders. "Okay." He swept his highlighted hair into a sweatband. "I'm going to go through it one more time. Except this time I'm going to stress every *fourth* syllable instead of every . . . *hello*."

"I'm listening," Charlotte assured him, resting an ice cube in the hollow at her throat.

"No, no . . . ," Don John murmured. "Methinks we have a guest." She propped herself on one elbow and twisted around. The ice cube clattered to the deck.

Great, Charlotte thought. *What was* she *doing here?*

"Have you or have you *not* received my texts?" Melissa asked, folding her arms across her bountiful chest. She stood right between two verdant banana trees, both of which bowed toward her like servants. She wore crisp white cotton shorts and a navy-and-white-striped silk tank with enormous gold crests and fringe at the shoulders. Her hair was tied into a blood-orange silk scarf that read VERSACE in splashy black letters. In contrast, Melissa's face appeared uncharacteristically pale and drawn—as though all the color had migrated from her complexion to the bandana around it. Charlotte might assume she was hungover, but everyone knew Melissa didn't drink. She was the president (and sole member) of Winston Women for Temperance.

"I'm sorry." Charlotte frowned as Don John excused himself to the gazebo. "I missed the part where I said you could come over."

"You think I *want* to be here?" Melissa scoffed.

"What are you saying? Is this a court order?"

"I left a million messages for you." Melissa narrowed her eyes. "I e-mailed. I texted. I did everything possible to contact you without having to see your ugly-ass face in person. *Obviously,* you left me no choice."

"I turned my phone off for the weekend," Charlotte answered coolly. The truth was a bit more complicated. She hypothesized that—just as watched kettles never boil—watched phones never ring. So, in addition to turning it off, she locked her cell in a drawer, asked Blanca to hide the key, and "forgot" about it. All she had to do was convince the universe she didn't care whether or not Jake called, and *then he would call.* It was classic reverse psychology.

"You turned off your phone?" Melissa gasped in disbelief. "Why would you *do* that?"

"It needs its beauty rest," Charlotte snipped. "Can you relate, Meliss? 'Cause you *look* like you do."

Melissa pressed her lips together and nodded. "So," she observed with a chilling laugh. "You think I could use some sleep."

Don John appeared with Charlotte's peach silk bathing kimono draped on his arm and a fresh mimosa in each hand. "Somemosa mimosa?" he chirped.

"Do you know how hard it is to plan a launch party all by yourself?!" Melissa exploded, blowing Don John two steps back by sheer force of volume.

"This is about Special Studies?" Charlotte's amused eyes sparkled. Don John fluttered his eyelashes, stunned. "Melissa. The meeting's on *Wednesday*."

"So?"

"Today is *Sunday*," Don John whispered, biting the tip of his straw.

"I *know*"—Melissa registered Don John's spandexed bulge with unadulterated disgust—"what *day* it is." She returned her attention to her classmate. "Let me explain something, okay? This class means a lot to me."

"That's really *très* touching," replied Charlotte.

"It means a lot more than some stupid once-a-week commitment."

"Well, a stupid once-a-week commitment is all I signed up for."

"How can you *say* that?" Melissa's fury boiled over. "Haven't you *ever* felt an *ounce* of passion about *anything* in your entire *life*?!"

"Oh no, she didn't!" Don John cried, bobbing his head around like a rooster. Charlotte, meanwhile, did not reply. She slipped into her kimono, knotted the ribbon at her waist, and shook her hair across her shoulders. If Melissa's flesh-melting glare made her the slightest bit uncomfortable, you'd never know it. She moved with the unhurried calm of a Buddhist monk.

Once her robe was secure, Charlotte turned to Melissa and cleared her throat.

"In regards to my 'ounces' of passion. That is a) none of your business, and b) just because I don't feel passion for a silly class does *not* mean I don't feel passion *en général,* and c) I am not used to measuring things in *ounces,* passion or otherwise. Unlike *you,*" she continued, raising her chin as high as it would go, "*I* was not raised by *drug dealers.* Now . . ." Charlotte waited for Melissa to move aside. "If you would please . . . *excusé-moi.*"

But Melissa Moon would not *excusé moi.* Instead, she swept her foot across the French terracotta tile, tipped Charlotte over her ankle, and shoved her face-first into the glittering blue pool. Don John clutched his face and screamed like a B-movie starlet. When Charlotte emerged, sputtering and gasping—her kimono *ruined*—he screamed again. Melissa lined the toes of her Valentino pumps at the pool's edge.

"Let's try this again," she said in the politest tone she could muster. "Charlotte. I need your help."

"Don John?" Charlotte gasped, pushing a slop of wet hair off her face. "Fetch Blanca."

Melissa stamped her foot. "Your *help,* Charlotte. Not your maid!"

"Blanca is a *dame de la maison*," Charlotte corrected, lifting her arm in the air. Don John pulled her to the deck like a clump of tangled seaweed. Charlotte staggered to her feet and squared her thin shoulders. A gray bead of mascara slalomed down her left cheek. "Fine," she sniffed. "I'll help you."

"Really?" Melissa gaped in surprise. She'd been expecting more of a fight. Don John looked appalled.

"Ask me now before I change my mind," Charlotte added.

Melissa cleared her throat. "Your mom's tight with Prada, right?"

"Well, she *is* the face of their fragrance."

"Do you think she could ask the Prada store on Rodeo to be the venue for our launch?"

Charlotte raised an arch eyebrow and paused. But for the dripping sound of pool water, the world was quiet.

"I can't promise anything," she answered at last. "But I can ask."

"*Thank you.*" Melissa breathed a sigh of relief. And then, with a final withering glance at Don John's repulsive bulge, she turned to go.

"Are you crazy?" Don John hissed once they were alone. "That girl pushes you into a pool and you give her what she *wants*?" Don John shook his head in quiet dismay. "Honey, that is *not* how it's done on *Desperate Housewives*."

Charlotte shrugged, pleased with her decision. All weekend she'd wanted nothing more than to not think about Jake Farrish, with no success. But then Melissa pushed her in the pool. For six glorious, transcendent seconds, Jake hadn't entered her mind once.

For that luxury, Charlotte would have given Melissa the world.

The Girl: Vivien Ho
The Getup: Frankie B. jeans, pink Uggs, pink shrunken driver's cap, white HO BAG baby tee, pink lace La Perla thong, and a rock the size of the Ritz

"So then he opens the door . . . and we walk inside . . . and there are pink rose petals *everywhere*. And, like, a million candles. And oh, the candles? Are all shaped like roses. I *know!*"

As challenging as Charlotte proved to be, the girl was small edamame compared to Melissa's ultimate nemesis. She could no longer hear Vivien Ho's voice without wincing. Every rose-petaled word out of Vivien's mouth pricked her like a thorn.

Vivien had been on the phone, relating the details of her marriage proposal to everyone from her mother to her manicurist, for eight hours straight. The marathon conversation began in her bedroom, worked its way into the kitchen, the elliptical trainer in the gym, back to the kitchen, and eventually into the front room, where she lay sprawled in the middle of their newly imported zebra skin rug. Melissa crossed the floor, stepping over Vivien as gingerly as she would a newly imported zebra turd.

"So then, he's like, 'Baby — every one of these rose petals represents a beat of my heart. Every beat of my heart belongs to you.' And I'm like, 'Seedy! That is so sweet, but *get to the point!*'

A-hahahahahahhahaha! Yeah, so he gets down on one knee and says, 'Vivien...'"

Melissa did not wait around to hear the rest. She'd heard the story so often, she could repeat it back word for word. She knew, for instance, that in any average telling, the word "baby" appeared eighteen times. The words "rose" and "petals" appeared ten times each. The phrase "I swear I was, like ..." appeared five times. As did the words "heart," "yes," and "love." The only words to appear one time each were (in order): "twenty," "six," and "carats."

They were also the only words Vivien screamed out loud. Which is why, less than two minutes later on the other side of the sprawling Bel Air estate, Melissa heard them clear as a yodel: "TWENTY-SIX CARATS!!!"

Melissa could not believe that, of all the women in the world, her father chose Vivien Ho. Vivien had been a featured background dancer in Seedy's "Lord of the Blings" video. *And she couldn't even dance.* The most she could do was stand by a wind machine and point. Still, okay. Vivien had a "look." She was a six-foot-tall, smokin' hot Korean chick with fake boobs and violet eyes that (she insisted) were 100 percent real, "just like Elizabeth Taylor's." Melissa knew better. Vivien stocked enough Bausch & Lomb for an eyeball the size of the Epcot Dome.

Melissa hadn't seen her real mom, Brooke, since she was ten years old. The courts wouldn't grant her mom visitation rights unless she proved she could hold a job and stay sober for a minimum of six months. Whenever her mother entered rehab, she sent Melissa letters on bright pink stationary — sometimes as many as three a day. She wrote in bubble handwriting, just like Melissa. She cut out pictures of celebrities and glued them to the page. *"She looks like you!"* she'd write next to a photo of Halle Berry. Or Jessica Alba. Or Lindsay Lohan. Or Lucy Liu. She ended every letter the same: *"Misses and kisses for my baby Melisses!"*

She'd promise to see her soon.

Melissa scooped up the dozing Emilio Poochie and flopped into her father's favorite chair: a custom-upholstered La-Z-Boy by Louis Vuitton (Seedy christened his creation the "Louie Boy"). She kicked off her heels and reached for the remote. There was only one escape from Hell with Vivien. TiVo.

"Excuse me!" Vivien invaded the living room wearing jeans tucked into pink Uggs, a shrunken driver's cap, and a baby tee that read STICK IT IN YOUR HO BAG. "What do you think you're doing?" she asked, snapping her jewel-encrusted cell phone shut.

"What does it look like?" Melissa punched the remote. A row of automatic window blinds clicked into place like dominoes, shutting out the stream of sunlight. An enormous plasma screen emerged from the floor.

"Muh-*lissa!*" Vivien cried. "The event planner's going to be here any minute."

"So?"

"So, you can't be in here!"

Melissa punched the remote a second time.

"I am paying this man by the minute!"

"*You're* paying him," Melissa repeated, cranking up the volume. She didn't care what was on. As long as it was loud.

Vivien stamped her foot. "I am serious!"

"Sorry, what?" Melissa increased the volume another notch. On the screen, two women with pixie haircuts and khaki capris curled up on a couch. They dipped spoons into small containers of yogurt.

"Melissa!" Vivien yelled.

The television blared: "THIS YOGURT IS *DATE WITH THAT CUTE BARTENDER* GOOD."

"I can't hear you," Melissa mouthed, pushing two fingers to the back of her ear.

Unfortunately, her father heard every word.

"Are either of you aware of something called THE MOTHER MCMUFFIN CREATIVE PROCESS?!" Seedy Moon exploded from the confines of his second-floor office like a crazed cuckoo bird. Melissa scrambled for the remote as her five-foot-six and extremely cut father paced the length of the second floor, robe flapping. Melissa and Vivien glanced at each other — briefly united by fear. Seedy just used "McMuffin" instead of the F-word. And her father only watched his language when he was truly pissed.

"How the HECK am I supposed to write — let alone maintain my DOGGONE SANITY — with you two goin' at it like MOTHER MCMUFFIN O.J. AND NICOLE?!"

"Baby," Vivien began, "we were just . . ."

"Yeah, I don't give a FRYING DUCK!" Seedy quaked at the top of the stairs. He was wearing his writing uniform: gray sweats, no shirt, a black silk bathrobe with the Korean flag on the back, and the Bugs Bunny slippers he'd worn since eighth grade. Between the two slippers, only three teeth, one eye, and three ratty ears remained. Melissa cringed as her father Hapkido-kicked the air. One slipper flew to the wall.

The two yogurt ladies closed their eyes, mouthing their ecstasy in muted silence.

"Okay . . ." He panted himself into relative calm and sat on the top stair, kneading his glossy, bald skull. "I apologize for losing my temper."

"It's okay, Daddy," Melissa assured him.

"The last thing I want to do is yell at the people I love!"

"Oh baby," Vivien replied, walking up the stairs to him. She ran her fingers under the collar of his robe, fixing him with her narrow violet eyes. One look and that was it: Seedy belonged to her. "I *tried* to talk to her," she murmured under her breath. "She won't listen."

Vivien left the room and Seedy sighed, getting to his feet. As he walked downstairs, Melissa set her jaw. She refused to look at him. Seedy cleared his throat and prodded her with his foot. Nothing. He squeezed in beside her. The leather cushion released a low ripping sound. Seedy grinned, nudging his daughter in the ribs. "That you?" he teased.

Melissa was not amused.

"'Lissa. I know how hard this is for you."

"I don't think you do."

"Vivien isn't the insensitive person you think she is," Seedy insisted. "She's just excited. And it makes her not think about stuff."

"Daddy, that woman has no problem thinking about *stuff*. It's *people* she don't think about."

"That is *not* true!" Vivien's voice yelled from somewhere down the hall.

Melissa turned to her father and continued in a whisper. "First, I'm not allowed to throw a party. Now I'm not allowed to *watch TV*? It's like you're getting married and I'm not allowed to exist!"

"You can exist," Seedy confided in a low voice. "Just exist on the DL."

"Daddy, *what*?" Melissa's jaw dropped. "How am I supposed to do that?"

"If you gotta watch TV, watch it in your room. And I told you, if you wanna have a party, go ahead! Have a party. Just not at the house."

"You know," Vivien reappeared with a Diet Coke in her hand. "I was thinking about that party of hers. . . ."

"That party of 'hers,'" Melissa repeated for her father. "Hear that? She talks like I'm not even here!"

"Like *she* doesn't?!" Vivien gasped, pointing her fire engine–red finger-talon. "She just called me 'she'!"

"Okay stop!" Seedy yelled. Two more seconds of this and he might implode. He gripped his head in his hands and visualized a quiet stream. "Vivien," he continued in a calm voice. "You were saying?"

"I was saying," his soon-to-be-bride continued, "since she can't have the party at the house, she could try reserving some tables at the Bel Air Public Park. People have parties there all the time."

"At the *park*?!" Melissa trembled with rage. "Are you for real?!"

"Vivien's just trying to help." Seedy patted her arm.

"Daddy!" Melissa whirled on her father. "I am launching a label! *Not* a piñata!"

"Well she can't have the party here!" Vivien declared.

"I'm *not* having it here!"

"Seedy!" Vivien pleaded.

"Would you please listen to me?!" Melissa screamed at the top of her lungs. *"I'm having it at the Prada store!"* Her announcement exploded across the family room like a sonic boom. The three of them stared at each other in silence. Vivien stood upright and perfectly still, like a diver at the edge of the board.

"What did you say?" she whispered.

In last month's issue of *Vogue,* Prada described their spring handbag collection as, "chic, intelligent . . . very modern. Simply put: the Anti–Ho Bag." For days, Vivien staggered around in shock. She felt like she'd been spiked through the heart. To make her feel better, Seedy banned everything Prada from the house. Even the word itself.

"I'm sorry," Melissa apologized to her father, only his head was back in his hands. "I meant to say the P-word store."

"Did you put this together for her?" Vivien squeaked with an accusing glare. Seedy held his hands up in surrender.

"Don't look at me."

"Okay." Vivien nodded. "I won't." She turned on the heel of her pink Ugg and headed for the doorway. "I'll never look at you *again*!"

Seedy got to his feet, fixing his daughter with a severe stare.

"It was Charlotte's idea," Melissa blurted. "Please don't be mad."

"Charlotte?" Seedy furrowed his brow. "Who's Charlotte?"

"My colleague. For my, I mean, *our* fashion label."

"Your *colleague,*" Seedy repeated, his face melting with gradual pride. He shook his head and planted a kiss on the crown of his only daughter's head. "Alright," he said.

As her father shuffled off in the direction of his high-maintenance fiancée, Melissa smiled. Without wasting another second, she pulled her white Special Studies binder from her black Fendi tote and flipped it open. At the top of the page she'd written *"Word Ideas for New Label."* She pressed her purple pen to the end of a growing list. She had one more word and letter to consider. *T.*

For *Triumph*.

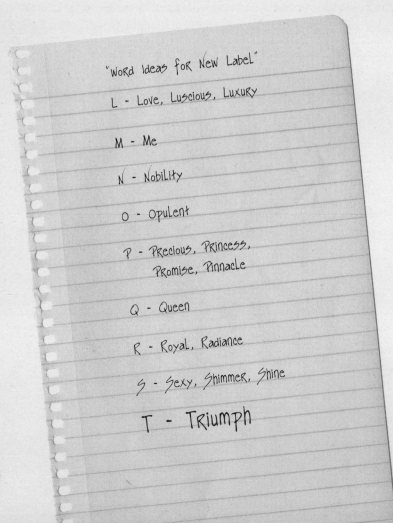

"Word Ideas for New Label"

L - Love, Luscious, Luxury

M - Me

N - Nobility

O - Opulent

P - Precious, Princess, Promise, Pinnacle

Q - Queen

R - Royal, Radiance

S - Sexy, Shimmer, Shine

T - Triumph

The Girl: Janie Farrish
The Getup: Used Diesel jeans, army-green Converse All-Stars, Joe Peep's Pizza 100 percent cotton t-shirt, bright orange baseball helmet

If you're a Valley kid, chances are you've spent a few birthdays of your life at the Sherman Oaks Magic Castle. Among its many treasures, the Magic Castle counts three miniature golf courses, an arcade, bumper boats, batting cages, a few half-dead, squawking ducks, and a moat. Everything, including the ducks, dates back to 1976. The grounds smell like chlorine, peanut shells, Dr Pepper, and sweat. The only thing castle-like about Magic Castle is the moat and drawbridge. The only thing magic about it is nothing.

Can you blame Janie for being surprised when her brother stopped by her bedroom door and asked her if she'd like to go?

"What about Tyler?" Janie asked, looking up from her desk. "Don't you have guy friends anymore?"

"Do you wanna come or what?"

Fifteen minutes later they were there.

"So"—she smirked, tucking her glossy brown hair into her rented baseball helmet—"this is what you do with your Sunday nights."

"Whatever, dude." Jake pointed at her with his bat. "You're here too."

"What about *Charlotte*?" Janie minced, tossing her brother a token. "Shouldn't you be with her?"

The coin ricocheted off Jake's hand.

"I don't know." He swept the coin from the ground and dropped it in his worn-out jeans' pocket.

"Is it true you're ignoring her?"

"What?" Jake stepped into a fierce-looking practice swing and frowned. "Who told you that?"

"She did."

"Great." He sighed. All he'd needed was a *little* time to think. Now he was "ignoring" her?

Jake swung the gate to the batter's box and slammed his way inside.

"Hell-*lo*?" His sister pointed to the sign above the gate. "You're in the one-hundred-miles-per-hour zone?"

"Yeah." Jake shook the token into the meter. "I can read."

The batting machine whirred to life like an enormous electric fan. Jake readied his bat and stared ahead. He could hear the ping of distant pitches, the rattle of the chain-link fence, the clap-'n'-holler of nice dads, the clap-'n'-holler of jerk dads. Jake blocked it out, focusing until — all at once — the ball popped, hurtling toward him like a comet. He swung.

He missed.

"This is way too fast!" Janie yelled, clutching the fence behind him.

"Thanks for the report, Dr. Obvious!" Jake scowled, tapping

the plate. The second pitch sang by him before he could even lift the bat. He clenched his jaw. He could do this. He could do this. All he had to do was *want it*.

Ten minutes later the batting machine rattled and slowed to a wheezing stop. Jake tipped his head back, staring through the ratty veil of black netting to the sky. Twenty-five pitches. Twenty-five chances.

He had missed every one.

"DAMMIT!" He threw his bat to the ground. Janie peered around anxiously. One did not just throw their bat at Magic Castle. Throwing one's bat at Magic Castle was like an act of high treason. People got *kicked out*. Jake glared at the 100 mph sign and balled up his fist.

Janie gasped.

But it was too late. He had already sent his fist flying. "OW!" he warbled, wringing his hand like a limp dishrag. Janie blinked at the battered sign, wondering which of the many small dents was the one left by her brother. She couldn't believe he'd just punched a sign. What did he think this was? A musical number in *West Side Story*?

"Are you okay?" she asked once her brother stopped cursing. She unlatched the gate, approaching him in timid steps.

"I'm fine," he muttered, picking the balls out with the toe of his Converse. They rolled down the long slope of concrete like beads of sweat.

"Well, don't be upset. No one can hit a hundred miles per hour."

"Some people can."

"Not unless they practice," Janie pointed out.

"I don't have enough time to practice!" Jake cried in pure wolf-man despair.

She stepped aside, allowing him to steam through the parking lot, hands heavy in his pockets, kicking bottle caps, ticket stubs, candy wrappers — any little thing that got in his way. What had gotten *into* him?

When Janie found Jake, he was slumped in the driver's seat with the windows rolled up, picking at a patch of duct tape on the lower left-hand dash. She opened the passenger door and slid into the seat. "Jake," she began quietly, watching her brother clench and unclench his jaw. "What's going on?"

He hooked his finger to the lip of the steering wheel and sighed. "Nothing."

"Jake." Janie leaned in confidentially. "You're listening to *Jewel.*"

He laughed. "I know, dude."

"You *hate* Jewel," she reminded him. At this point, she was truly concerned.

Jake didn't respond. He was too busy thinking about Nikki. Nikki and her shy smile. Nikki and her big blue eyes. Nikki and her little red team shorts. She was nowhere near as hot as Charlotte, but wasn't that exactly the point? Nikki made him feel safe. Like he could kiss her without shaking. Like he could touch her and not pass out. Like he might be able to see her naked without dissolving into a completely spastic dork-meister.

The more he thought about making out with Nikki, the better it sounded. Which wasn't to say he didn't want to be with Charlotte. He did.

He just needed to get some practice in first.

"Jake," Janie interrupted his thoughts, "I think we should go?"

He reached for the door. "Just one more round, okay?"

"I don't know." She hesitated.

"Relax." Jake smiled, cracking the door. "I'll stick with the easy pitches."

there was a little girl
who had a little curl
right in the middle of her forehead...
and she sucked.

fresh water pearl necklace
(I bet she killed the
oysters herself)

CHARLOTTE BEVERON

THE FRENCH WENCH

Louis Vuitton clutch
(for evil clutches)

Assume
"FIRST POSITION"

← L'autre Chose boots

YM

"The second session of The Trend Set—*which is a working title, subject to change*—is now in session," Melissa announced, rapping her wooden desk with a small silver Tiffany hammer.

"Okay, what is *that*?" Charlotte asked from her designated spot on the windowsill.

"It's a gavel," Melissa answered with a hard look. "In case certain people get out of order."

"Whatever do you mean?" Charlotte replied innocently, smoothing the skirt of her black lace baby-doll pinafore. She'd paired the pinafore with a silk shirt with cap sleeves and a mao collar. The collar was marcasite gray, the same as her peep-toe flats. Everything else was black. It wasn't conscious, but—ever since Jake went AWOL—Charlotte's outfits grew progressively darker, swallowing her up like a cloud. Her red patent leather belt and matching Hermès clutch were the only evidence of a happier, sunnier life. It was just a matter of time before they were swallowed up too.

"So," Melissa continued, hooking the silver gavel to her new Gucci tool belt. The belt sat low on her hips, emphasizing the waist of her pink faded Joe's jeans. To complete her "construction worker goes to Milan" look, she tucked the jeans into her tan Manolo Timberlands with the spiked heels. "Did everyone come up with a super-great word for our label?"

She picked up a piece of bright blue chalk and turned toward the wall. "Mine's *D*," Melissa announced, scrawling the letter on the board. She brushed her hands. "For *Diva*."

When no one volunteered to go next, Melissa looked at Janie.

"Oh, mine's *T*," Janie coughed up. "For *Tall*."

"Tall?" Melissa fluttered her eyes shut and tried to breathe. How boring could one person get? Before she could object, Petra made things ten times worse.

"Mine's *U*," she announced. "As in *Ugly*."

Melissa stared in disbelief. Petra was wearing a paint-smeared blue canvas smock over jeans and brown pleather "goddess" sandals. Her shoes looked comfortable, a quality Melissa found deeply suspicious. After all, what was *comfortable* but another word for . . .

"Ugly," Melissa repeated. "You want the word *ugly* to be associated with our label."

"Yeah, I do."

"This is a *fashion* label, okay? The whole *point* of fashion is, like, the *opposite* of ugly."

Petra held her ground. "I guess that's a matter of opinion."

"*Fine,*" Melissa surrendered, wielding the blue chalk like a dagger. She slashed the board in angry strokes. By the time she finished, the chalk had broken twice. She turned to Charlotte and braced herself. "Please have something good."

"Mine's *R*." Charlotte shrugged. "As in *Rich*."

Melissa exhaled. "*Thank* you."

"Typical," Petra grumbled from her place on the floor. "All anyone cares about at this school is money."

"I'd like to point out *rich* can also mean *decadent,*" Charlotte replied. "As in *this crème brulée is so rich.*"

Petra rolled her eyes. "I'm sure that's how you meant it."

"Okay," Melissa began, going over their list of words. "We got a *D,* a *U,* a *T,* and an *R.* Anyone get a word from that?"

The girls stared at the letters for what seemed like a very long time. Outside the closed door, the high-pitched shrieks of a few ninth-grade girls rose and fell. Then, after a moment of passing footsteps, it was quiet again.

"Oh," Janie exclaimed, instantly regretting it. She really didn't mean to say "oh" out loud.

"What?" Melissa asked, moving to the front of the desk.

"No." Janie shook her head. "Never mind."

"Oh, come on." Melissa stamped her work-boot heel. *"What?"*

"Um . . ." Janie stuttered after a tense pause. She couldn't take the pressure of Melissa's stare much longer. "It, um . . . it kind of spells . . . you know . . ."

"Oh, spit it out!" Charlotte groaned.

Janie swallowed. "It spells *turd.*"

"What?" Melissa whirled toward the board. "It does not!"

"It totally does." Petra cackled with delight. "Omigod, that's awesome."

"No, that is *not* awesome!" Melissa sputtered. Here she was, organizing the launch party of a lifetime, and for what? A start-up fashion company called Tall Ugly Rich Diva? Aka *TURD*? No, no, no, and *hell's no*! "We have to come up with a new set of words. Right now."

"Do we have to?" Petra whined. "My brain hurts."

"Wow, I feel for you." Melissa frowned with contempt. "I really, *really* do. But *unfortunately,* no one *else* is gonna do the thinking for us!"

"Well, maybe they should," Charlotte replied, failing to contain her exasperation.

"Is that supposed to be funny?"

"Not unless you think good business strategy is funny."

Melissa sighed and collapsed into her seat. "Okay. I'm listening."

"Alright." Charlotte nodded. "Since we're having so much trouble with a name, why don't we do something like hold a contest? Whoever comes up with the best name for our label could, like, get something."

"Like what?" Petra asked, lifting her disheveled head from her folded arms.

"I don't know." Charlotte shrugged. "Like a t-shirt?"

"A t-shirt." Melissa nodded in agreement, pacing the room. "Like, a couture t-shirt with the name of the label?" Melissa drew an imaginary line across her chest, indicating the label in question.

"Exactly." Charlotte also nodded. "Not only do label t-shirts look professional and designer, they also provide free advertising."

Melissa clapped her hands. "Whoever wears the shirt will become a walking billboard!"

"As long as the shirt's one hundred percent cotton and sweatshop labor–free . . . ," Petra began.

"Yeah, yeah, of course," Melissa consented hurriedly. "So," she continued, "we're all agreed on the t-shirt?"

"Yay," Charlotte sang.

"Yay," Petra chimed in.

"Um . . ." Janie stared into her lap. *What about making a couture dress?* she couldn't help thinking. Not only was a couture dress a *much* better item than a t-shirt, she could secretly lend it to Amelia. Amelia would have her dress for Spaceland, The Trend Set would have their "thing," and everyone would be happy. Then again, the t-shirt idea had been Charlotte's. If Janie dissented, she could only imagine what Pompidou-themed ills were in store.

"Well?" Charlotte asked with a catlike smile. Janie's heart fluttered like a canary.

"Yay," she answered in a weak whisper.

Melissa thwacked the desk with her silver gavel.

"Alright!" She pumped her fist. "If you guys wanna e-mail me your guest lists tonight, I'll go ahead and put the invitations together. You can reach me on my Web site: *www.MoonWalksOnMan .com.* Peace."

As Melissa sashayed toward the exit, the bell rang long and loud and clear.

The Girl: Amelia Hernandez
The Getup: Oversized vintage red-and-white striped shirt, white leather belt with silver hoop buckle, gray skinny Lux jeans, vintage red pointy-toe pumps, silver bangles, red plastic hoop earrings

"What do you think?" Amelia asked, tilting the Goodwill's rickety mirror to get a better view of her black leather–clad ass. "I'm looking for a Debbie Harry in her heyday sorta thing."

When Amelia started Creatures of Habit, her first priority — after securing actual living, breathing band members — was to buy a badass pair of black leather pants. But after eight months of solid searching, she remained without a badass pair of black leather pants. She was an embarrassment to her profession. A doctor without a lab coat. A sailor without a cap. A drag queen without a frosted wig.

Whenever she got close to giving up, she'd settle down to a long night of VH1's *We Love the Eighties,* and that was all it took. Her craving for leather would start all over again. With one eye on the TV, she'd call up Janie and demand they meet on Melrose, Venice Beach, or — in today's case — the Goodwill on Magnolia Boulevard.

"Who's Debbie Harry?" Janie asked, peering from behind a rack of old summer camp t-shirts. She'd been considering a sky-blue t-shirt with a picture of a beaver, a boat, and a rainbow.

"Are you kidding me?" Amelia stopped, appalled at her ignorance. "The lead singer of Blondie!"

"I thought her name was Blondie."

"Omigod." Amelia pressed her hand to her head and a collection of bangles slid down her wrist. "Who *are* you?"

"Whatev." Janie frowned, her hand on the t-shirt rack. "You look like Ashlee Simpson in those pants."

Amelia gasped. "I do?" She darted into the fitting room, slamming the door behind her. Janie laughed at the sight of her staggering feet under the door. When it came to removing Ashlee Simpson from her body, Amelia refused to spare a single second.

"Oh! I forgot to tell you!"

"What?" Janie asked.

Amelia emerged from the fitting room in less than ten seconds. "I got the invitation to your launch party last night."

"Oh no. Don't laugh."

"I'd never," Amelia said, re-examining her reflection *sans* pants. "It's just . . . you realize I can't make it."

"What?" Janie fought off a spasm of panic. "Why not?"

"It's the same night as my show."

"What?!" Janie squawked.

Amelia shook her head. "I had a feeling you didn't realize."

Janie wandered to a corner bench and collapsed. She stared ahead in a daze. "I can't believe this."

Amelia put her arm around her friend. A single tear formed in the corner of her right eye. She couldn't *believe* she was missing

Amelia's show. She might as well give up on seeing Paul Elliot Miller ever again.

"You can always come *after* the fashion thing. We'll still be hanging out." Amelia looked sympathetically at her friend.

"Really?" Janie exhaled with trembling relief. When Amelia saw how quickly her friend was consoled by the option of hanging out after, she removed her arm to smack her on the shoulder.

"All you care about is Paul!"

"No! I really am upset about missing your show. Besides," Janie pointed out, "it's not like you've said anything about missing my launch party."

"Point." Amelia got to her feet and stretched. "You ready to go?"

"Sure." Janie nodded. But then her eyes widened and she grabbed Amelia's arm and yanked her behind a skirt rack.

"Ow!" Amelia yelled, rubbing her abused arm.

"Shhhhh . . ." Janie crouched low to the floor, pulling her best friend down with her.

"What's going on?" Amelia whispered, craning her neck to get a look. "Is there . . ."

She yanked her down again. *"Don't,"* she ordered through clenched teeth.

"Janie?"

Janie and Amelia glanced up at the same time. Even though she'd never met him, Amelia knew exactly who it was. He was wearing a distressed blue SEX WAX t-shirt, brownish cords, and black flip-flops. He forked his fingers through his golden hair until it sat like a lopsided thatch of straw. His skin had the smooth luster of a beach stone, and when he smiled, the sandy stubble on his well-defined jaw caught the light. He actually glittered.

"Thought that was you." He smiled.

"I'm just . . . I dropped something," Janie explained, making a show of searching the dusty floor. Amelia brushed her hands and got to her feet.

"I'm Amelia," Janie heard from above.

"Hey . . . Evan."

"Found it!" Janie swept something invisible into her pocket and got to her feet.

"Okay," she said, taking Amelia's hand. She nodded to Evan. "Well. Bye."

"Wait!" Evan laughed. Janie frowned. She knew Evan only talked to her because of Charlotte, so why talk to her now? She looked into his pool-green eyes for some kind of clue. She looked away. His eyes were far too similar to Charlotte's for comfort. It was like she was *in* there, watching.

"What?" she asked.

"I don't know." Evan scratched the back of his ankle with the toe of his flip-flop. "I just . . . um . . . what are you doing here?"

"Shopping," Amelia replied from behind a nearby rack of tartan kilts.

"No, we are *not* shopping," Janie blurted. She could *not* believe Amelia just admitted to shopping at the Goodwill! "She's totally joking," she explained, avoiding Amelia's confused expression. "We're donating."

"Me too," he replied, hugging a Barneys shopping bag to his chest. "Can I ask you guys a question?" They watched Evan crouch to the ground and dig through the bag. He pulled out a lavender silk Chloé halter and a beautiful Cacharel skirt in white cashmere, discarding both in sad, crumpled heaps. And then, just when things couldn't get more painful, he pulled out a pair of pants. And not just any pair of pants.

The perfect pair of badass black leather pants.

Amelia stared at Janie with the plaintive look of a starving animal. Janie shook her head. No *way* would she allow her friend to dig through Charlotte Beverwil's hand-me-downs. Especially in front of Charlotte's not-to-be-trusted brother.

"Do you guys know what this is?" Evan pulled a jade green something from the bag by a long, silky ribbon.

"It's a corset," Amelia answered, still staring at the leather pants.

"Cool," Evan replied, smoothing a Goodwill donation form across his knee. He clicked his pen, crossed out the word *"vest"* and replaced it with *"coursette."*

No one bothered to correct his spelling.

"Well, thanks," he said, refolding the form. Then he re-forked his fingers through his hair and flashed his most devastating, shamelessly dimpled smile to date. Janie picked dirt from her fingernail and stared into space. Evan sighed. It was weird. The more this girl ignored him, the prettier she got.

Why *was* that?

"Late," he surrendered with a lift of his chin.

Janie and Amelia watched Evan exit and lope along the front window in the direction of his mud-splattered forest green Range Rover. As soon as he was gone, Amelia clapped her hands and did a little jig. "Yay! I *have* to try those on!"

"You're not serious," Janie gasped in disbelief.

"Did you *not* see those things?" Amelia spluttered, her disbelief equal if not superior to her best friend's. "They were perfect!"

"Amelia," Janie commanded. "No!"

"But *why?*"

"Um . . . your dignity?"

"Dignity has nothing to do with this!" Amelia fumed, storming for the exit.

"Omigod, 'Melia!" Janie followed her through the exit and out onto the sidewalk. The door slammed behind her with a joyous jangle of bells. "What if someone saw you wearing those pants?! What if they like, *recognized* them and Charlotte *found out?!* Don't you see how humiliating that would be?"

"Omigod," Amelia groaned. "For *who?* You or me?"

"It doesn't matter!"

"Yes, it does! See, I don't *care* what that girl thinks. *You* care! It's all about *you!*"

"Well, easy for you to say!" Janie defended herself. "*You* don't have to be in class with her. You don't know what it's like!"

"Like that's my fault?!"

"Yeah, actually! IT IS!" Janie exploded on the street corner. "I wouldn't even be *in* that class if it weren't for you!"

Amelia walked until she found her bus stop and plunked herself down. A million posters of Britney Spears plastered the face of a stucco wall. Her front teeth were blacked out with marker. Her foreheads were marked with *SLUT* or *SKANK*. The posters curled and cracked in the sun. Janie and Amelia stared ahead, frowning in the face of Britney's million mutilated smiles.

"If you hate it so much" — Amelia finally broke the silence — "why don't you just drop out?"

Janie stared at the ground. A clump of tough yellow grass sprouted through a crack in the concrete and she touched it with the toe of her Converse. "We were gonna make that dress."

"Were we?" Amelia asked. Janie kept staring at the ground. She'd made no plans to make that dress, and Amelia knew it.

"See?" Amelia shook her head. "I got you into this grossness, but the reason you're still in it has nothing to do with me. It's *you*, Janie. You devote yourself to people who reject you."

"*That is not true.*" Janie's eyes smarted with tears.

"Whatever."

As the Metro rounded the corner, Amelia got to her feet. Within moments, the grumbling bus pulled to the curb, sounding a long, high-pitched whine. The tall vertical doors hissed open and locked with a snap. Janie watched her friend climb the dirty black stairs and clamber along the aisle. She ducked into a seat on the opposite side, disappearing from view. As the bus pulled away, Janie swallowed. A bead-sized lump lodged inside her throat.

For the first time in the history of their eight-year friendship, Amelia hadn't waved goodbye.

The Girl: Charlotte Beverwil
The Getup: Sacred Ceremonial Garb

Charlotte liked to claim she was born a century late. She imagined herself as a drowsy-eyed courtesan in 1910 Paris, or perhaps a depressive ballerina, or perhaps a rosy-cheeked nun who runs off with a daring young sculptor named Sebastien-Pièrre du Pont. "But you wouldn't have *liked* it, Blue Bear," her father declared in his booming, theatrical voice (he'd invited Charlotte into his study for one of his monthly fireside chats). "All that disease! The bad teeth! The horse shit in the streets! And besides," he chortled to himself, "a hundred years ago, actors were treated no better than whores!"

Charlotte added "actors treated like whores" to her list of positives.

Toward the tail end of eighth grade, Charlotte's romance of times past began to show up in her closet: silk stockings and chemises, hunting coats and corsets, velvet capes and lace gloves, a bustle. Not that she ever wore this stuff. Not in public anyway. She dressed up in the privacy of her own room and stared deep into her own reflection. "Sebastien-Pièrre," she would whisper with all the longing she could muster. "Take me away from this place." And then she'd press a hand to the mirror, kissing the glass until it fogged.

Seriously.

Of course, as soon as Charlotte landed her first real-life boyfriend, she broke up with the mirror and never gave their time together another thought. But then Jake Farrish stopped calling, and Charlotte reconsidered. With careful, measured movements she'd draped herself in a black widow's veil from 1905, clutched a rosary from 1906, and faced her first and only dependable love: herself.

"I loved you, Jake," she sighed, staring deep into her mirror. "But you have parted for another world. And so I say . . . *adieu*."

The next day she bounded out of bed, blasted an old Beck CD, and danced until she actually laughed out loud. Her little funeral had done the trick! Now that the relationship was officially dead and buried, that was it. She was free!

Charlotte slipped into her newest Blumarine dress and headed for school with all the sparkle of a freshly corked bottle of champagne. Sometimes, she realized, the future wasn't so bad.

The Girl: Nikki Pellegrini
The Getup: Paige "Laurel Canyon" jeans, Ella Moss
extra-long magenta cotton tank, silver Joie ballet
flats, Kate Spade wicker lunch tote

Jake leaned against a tree, cracked open his Physics text, and
cursed, quietly, in the key of F. Jake, like many Winston students,
studied according to the time-honored Procrastination Method.
If you saw him studying at 7:48 a.m., his test, most likely, was
at 9:00 a.m. He dropped into his books like a bomb, his heart
ticking like a countdown. And the slightest disturbance — from a
mild *good morning* to a locker *click* to a gentle *purr* of a far-off
Jaguar — could set him off.

As Charlotte pulled her cream-colored Jag into the Showroom,
and the purr grew into a full-fledged growl, Jake's hair-trigger panic
exploded. Without thinking, he stopped, dropped, and — clutching
his Physics text to his chest — rolled into a nearby hedge. He
wished he could say this was the first time he'd ducked for cover.

It wasn't.

Of course, hidden as he was, Jake could still hear. At the ring-
ing chime that was Charlotte's laugh, he pushed aside the dense
branches, picked a leaf from his hair and squinted. She stood at a
distance of twenty feet, leaning against her left fender, her foot
against the wheel. The morning sun shone through the flimsy fabric of her flowery dress. A triangle of light glowed behind her

knee. Jake swallowed, hard. He had never seen anything so beautiful, so pure. . . .

And so *completely* surrounded by tools.

Tim Beckerman crouched at her feet, tilting his head and brushing back his sensitive, emo-boy bangs. *Tool.* Theo Godfrey sat up on the hood, his skateboard in his lap. *Tool.* Luke Christie pushed up his shirtsleeve, indicating a small space on his bulging bicep. (Luke was forever inviting girls to brainstorm his next tattoo.) *Tool.* But Charlotte allowed them to crowd her; she even seemed to enjoy it. Jake frowned. Why the hell was she giggling so hard? It's not like any of those guys were funny.

"Hi, Jake."

Jake tore himself from the overpowering spectacle of Charlotte to find his new little friend, Nikki Pellegrini, smiling down at him. He blinked.

"I was wondering," she began in a rush, "would you wanna have lunch in the projection room today? It's empty on Fridays." *And dark,* she thought with a deep, happy blush.

To Nikki's increasing amazement, she and Jake had been having lunch together for a week straight. It started when he invited her to the roof of the gym so she could educate him a little on the subject of Jewel. At first she thought he was joking. He wasn't. Nikki talked music for twenty minutes (in addition to Jewel she really liked Sarah McLachlan), and Jake totally listened to what she had to say. When she was done, they gazed down at the glinting river of cars in Coldwater Canyon, the long slope of the hillside, and the cityscape beyond. Never had the wide plain of telephone poles, billboards, and traffic looked so beautiful. After a long pause, Jake cleared his throat. "Wouldn't it be awesome if the iPod people, like, came alive and leaped down from the billboards, wreaking havoc on Los Angeles?" It wasn't the kind of line that worked for everyone.

It worked for Nikki.

For the rest of the week, the lunches didn't stop. Tuesday, they sipped sodas on the roof. Wednesday, they shared bags of chips in the stairwell. And Thursday, in the quiet shade behind the lockers, they split a pastrami sandwich. For some reason, Jake insisted they keep their lunches secret (they ate where they would not be seen). As much as Nikki found the secrecy of their lunches confusing, it also gave her a thrill. She felt special somehow, chosen — like a sacred cow.

"Not now, Nik," Jake muttered, his eyes still fixed on Charlotte. Why the hell was she scruffing Tim Beckerman's hair? The whole notion of Charlotte's hand on Tim's body made Jake sick.

"Oh." Nikki panicked. Maybe she should have waited for Jake to invite *her* to the projection room. Then again, she'd waited *all last week* — and *someone* had to ask. The projection room was the perfect spot: dim and quiet, warm and cramped — private. It was where lunching types went to share *more than just a sandwich*. If her instincts were correct, her hair soft, and her lips freshly glossed (she picked Lancôme Juicy Tube in Caramel Delight), Jake would just *have* to kiss her.

"You wanna take a rain check?" she asked with a brave smile.

"Huh?" Jake said in a semi-absent way. Before she could respond, he moved past her. Nikki followed him with her eyes, her heart sinking. She knew where he was headed. Charlotte Beverwil wore a sun-drenched flowered shift dress and brown leather boots that laced to the knee. Her hair fell in shiny dark ringlets around her laughing face. Nikki had never seen anyone more gorgeous. As Jake broke into a trot, she wiped the slick of gloss from her lips. The message was all too clear: she was nothing more than procrastination.

Charlotte Beverwil was the big exam.

Jake paced around the Showroom in easy, measured steps. He had to give her ample time to look up and happen to see him. He would happen to see her too, smile, wave, and approach. After two laps, however, Charlotte had yet to glance in his direction. Jake opted for an alternative tactic.

"Hey," he began, clearing his throat. Charlotte didn't seem to hear him. She was too busy listening to Joaquin Whitman.

"So I'm staring into this cup of noodles, right? And fuggin' Ziggy's jammin' with all these cellos and shit, and I'm, like, totally trippin', cause all of a sudden the noodles turn into these craaaazy dreads, and the little dehydrated carrot things are, like, his *eyes*—"

"Shut up, Whitman," Luke said. Charlotte tilted her head back and laughed.

"Dude, I'm serious!" Joaquin insisted. "That shit's, like, instant cup of *demon,* man."

The bell rang and the tools dispersed to opposite sides of the lot, unlocking their luxury cars with electric chirps and grabbing books from their places in the trunk. Jake followed Charlotte around her car. She popped open the back, located her notebook, her organizer, her *L'Étranger,* and dropped them into her black vinyl Chanel shopper.

"Hey," Jake said again. Charlotte slammed her trunk shut. Her eyes fixed into the depths of her bag; she walked right past him. "Charlotte," Jake walked to keep up with her. "Are you gonna talk to me?"

"Why should I talk to *you?*" she flashed. "Do I look crazy?"

"A little," Jake teased. She pinned him with a warning glance and steamed ahead. "Did I mention you look like an extremely *attractive* crazy person?" he added, his tone hopeful. If Jake ever realized the error of "taking some time to think," he realized it now, trailing in the wake of this fed-up, fuming, and furious female.

"Ugh!" Charlotte groaned. "You know what you are, Jake? You're like that guy in *A Beautiful Mind.* The guy Russell Crowe *thinks* is his best friend, only to find out . . . wait! *He's a hallucination.*"

Jake knit his eyebrows. "I think you've been talking to Joaquin too long."

"No, I've been talking to *you* too long," she snapped, shifting the strap of her shopper from one shoulder to the other. "If you'll excuse me. It's time for me to take my little Russell Crowe pill and make you disappear."

"You have a Russell Crowe pill?"

"Of course I don't. But if I did, I would take it like *that*." She snapped her fingers in his face.

"Okay." Jake unzipped his backpack. "Just wait a second." Sometime last year, if he remembered correctly, he'd spilled a box of Sweet Tarts and never bothered to clean them out. Sure enough, the Sweet Tarts were still there, buried in the darkest, lintiest corner of the pocket. He pinched one between his fingers. Once upon a time the Sweet Tart was a bright green — now it was more of an algae gray. Jake rubbed the candy on his cords. He reached for Charlotte's hand.

"Charlotte," he began, trying to ignore his trembling fingers. Charlotte stared fiercely at the ground. "I'm sorry I've been . . ."

"An utter and complete jerk?!" she erupted. Jake's mouth fell open, and she couldn't resist a smile, pleased to have finally put him in his place. Little did she know, far from feeling wounded, Jake felt flattered. *Excited,* even. There is no greater moment in a guy's life than the transition from "nice guy" to "jerk." Jake smiled a little himself, cherishing the moment.

"I just . . ." He sighed to communicate the weight of his confession. "I kind of freaked out."

Charlotte nodded with cold comprehension. "Because of your sister, right?"

"Actually, she had nothing to with it."

"She didn't?"

"I'm telling you," Jake insisted, "I just freaked out. And I thought if I put some, like, distance between us . . . I would feel *less* freaked out. But instead I got *more* freaked out."

"Really?" Charlotte looked perplexed. "Why?"

"Because . . . ," Jake continued after a soulful pause. "I *missed* you."

Charlotte raised her eyes from the ground and, for the first time during their conversation, looked directly into his. All she wanted to do was trust him. To bury her face into the soft cotton of his faded plaid cowboy shirt and breathe in until her lungs were full and her heart was bursting. But she was scared. Just when she'd gotten over him, here he was — reeling her back in. It wasn't fair.

Jake pressed the gray Sweet Tart into the palm of her hand. "Here."

"What is this?"

"It's, um, a Russell Crowe pill."

Charlotte rolled the little disk between her finger and thumb. "It's a Sweet Tart, Jake. A really gross, really old Sweet Tart."

"It's a Russell Crowe pill," he cried out with mock severity. She cracked a small smile. "If you take this pill," he instructed, "I promise you — I'll go away. I will disappear into the ether. Just like Russell Crowe's Australian roommate dude."

"*British* roommate," she corrected.

"British roommate dude. Whatever."

Charlotte looked at Jake for what felt like a long time. And then, with a small but significant bob of her perfect, arched eyebrows, she popped the pill into her mouth. She touched him on the arm, turned on the hard, brown heel of her L'Autre Chose boot, and walked away. Jake watched her go, stunned. There was nothing he could do. Nothing he could say.

He had lost.

But then he had a thought.

"You didn't swallow!" he yelled at the top of his lungs.

A crew of passing skaters slowed their boards. A nearby basketball game called time-out. Two ninth-grade girls shared a glance. Everyone was thinking it: *Drr-rama!*

Charlotte shot Jake her best *how-dare-you* look. "*Yeth, I didth!*" she replied.

Which was all the evidence he needed. In three swift steps he was at her side, pulling her to him. He wasn't sure if he felt like a baller or a total doofus, but he crossed his fingers for baller and went in for the kill. He took her small, sweet face in his hands and he kissed her. He kissed her until the whole world shrunk to the size of a laundry room and the laundry room became the whole world.

The Showroom erupted into whoops and hollers. "Get a room!" some guy yelled.

"*That's* original!" some girl replied.

"Yeah, you're *face* is original!" the guy shot back.

Embarrassed, Jake and Charlotte broke apart and started walking toward Assembly Hall. "By the way," he said, pulling on one of her curls. "You're a really bad liar."

"I am?" She looked up. She was still a little dazed.

Jake opened his mouth. The stolen Sweet Tart stuck to his tongue like a button. *"Ew,"* Charlotte laughed, realizing what he'd done. He crunched down on the candy and chewed. His chews were loud, grotesque — triumphant. "You're disgusting," she declared. Jake dropped his arm across her shoulder and beamed.

They walked to Town Meeting together.

The Dog: Emilio Poochie
The Getup: Blue rhinestone-encrusted
Louis Vuitton collar

At three and a half months of dating, Melissa informed Marco she refused to have sex until marriage. Marco respected her decision, especially since it had to do with Jesus, and Marco respected Jesus. "We can do other stuff though, right?" He had to ask.

"Of course," she replied, smiling in a way Marco found promising. They were lying in bed and talking. After a few minutes, talking turned to kissing. And then, just as he got his hands on the piranha-like hooks of Melissa's double-D bra, she pulled away.

"Would you just *look* at him?" she gasped. Slowly, reluctantly, Marco turned around. Sure enough, there he was: Melissa's dog. Emilio Poochie propped himself up on his hind legs and peeped his head over the edge of the overstuffed mattress. He smacked his lips.

"He misses us!" Melissa crooned with a pouty face.

Before Marco knew what was happening, Emilio Poochie was in bed with them, sandwiched between their bodies like a fuzzy burger. "Who's my little badabing?" Melissa gurgled as Emilio pushed his butt into her cooing face. Emilio stared at Marco with his black button eyes. Marco stared back.

"*I'm* her badabing," Emilio Poochie gloated, sticking out the tip of his pink tongue. (More and more Marco found he could read Emilio's thoughts.)

Marco turned over on his back and blinked at the ceiling. Emilio Poochie's room was just sixteen feet down the hall. And yet. His miniature princess bed, with its impossibly tiny floral comforter and candy-striped sheets, had yet to be slept in. The éclair-shaped, pink-frosted dog treats were still on the pillows. His gold-framed flat HDTV screen, with copies of such dog-friendly classics as *Homeward Bound* and *Lady and the Tramp* in the built-in shelves, remained unwatched. His Christmas present, a stroller-sized treadmill with a built-in recording of Melissa's voice ("Emilio, come! Good *boy,* Emilio!") remained unwrapped. And yes, he even had his own bathroom. Emilio's *salle de bain* came with bowl-sized sinks, a ten-gallon porcelain tub with baby claw feet, a mini crystal chandelier, a flushable toy toilet, and a matching set of pink towels with embroidered gold crests. The two-foot-high vanity (with ruffled skirt and heart-shaped mirror) was fully stocked with a complete set of travel-sized BIG SEXY HAIR products. It was all a two pound ball of fluff could ask for, and Emilio had never so much as stepped inside. Why would he? Melissa's room and his were *exact replicas of each other* — except Melissa's was, in comparison, huge. Emilio was no fool. He knew the rules. And what's the number one rule of *livin' it up*?

BIGGER IS BETTER.

"Baby" — Marco squeezed Melissa's smooth hand — "I've been thinking. Maybe it's time Emilio slept in his own room."

"What?" Melissa clutched Emilio close. "Why?"

Marco sighed. What could he say? That Emilio Poochie was slowly but surely ruining their (everything but) sex life? That Emilio beamed evil dog–thoughts into Marco's brain twenty-four-seven? Could Marco say he was sick of leaning in for a kiss and coming up with a mouthful of fur? That he was beginning to wonder if his girlfriend's virginity had less to do with God, and more to do with . . . Dog?

"Melissa," he began, working up his nerve, "it's just, some-times I feel . . ."

"Oh baby," she cut him off. Her phone was alerting her to an Unknown Caller. "Will you see who that is? I don't want to move Emilio."

"It's Charlotte," Marco groaned, reaching for the phone.

"Pick it up, pick it up!"

"Melissa!" he repeated. "I am *trying* to communicate!"

She pushed Emilio from her lap and leaped across the bed, snatching the phone from Marco's hand. "Hello?" she answered. Marco shook his head in slow disbelief. Melissa rolled her eyes, pressed the phone to her chest and hissed, "It's *business.*"

"Hey, Melinoma," sang a melodious voice on the other line. *"Comment allez-vous?"*

"Did you ask your mom about Prada?" Melissa burbled in reply. During her blow-out with Vivien, Melissa had behaved as though Prada was a done deal. In fact, in the heat of the mo-ment, she'd *believed* it was a done deal. Only in recent days had it occurred to her: she'd never had Prada confirmed.

Charlotte flopped across her mint and yellow pastry bed and yawned. She'd just returned from ballet and was dead *fatiguée*.

"Do you know the painting, *Le Petit Déjeuner sur l'Herbe?*" she asked.

Melissa frowned. "What?"

"It's a famous painting of a picnic," Charlotte explained, fingering a small hole in her tights. "The guys have their clothes on, but the girl they're with? Completely naked." She smiled dreamily. "Don't you just *love* picnics?"

"Sorry . . ." Melissa looked at her phone and scowled. "What does this have to do with Prada?"

"Oh yeah. *Prada*," Charlotte said. "My mom put in a call."

"And?"

"They're happy to do it."

"Omigod, YES!" Melissa screamed. Emilio dipped his head and flattened his ears. "Yes, yes, yes, yes, *yes*!"

After the third "yes," Marco's jaw dropped. He'd *never* seen Melissa this excited. In fact, up 'til then, he'd pegged his girlfriend as a non-yessing kinda girl. But he was wrong. Defeated and demoralized, he pointed to the door and mouthed *I'm out.*

Melissa didn't notice. She was too busy taking in a new, less promising piece of news.

"No, no, no, no, no," she moaned into the phone, sitting on the edge of her bed and switching her phone to a fresh ear. "What do you mean 'there's a catch'?"

"It's no big thing." Charlotte pulled her peach nylon-clad knee to her nose and stretched. "You just need one more person's approval."

"Who?"

Charlotte slid her legs apart, fell into a perfect split, and grinned. *"Moi."*

"You?" Melissa grimaced. "I thought I *had* your okay."

"And you *do*. Assuming you give me something in return."

"Okay. What do you want?"

"When I was in Paris," Charlotte began, "I saw this couple sitting in a park. I forget which one. *Le Jardin des Tuileries?* Anyway. They were having a picnic. Sitting under a tree on a checked blanket. The whole clichéd spread: baguette, brie, blueberries . . . but the best part had to be the water guns. They filled them with champagne. I'm not joking. I *saw* them do it. They sat there, squirting each other for hours. They were having *so much fun*. I just thought . . . that has to be it. That has to be *love*. I swore one day, when I met the right guy, I'd have a picnic like that. Except better. 'Cause me and my boyfriend would be cuter."

"Okay," Melissa replied, swallowing her frustration. She hated conversations like this — you ask someone what time it was, and they answer with a detailed explanation of the weather. "So . . . what is this about?"

"Well, according to *Cribs,* your father bid on a case of 1990 Cristal Brut Millennium 2000 at Sotheby's last year, and I was *thinking* . . ."

"No." Melissa paced a small circle in the middle of her white

Berber carpet. "You want my dad's *Cristal*?" Melissa shook her head at the impossibility of the request. "Those bottles are worth, like, seven thousand dollars each!"

"Really?" Charlotte tsked with fake sympathy. "The water guns are only a dollar ninety-five."

Melissa swallowed. Not only were those bottles worth seven thousand dollars each, her father was saving them for his wedding. *I do this and I'm dead,* she realized, a great bubble of panic bursting in her gut. But then, just as suddenly, she imagined launching her label at the *park* instead of at Prada. She imagined the paper plates, the plastic cups, the stupid bouncing balloons. The horrible, smug look on Vivien's face.

Probably her father wouldn't notice if *one* bottle was missing?

"Fine. I'll do it."

"Formidable," Charlotte gushed into the phone. "You won't regret it, Melissa. The Prada store on Rodeo is amazing this time of year."

Melissa clicked off the phone, sat on the edge of her bed and stared numbly into space. "Marco?" she called. "Marco?"

Whenever she needed him most, Marco was gone. Emilio Poochie bounded into her lap and nuzzled into her stomach. "At least I have you," she whispered into his ear. Emilio lapped her nose in agreement.

The Girl: Barney's mannequin
The Getup: "Carcass Fantasia"

Rodeo Drive begins at the world famous Beverly Wilshire Hotel and extends to Santa Monica Boulevard at a gentle incline, like the first half of a bridge. The sidewalks are bleach white and dinner-plate clean. Well-groomed camellias and elegant palms divide the street. Hundred-thousand-dollar cars glide by like floats in a parade: Ferrari, Porsche, Lamborghini, Aston Martin, Bentley. People stare at them and they stare back—except the Rolls Royce Phantom, which sneers with perceptible contempt (if you think the grill's resemblance to an upturned nose is accidental, think again). Men sport deep tans and designer active wear. Women flash white teeth and four-inch heels. They emerge from plush leather drivers' seats, frown into cell phones, and slam doors behind them. They take off down the street at the vigorous pace of the tread-mill-trained. And they never stop to feed the meters, preferring to dangle handicap placards from their rearview mirrors instead.

After Melissa's relentless petition, Miss Paletsky granted The Trend Set leave for an "educational field trip" to Beverly Hills' most famous street. The girls had a ton of ground to cover in a short amount of time, and—to Melissa's endless frustration—Petra kept slowing them down. At the first sign of silicone, saline, Botox, or collagen, she stopped and stared—not because the sight surprised her, but because she had a *duty*. A duty to communicate disgust.

"Petra!" Melissa stamped her foot. "Sometime today, puh-lease!"

At the moment, Petra could not take her eyes off the white mannequin in the Barney's department store window. The mannequin wore a camel-hair skirt with darts at the hips, glossy alligator skin knee-high boots, a wide patent-leather belt with gold buckle of interlocking Cs, and a black cashmere sweater with fox fur collar and cuffs. The collar was so huge it resembled a platter—like a serving plate for decapitated heads.

In Petra's humble opinion, decapitation was exactly what this mannequin deserved.

"I refuse to go in there," she informed the other girls.

"What?" Melissa snapped. For Melissa, the world was pretty much divided between two drives: sex and Rodeo. But while *sex drive* referred to the overriding impulse to bonk (an urge Melissa couldn't, for the life of her, understand), *Rodeo Drive* referred to the overriding impulse to *spend* (an urge Melissa lived for.) So far, Petra's low-level Rodeo was serious cause for concern. Melissa wondered if she was some kind of pervert.

Petra paused to do a quick tally in her head. "Do you realize that mannequin is wearing a total of FIVE animals on her body?"

"Pet, darling," Charlotte rolled her eyes. "*That's* why they call it the Rodeo."

"It's disgusting and it's cruel!"

"You wanna know disgusting and cruel?" Melissa slapped her notebook to her knee. "Keeping us out in eight-hundred-degree heat, when we could be enjoying ourselves in something called air-conditioning." In addition to air-conditioning, Barneys carried a wrap-around Ella Moss dress in a purple and black leopard print that Melissa *had to have*. She'd seen it in her fall issue of *Teen Vogue:* "Forget About Prince Charming," read the headline. "Fall in Love with Charming Prints!"

"I'm goin' in," she announced.

"Go ahead," Petra folded her arms. "Shop until you drop dead. Like one of those poor, innocent animals."

"I can not believe you just said that." Melissa cringed, her hand on the brass door handle. "We are not *shopping*. We're *researching*."

"Oh please."

"When I bought my Dolce & Gabbana heels, did I *not* find out they have a better marketing strategy than Lanvin? Whose heels I did *not* buy?"

"Yes." Charlotte lit up her second Gauloise of the afternoon. "And I found out *certain* consumers prefer trashy trends to plain good taste."

"See?" Melissa agreed, oblivious to the insult. *"Research."*

"Well, I'm with Petra," Janie interrupted from her seat on a nearby marble fountain.

"Sorry"—Melissa knit her eyebrows together—"was some-one talkin' to you?" Under normal circumstances, Melissa's knit eyebrows were Janie's cue to mumble an apology and move on. But today Janie had greater concerns than Melissa's fluctuating mood, like the fact that she and Amelia hadn't talked for a record *three days.* While the other girls tried on sunglasses and sucked down smoothies, Janie walked around in a stupor of sorrow and regret. She hadn't said a single word all day, not that anybody had noticed. They'd long grown accustomed to her quiet. What Melissa, Petra, and Charlotte didn't know was, outside the world of The Trend Set, Janie wasn't shy at all. Imagine their surprise when, instead of the repentant whisper, Janie launched into a full-fledged rant.

"We're about to throw some huge launch party for a label that exists *why?*" she bounded to her feet. "Because we *say* it does? Do you realize how incredibly lame that is?! It's like NASA announcing the launch of a space shuttle and then everyone shows up and they like, *fly a paper airplane!* Except, wait. We don't even have a paper airplane. We don't have *anything!*"

The three girls stared at Janie with a mixture of awe and disbelief. She was like a magic lamp, ignorable until you rubbed her the wrong way. By then a genie was released: an explosive, unpredictable, *step-back-before-I-beat-your-ass* genie. Charlotte glowed with admiration. Crazy Genie Janie was a major improvement to Mousy Suck-up Janie. Crazy Genie Janie was someone she could actually learn to respect. Which was convenient because, since she and Jake had gotten back together, Charlotte had renewed her vow to be nice.

"Janie has a point," Charlotte nodded.

"*Yeah,* I have a point!"

"Okay, fine," huffed Melissa. "But what are we supposed to

do? The party is this Saturday and don't *even* ask me to reschedule. You have no idea how much work I put into this." She narrowed her eyes at Charlotte. "Not to mention champagne."

Charlotte raised an invisible glass. "Chin Chin!"

"Okay . . ." Janie took a deep, calming breath. "How much are you guys planning to spend on new outfits for the party?"

"Do we have to discuss money?" Charlotte asked with wincing sweetness. "It's a little *gauche*."

"You wear Chanel sunglasses and drive a *Jag*," Petra scoffed. "If that's not 'discussing money' I don't know what is."

"Sorry, what was that?" Charlotte feigned incomprehension. "I don't speak *hippie*."

"Okay, stop!" Janie flared. She tore through her army green canvas tote and fished out the crumpled twenty she made babysitting the Longarzos. "This is what I plan on spending."

"That's *it*?" Melissa gasped. "What are you planning on wearing? A gumball?"

"This is what we're going to do, okay?" Janie smiled through clenched teeth. "We are *not* going to spend money on new clothes with *no personality*. We are going to hire *each other* to design something *unique*."

"But . . . ," Charlotte began.

"It doesn't have to be the most amazing thing ever!" Janie cut her off. "Just *something*. Something that shows our potential. Assuming we even *have* potential."

She kneeled to the ground and scribbled their names on four

small squares of notebook paper. Then crumpled the squares into tiny spitballs, cupped the paper wads in her palms, and shook. "Okay. Whoever's name you get, that's your design partner."

She uncupped her hands, and the girls picked one spitball each. After a moment of uncrinkling, Melissa began the reading of names.

"I'm supposed to trust *her* with my outfit?" She pointed at Petra in horror. "No! No way!"

"Oh, just deal with it, Melissa." Charlotte tsked, unclasping her pink Chanel coin-purse. She pulled out a few crisp hundred-dollar bills and handed them to Janie. Janie accepted the money, counted the bills, and promptly lost her ability to breathe. *Five hundred dollars? Was she serious?* Janie glanced at Charlotte for signs of trickery.

"Just make me something good," Charlotte requested.

"Of course," Janie replied. But she could barely contain her excitement. She folded the bills into tight squares, and tucked them into her dad's old wallet. When she dropped the bloated billfold into her bag, it tugged with new weight, heavy as a sack of gold.

"Thanks."

Charlotte pinched Janie's twenty between her fingers like a used Kleenex. "No . . . ," she smiled. "Thank *you!*"

"Fine!" Melissa stormed off. "If that's how it's gonna be!"

"Where are you going?!" Petra called.

Charlotte checked her platinum Bvlgari wristwatch. "Barneys closes in twenty minutes."

"I'm returning my shoes!" Melissa hollered from the curb.

The remaining ladies looked at each other in surprise. Melissa had just spent the last hour and a half gabbing about the "fabuliciousness" of her latest "necessary" purchase: a pair of black, brass-studded Dolce & Gabbana wedge platform heels—the very last pair in the store.

"Why?!" Charlotte yelled after her.

"So I have enough money!" Melissa cried bitterly. "To give to Miss Animal Rights over there!"

"That's perfect." Petra plopped down by the fountain. But Janie smiled, proud of herself.

Her plan had totally worked.

Nikki Pellegrini was one of those girls everybody liked. She was the Amanda Bynes of the eighth grade—pretty (but not *too* pretty), smart (but not *too* smart). And she was *sooooo* sweet. As her chain-smoking grandmother, Nikki the First, concluded in a frog-like rasp: nicotine's the world's most addictive substance, but Nikki's a close second.

But the addiction people had to Nikki was no match for the addiction Nikki had to people. From cool kids to wannabes, jocks to jokesters, brainiacs to hacky-sacks, suck-ups to stuck-ups—no one escaped the click of her mouse. A hefty 384 friends belonged to her MySpace account alone. (Of course, her tally excluded bands, celebrities, and MySpace Tom.)

Having virtually recruited every member of the seventh and eighth grades, Nikki realized it was high time she conquered the ninth. She figured out a shortcut: she would befriend one supremely popular person in the *tenth grade*. Once Supremely Popular Tenth Grader was in place, Nikki would place her in the Top Eight, where she would serve as indisputable evidence of Nikki's coolness. Curious freshman would have to wonder: who *was* this Nikki? And if Supremely Popular Tenth Grader was her friend, why then, weren't they?

Nikki logged onto MySpace.com and entered her Supremely Popular Tenth Grader of choice. She scrolled down the list of inevitable Loser-Charlottes (there was *Charlotteandkey,* a forty-two-year-old swinger from Austin, *CharlotteKisses,* a thirteen-year-old cheerleader from Boise, and *"ShootingChars,"* a fifteen-year-old Scientologist from Tampa), until she found her target: *Charlotte_ Beaucoup*, a ninety-nine-year-old "Other" from Los Angeles. In her thumbnail pic, Charlotte held her cat, a scowling Burmese named Monkey, to her cheek. Charlotte was dressed as a French maid. Monkey was dressed as a feather duster.

Ever since Jake kissed her in the Showroom, Charlotte had become Nikki's new obsession. Charlotte had beauty, brains, style, and wit. But most of all she had *experience.* Behind that sly half-smile was a world Nikki could only dream about — a secret world of jets, Jaguars, and (most of all) Jake. Nikki scrutinized Charlotte's pic for some kind of clue, analyzing her face like a tarot card. She outlined Charlotte's features with the point of her cursor. If Nikki couldn't be close to Jake, then at the very least, she would be close to the girl he loved.

Do you really want to add Charlotte_Beaucoup as a friend?

Click "Add" only if you really wish to add Charlotte_Beaucoup as a friend.

Nikki moved her cursor across the screen and held her breath. She vowed not to exhale until she clicked. She used this technique whenever she had to do something that scared her.

After twenty-one seconds, Nikki clicked ADD. And then she gasped for air.

The next day, Charlotte_Beaucoup accepted her as a friend. Within a week the entire ninth grade class and a quarter of the tenth joined Nikki's network. She now had a staggering 451 friends to her name, including—to her unparalleled joy—Charlotte Beverwil herself. Things couldn't get better.

And then things did.

"You are so lying!" Carly gasped once she shared the news. Nikki, Carly, and Juliet (aka "The Nicarettes") had spread their bagged lunches on the steps outside the breezeway. The breezeway attracted a lot of foot traffic, which gave Nikki ample opportunity to greet friends should they happen to walk by.

"She's not lying," Juliet sighed, staring into her Smart Water. "I saw it with my own eyes."

It referred to nothing less than Nikki's personal invite to The Trend Set's highly anticipated "Tag—You're It!" Party. As far as Nikki knew, she was the only eighth grader to have received one (she chalked it up to the Pellegrini charm). The stiff white envelope had arrived sealed with a dollop of pink wax stamped in the shape of a rose. The card inside was a matching shade of pink with a lacquered black border. Nikki ran her fingertip across the raised calligraphy letters. So accustomed was she to evites, an actual invitation was an event in and of itself.

"What did it say?" Carly asked. Nikki cleared her throat. She'd committed every word to memory.

As further evidence, she grabbed her new 9502 Caramella bag by LeSportsac, unzipped the front pocket, and slipped out the tag. Carly and Juliet passed it between them, their mouths hanging open. They both looked a little like Nikki's grandmother after the stroke.

"I like 'Shotgun,' don't you?" Nikki asked. Her label choice referred to the day she sat shotgun with Jake at the wheel. She licked the foil lid of her peach yogurt and sighed. "I hope I win."

Carly pitched the tag into Nikki's lap. "*How* were you invited to this?!" It was less a question than an accusation.

"MySpace. Charlotte's one of my friends."

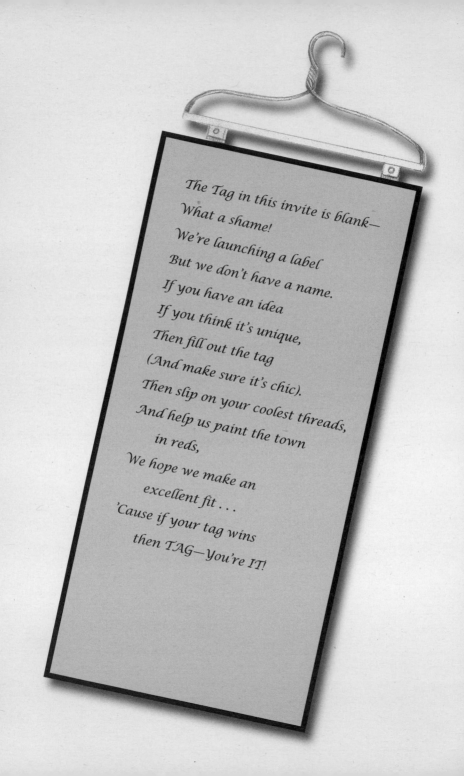

The Tag in this invite is blank—
What a shame!
We're launching a label
But we don't have a name.
If you have an idea
If you think it's unique,
Then fill out the tag
(And make sure it's chic).
Then slip on your coolest threads,
And help us paint the town
in reds,
We hope we make an
excellent fit . . .
'Cause if your tag wins
then TAG—You're IT!

Carly stared at Juliet, like, *how is that possible?*

"How is that possible?" Juliet asked. Her grilled tofu wrap levitated at her lips.

"Um . . . I asked her?"

"B-but," Carly sputtered. "She just accepted?!"

"Obvie," Nikki replied, exasperated.

As if on cue, Charlotte and Kate Joliet emerged from the breezeway. Kate was wearing a butterfly-print thermal, a distressed denim mini, and tan Frye harness boots. Charlotte was wearing an emerald green camisole, "Ava" skinny jeans, and silver eyelet Twelfth Street flats. "He is *not* my boyfriend!" She giggled, smacking Kate's bony excuse for an arm.

"O-ow!" Kate whined, raising her arm to her lips. She gave herself a get-well kiss. "If he's not your boyfriend," Kate said, returning her attention to Charlotte, "then what is he?"

"My *friend,*" Charlotte answered. "Who happens to be . . . a boy." At *boy,* she closed her eyes, savoring the word like candy.

"You are so full of it." Kate grinned.

Charlotte clapped her hands in delight. "I know!"

As they waltzed by her, Nikki tried to smile, but she felt slightly stunned, like a baby in the presence of two larger-than-life dogs. Charlotte seemed to barely register her presence.

"Wow, Nikki." Juliet smirked once the two older girls were gone. "You guys seem *pretty* tight."

"Aka—she has no idea who you are," Carly snorted in triumph.

"I look really *different* in person," Nikki protested, hoping it was true.

"Omigod!" Juliet gasped, slapping her hand across her mouth. She looked over at Carly. Her eyes bulged.

"What?" Carly snapped.

"Remember seventh grade?" Juliet asked, removing her hand. "When Molly Berger came to my bat mitzvah?"

"Ew-uh . . . yeah." Carly cringed. "Why did you invite her? That was so *awk.*"

"Because . . ." Juliet paused for effect. "I told my mom to invite everyone on my MySpace list. But I completely forgot I'd accepted Molly Berger as one of my friends. And then, once I remembered, it was too late."

"Wait." Carly frowned. "You accepted her as a friend?"

Juliet executed her best Sad Face. "I felt *bad.*"

"That's the problem with the Internet," Carly sighed. "It makes you too nice."

"Totally," Juliet agreed. She turned to Nikki. "You, like, *get* the moral of this story, right?"

"I guess." Nikki frowned. Carly and Juliet shared a knowing glance. They could tell she didn't have a clue.

"The moral of the story is"—Juliet touched Nikki on the knee—"Charlotte looked at her MySpace list and invited you by mistake."

"And she only accepted you in the first place because she was being nice," Carly added.

"Aka—she pitied you."

"You're, like, a random."

"A Pity Project."

"A Charity Chum."

"If you go to this party?" Juliet shook her head. "Everyone's gonna look at you and be like . . ."

"What is *she* doing here?" Carly groaned.

"Just like Molly Berger," Juliet finished in her best ghost-story tone.

Nikki frowned into her lap. Her friends had a point. She probably *had* been invited by mistake. But was that any reason not to go? What was "mistake" but another word for "incredible stroke of good luck?" What was "incredible stroke of good luck" but another five words for Fate? How could she pass up an opportunity to be near Jake Farrish? And what's more, be near him in a pretty dress, on a warm September night, at a glamorous party in Beverly Hills? And besides. Maybe she *wasn't* invited by mistake. Maybe Charlotte actually wanted her to go!

"I don't care," Nikki declared. "I'm going."

"Fine," Carly shot back with unadulterated contempt. "I would so not go if I were you but that's just me so whatever."

Nikki turned to Juliet. "Do you wanna come? I'm allowed a plus one."

Juliet gasped like Miss America. "Are you *kidding* me?!" she cried, throwing her arms around Nikki's neck. Carly croaked like she'd swallowed a fly.

"You asked *her?*"

"You said you didn't want to go," Nikki reminded her with a tiny smile.

"Well, I don't!" Carly huffed, crushing her paper lunch bag into a tiny ball. She tossed it toward a trash can.

She missed by a mile.

According to local Valley lore, the tiny shop on the corner of Colfax Street and Riverside Avenue was cursed. It had started out as a shoe repair called "Cinderella's Shoe Repair." The elderly shoemaker wore tiny spectacles and a leather apron. Then the shoemaker died and his store got snapped up by a yogurt vender. Within days, the only evidence of the shoemaker's eighty-eight-year life was the small glass slipper decal on the old glass entrance door. Despite repeated applications of steel wool and nail polish remover by the new owner — the decal survived. His yogurt store did not. Neither did the the B-grade sushi restaurant, the gourmet dog treat bakery, the Boba tea lounge, the tapioca bar, the hammock hut, or the "happy" hookah parlor. Every business failed within three months.

Then came Bippity Boppity Beads.

Maybe there'd been a sudden boom in the bead industry, or maybe the store-name's reference to Cinderella appeased the shoemaker's ghost; whatever the reason, Bippity Boppity Beads broke the corner store curse. It passed the three-month mark in July and by September was still going strong. Which was very good news.

Because Janie was obsessed with Bippity Boppity Beads.

"Aren't those beautiful?" Elsa, the owner of Bippity Boppity Beads, had asked. Elsa weighed in at two hundred pounds and had the exact same haircut as Richard Gere. She wore a fringed black leather motorcycle jacket and called herself the Bead Baron. "They're from Moreno," she added, peering over Janie's shoulder. The beads in her hand were the murky blue of sea glass.

"I love them."

"They're ninety-five cents each." Elsa smiled, showing off her silver caps. "We got them in yesterday."

Janie had already made her purchase—fifty red beads from Morocco, fifty black beads from Egypt—but she didn't let that stop her. She stuck her hand into her canvas tote to scrounge for a few free-floating bills. She couldn't find any. She scrounged for a few quarters. She couldn't find any. In the end, she found four pennies, a Magic Castle token, two bobby pins, and a piece of blue lint.

Janie's stomach fell into her shoes.

"I'll be right back," she squeaked. She headed for the door, stepped outside, and took a deep breath. If that piece of blue lint meant what she thought it did, then Janie had spent every dime of Charlotte's five hundred dollars in a matter of *two and a half hours*. How was that even possible?!

"Of course it's possible," Jake now scoffed. "This is, like, old-school Galileo shit."

Whenever he chilled in his sister's room, Jake leaned against her closet. Leaning against the closet was the best way to avoid *looking* at the closet, which (let's be honest) wasn't so much a closet than a semi-fanatical shrine to Nick Valensi, the guitarist of the Strokes. Nick Valensi's "achingly perfect" face and "kill me now" forearms graced every inch of the door's surface, including the brass knob (Jake could only assume it was brass; the knob hadn't been Valensi-free for years).

Janie pushed aside her black star-shaped pillows and dumped her afternoon purchases on her bed. "What does Galileo have to do with this?" she asked, staring down at her loot.

"Well, you know about the theory of gravity, right?"

"Sort of," she replied, immediately resenting Jake's scientific prowess. It was like, how could her brother be so smart and yet so dumb?

"In the absence of resisting forces," he explained, "everything falls at the same rate. Same goes with money. In the absence of resisting force, you spend it. It doesn't matter if it's, like, two bucks or two thousand—it all goes at the same rate."

"Yeah, except—there's no force that stops people from spending," Janie pointed out.

"Yeah, there is. I'm a force."

"Omigod." She peeled with laughter. "Sorry, but you are *so* not a force."

Jake made a sound like a hyena flying around on a broomstick.

"I do not sound like that!" Janie pitched a bag of red beads at his head. He collapsed into the fetal position.

"I would've been, like: *don't do it,* Janie." Jake shook his head, his voice muffled. "Don't buy those little red bead things. They're dumb. And you would have been, like, wow, Jake. Indeed, you are a *force.* A force . . . of *reason.*"

Janie snatched her bag of beads and scowled. "They are *not* dumb, okay? They're a necessary component of my design."

He considered her point with a solemn nod. "Dumb."

"Get out," she ordered.

Jake got to his feet and shuffled for the exit. He paused at his sister's door and shook his head. "Dumb," he whispered.

"JAKE!"

In a flash, he escaped down the hall.

Janie shut her door and collapsed against it. She gazed at the mess of material, beads, buttons, safety pins, and thread on her red and black twin bed. Over the last year, she'd made sure everything in her bedroom was either white, red, black, or a combination of the three. Jake kept asking her if she'd invited the White Stripes over for a slumber party (he thought that was super-hilarious), but Janie didn't care. She thought it looked cool.

She slid open the top drawer of her white bureau (she'd painted the handles fire-engine red) and looked inside. The enormous vintage British flag she'd bought on eBay was folded inside. It was about twenty times more expensive than a brand-new one—

but it was worth it. New flags were made of stiff, synthetic fibers like nylon and polyester. New flags had no history or romance. The vintage flag was made from hand-stitched, 100 percent silk. The vintage flag belonged to a World War II veteran named Perry McCloud. Perry McCloud wrote Janie a personal congratulations upon the date of her purchase.

Dear Jane,

Special attention and care was given to the creation of this hand sewn silk flag. Due to the natural fiber, delicate stitching and the passing of time, some disintegration has occurred. Disintegration is characteristic of hand loomed fabric and not considered a defect. I hope you work to preserve the integrity of this superb Flag and great relic of British history. Congratulations on your purchase.

With many sincere thanks,

Perry McCloud

Janie sat down on her fluffy sheepskin throw rug and grabbed a pair of shears. She fixed them to a corner of the flag, right at the diagonal of the Union Jack stripe. She sucked in her breath and sliced into the fabric. The scissors stuttered with effort. Her heart beat like a drum. *There's no going back now,* she thought, splitting the silk at a faster clip. Suddenly, her vision was clear, so clear she could almost touch it.

The Girls: Melissa Moon, Charlotte Beverwil,
Petra Greene, Janie Farrish
The Getups: Handmade party frocks (to be revealed)

The "Tag—You're It!" party was set for Saturday night, which meant (unless you were planning to look like a total slob) primping prepped on Tuesday. Everyone knows the first rule in looking good is booking good. The coolest girls at Winston secured appointments with The Pore House, the trendy new spa on Robertson Boulevard. From buffing to blowouts, pedicures to paraffin, seaweed to salt scrubs, teasing to tweezing to professional squeezing, The Pore House promised everything short of a whole new skin, for a price that stopped just short of your soul.

And yes. That was debatable.

As a thrifty alternative, Janie convinced Jake to drop her off at Bloomingdale's. She spent Saturday morning floating from makeup station to makeup station like a nectar-binging butterfly. She lacquered her lashes in Lancôme, shimmered her cheeks in Chanel, boosted her brows with Benefit, and plumped up her pout with Prada. She even fortified her follicles with Frederic Fekkai (whatever that meant). By the time Jake picked her up, Janie's face boasted $360 worth of makeup. And (unless you count the mint gumball she bought at the Origins counter) she hadn't spent a dime.

Leave it to Petra to spend even less.

"I'm so excited you're having friends over," Heather Greene

said as she breathlessly arranged their formal dining room table. Already, she'd laid out every piece of her wedding silver and china. Their crystal wineglasses blossomed intricately folded linen napkins. The Arte Italica candleholders sprouted smooth white candles. Everything floated on lily pads of antique lace. "It's so nice to have people over," she remarked, polishing an impossibly tiny fork.

The Trend Set voted Petra's house as the most convenient place to congregate before the party. Petra had been too stoned to refuse. As she watched her mother flit about the table, she realized she'd made a terrible mistake.

"Why are you putting out crab forks, Mom?" Petra could barely contain her frustration.

"Aren't they darling?" Heather tenderly placed each fork next to a pair of hand-painted chopsticks. "They should have a chance to get out and *breathe*."

"Mom," Petra pleaded, glancing out the window. The others would be arriving any minute. It was one thing for her mother to discuss her fork's respiratory health in front of her own daughter, but in front of *them*? Petra felt the blood drain from her face. Her Potential for Embarrassment Quotient was through the roof.

"You know what we need?" Heather remarked, gazing about the gilded rose-and-cream room. "Fresh cut flowers."

"Mom! These kids are gonna be here for, like, *ten* minutes. You really don't have to do all this!"

Heather stared at the table, patting her hair like a bird that might fly away.

"Mom!" Petra covered her eyes with her hands. "Do you have *any* idea how weird and, like, *embarrassing* this is?!"

"How *dare* you talk to me in that tone!" Her mother blew up. Petra swallowed, storming from the table. She ran upstairs to her bedroom, the plush white carpet muting the thud of her angry footsteps. And still, for all her dramatics, she preferred it when her mother yelled. At least she sounded like a real parent and not some zonked-out mental patient.

Petra slammed her bedroom door. She yanked her underwear drawer open, clawed apart a chaos of cotton bras, underwear, and lavender sachets, and located her stash, which was kept inside a dented Sleepytime tea tin along with her collected seashells, Devendra Banhart ticket stubs, and a photo-booth picture of her parents in their twenties. They were laughing.

When she first starting smoking, in eighth grade, she'd been paranoid about getting caught. She took every possible precaution. She rolled up damp towels and shoved them beneath her locked door. She sealed her weed in film canisters and hid them in bottles of shampoo. She lit incense and stocked her room with munchies, preventing future (and possibly incriminating) runs to the kitchen. But then one day she got lazy. Joaquin, Theo, and Christina Boyd came over, and they started a round of shotgun. She started the game, exhaling a stream of smoke into Theo's mouth. Theo inhaled, smiling like a toad. As he turned toward Christina, Petra glanced at the doorway. Her heart skittered like a stone.

Her father had been standing there the whole time.

"Now I know why you're not picking up your phone."

"What do you want?" Petra snapped. She was weirded out by the amused expression on his face. It was like, *hello*. She was doing drugs under his own roof. Wasn't he supposed to be pissed?

"What do I want, what do I want . . . ," he began, his eyes resting on Christina. For the first time, Petra noticed the sheerness of Christina's paisley cotton blouse. Her father ran his hand around and around his trendy shaved head. "Do you know where the remote is?" he asked at last. "Lola can't find it."

"No," Petra answered. "I don't watch TV, remember?"

Her father nodded absently, shutting the door with a quiet *click*. Petra's shotgun buddies collapsed to the floor, clutched their sides, and rolled with laughter. "I don't watch TV!" Joaquin gasped, his red-rimmed eyes watering with joy. Christina crammed her face into a pillow and cackled.

Petra didn't think it was funny.

While her mother was undoubtedly polishing another crab fork, Petra stepped outside and lit up. Her bedroom balcony, which she'd decorated herself, was the only place in the house where she felt truly safe. The balcony was as big as some bedrooms. Watered silks fell along the walls and oversized Moroccan pillows cluttered the floor. Jewel-encrusted lanterns dangled from the ceiling, and at night the lanterns glowed their amber light, illuminating the needles of a nearby pine.

Petra rested her pipe on the banister and peered into her neighbor's vast yard. One night in late July, she'd glimpsed a guy her age strip down to his birthday suit and dive into the neighbors' pool. He swam one lap and got out, squeezing water from his dark hair. He looked up at the moon, still and pure and perfect as a statue. She couldn't understand it. Her neighbors, Miriam and George Elliot Miller, were pretty old — in their seventies at least. What the hell were they doing with a Naked Moon God in their backyard? Petra didn't have the nerve to ask. After all, what if she'd hallucinated the whole thing? What if she really had fried her brain, just like everybody said?

Petra's cell phone rang and interrupted her thoughts. She stared at the small flashing screen and frowned. She was supposed to do something now. What was she supposed to do?

"Hello?"

"Does everyone's phone need beauty sleep but mine?!" Melissa barked from the other end.

"What?"

"This is the fourth time we've called," Charlotte took over in calmer tones. "We've been on the sidewalk outside your house for, like . . . ten minutes?"

"What are we supposed to do out here?!" Melissa's voice squawked in the background. "Sell *lemonade*?!"

Petra peered around the pillar at the edge of her balcony, craning her face around the ivy-covered south wall. "Over here!"

she cried. The three girls looked around. She could see them squinting through the trees, using their hands as visors. They looked like a troop of tiny saluting soldiers. Petra giggled, flinging her arm in greeting.

Melissa snatched the phone.

"Are you gonna let us in? Or are we supposed to get to you by magic carpet?"

"Sorry!" Petra yelled. Melissa winced, holding the phone from her ear.

Petra punched the OPEN GATE button and ran downstairs. "What's going on?" her mother called from the living room, removing her noise-cancellation headphones. (She was listening to her Deepak Chopra tapes.) "Why are you running?"

"Didn't you hear the doorbell?" Petra asked. "Where's Lola?"

"What do you mean, *where's Lola?*" Heather fluttered with panic. "She's not picking up Sofia and Isabel?!"

Petra flung open the double French doors to a crowd of faces: Melissa, Charlotte, Janie, Lola, Sofia, Isabel, and some random guy with a Thai takeout flyer. They looked like a mob of angry villagers except, instead of torches, almost everyone carried a bulging shopping bag.

"Oh, Lola!" Heather pressed her hand to her heart. "Petra had me so *worried.*"

"*Mom,*" Petra pleaded in her best *please shut up* tone. Sofia and Isabel writhed away from their nanny and clutched Petra's legs.

They turned around, peering shyly at the three mysterious older girls.

"Come in," Petra said as Melissa stepped inside. Charlotte glided in her wake, and Janie followed soon after. Petra accepted the Thai takeout flyer, closed the door, and repeated her mantra: *No one can tell you're high, no one can tell you're high, no one can tell you're high.*

"*Finally.*" Melissa pushed her gold Roberto Cavalli sunglasses to the top of her head. She punched something into her metallic-pink sidekick. Emilio Poochie watched with interest from the crook of her arm.

"Look at the dog," Sofia whispered.

"Are you famous?" Isabel asked.

"Not yet," Melissa replied, bending to shake Isabel's tiny hand. "I'm Melissa."

Sofia stared into her shimmering cleavage, mesmerized. "OOoo . . . ," she breathed, pressing Melissa's boob like a doorbell.

"Sofie!" Petra's mother gasped while Charlotte snickered into her wrist. Heather lifted Sofia with her thin arms, balancing her on her hip.

"I am so sorry," she clucked, widening her eyes.

"It's fine." Melissa shrugged. Marco pulled stunts like that all the time, and *he* didn't have the excuse of being four.

"You have a lovely home," Charlotte said.

"Yes," Janie agreed, looking around. Her parents loathed houses like Heather's, and Jake and Janie were trained to agree. A minute inside the house, however, and Janie felt her hate subside into something like appreciation. Who cared if it was a McMansion? It sure beat a Happy Meal box in the Valley.

"I love the yellow wallpaper," she added.

"Well, *thank* you!" Heather smiled brightly. "Would you girls like some apple pie? I baked it myself."

"We actually have to go, Mom," Petra interrupted, pushing the girls toward the east wing stairs. Melissa turned around. She hadn't seen her own mother for almost six years. And still. Even when she *was* sober, Brooke was never the type to bake pies. Melissa didn't think moms like that existed. She watched Heather with a tourist's sense of wonder.

"Have fun, girls!" Heather chirped, ushering Sofia and Isabel into the kitchen.

"It was nice meeting you!" Melissa called, following Petra upstairs.

"Sorry about that," Petra groaned, kicking a wad of laundry under her rumpled futon. Melissa stared at Petra with contempt. Only kids with perfect, pie-baking moms had the nerve to complain.

"I like your mom," she bristled. "She's really nice."

"Oh," Petra said, pausing. "Yeah. She is."

Charlotte brushed the arm of Petra's overstuffed velvet chair and sat down. "Were you smoking pot?" she asked with a suspicious sniff.

Petra's face froze. "What?"

"Oh relax," Charlotte sighed. "I was just gonna ask if I could partake *un petit peu.*"

"It's on the balcony."

"Oh goodie," Charlotte said, retrieving the pipe. She held her platinum Zippo to the bowl and lit up. "Anyone want?" she asked, exhaling with the delicacy of a teakettle. Charlotte could make freebasing crack look like a subtle feminine art.

"I don't do drugs," Melissa snapped.

"Janie?" Charlotte asked, ignoring the previous comment with a dainty cough.

"Not today," Janie replied, as if on any other day she'd be game. The truth was, despite her increasing curiosity, she'd never tried pot before. And she didn't want her first time to be with *them.* What if she did something stupid?

"Okay," Melissa said. She shook her watch as if to wake it. "It's five o'clock."

"Petra?" Charlotte asked. "You have the pirate's chest?"

Petra disappeared into her walk-in closet and emerged with a medium-sized, jewel-studded mahogany box with four brass pad-locks. The chest — a prop from *Pirates of the Caribbean* — was a gift to Petra's father from a powerful Hollywood talent agent (Dr. Greene had squeezed her in for an "emergency" lip injection the night of the premiere). As Petra lowered the chest to her bedroom floor, Janie's hands went cold and clammy. She'd been dreading this moment all week.

Melissa flipped open her glittery white notebook and jotted something inside.

"Alright," she began, "as you know, we're here to exchange the outfits we designed for each other. And we agree to wear them with *pride*. . . ."

"Or at least a good imitation of it," Charlotte clarified.

"Exactly," Melissa agreed. "As extra insurance that we do *not* back out, we agree to lock the outfits we're currently wearing into the pirate's chest. That way, we have no choice but to wear each other's designs. Unless you wanna go naked."

"Okay, do we *have* to do this?" Janie blurted, folding her arms across her flat chest. "I mean, shouldn't we just trust each other?"

"Trust is something you earn over a long period of time. And we don't have *time* for time." Melissa crossed her arms and pinched the corners of her shirt. "Now *strip*."

The three girls pulled off their tops with the ease of Las Vegas showgirls. Charlotte tugged the silk string of her fuchsia disco skirt until it split apart, sliding to the floor. Petra and Melissa shimmied out of their jeans, lifting their dainty feet like ponies. Charlotte ran her slender fingers under the waist of her light pink Hanky Panky thong, making sure it lay flat on her hips. Janie couldn't help but notice her nipples through her matching pink La Perla pushup bra. She blushed and looked away, only to be bombarded by the more overwhelming sight of Melissa's enormous double-Ds. Petra's perfect in-between-B-and-Cs were cradled by light blue cotton, a simple United States of Apparel number Janie recognized. She happened to be wearing the same one. The bra looked different on her. A lot different.

"Hello?" Melissa said. "We don't have all day."

Janie realized she was the only one left dressed.

"Sorry," she whispered, slipping her arms inside her red t-shirt. She could feel the eyes of the other girls as she lifted her shirt over her head. In the confines of her cottony cave, Janie felt safe. *If I can't see them, they can't see me,* she reasoned like a two-year-old. But she couldn't stay in there forever.

Her head emerged from her t-shirt to find the other girls intent on folding their clothes. If they *had* been watching her, then they lost interest pretty fast. Janie exhaled, unsure if she felt relieved or insulted. She quickly folded her t-shirt and jeans and placed them inside the trunk, careful not to topple the other girls' piles.

Petra closed the trunk, turning the locks with four separate silver keys. She handed one key to each girl. In order to unlock the trunk, they'd have to be together.

"Okay!" Charlotte tried to smile. "Let's see what we have to wear!"

"You mean, *get* to wear," Melissa corrected. But even she didn't sound convinced.

They each reached into their shopping bags. The stiff paper crinkled like the sound of distant fireworks.

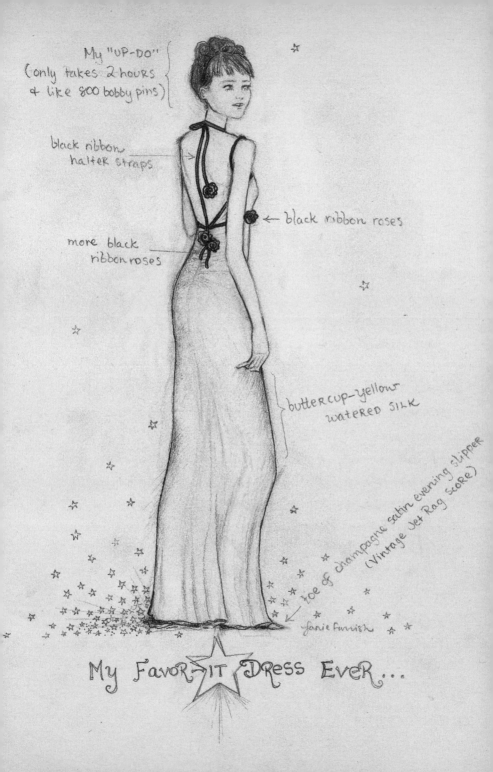

My "UP-DO"
(only takes 2 hours
& like 800 bobby pins)

black ribbon
halter straps

black ribbon roses

more black
ribbon roses

buttercup-yellow
watered silk

toe & champagne satin evening slipper
(vintage Jet Rag score)

Janie Furnish

My FavoRIT DRESS EVER...

Rodeo Drive was brighter than ever. Lampposts bathed the smooth sidewalk with a milky glow. Strings of white lights wound around palm trees, and bright beams shot into the indigo night sky. Janie looked out the tinted window of the Beverwils' Bentley Arnage and sighed. Her dad complained about city lights because they blocked out all the stars. But she didn't care. What good were stars on a night like tonight? What wish could they grant that hadn't just been granted?

Janie was wearing a floor-length, empire-waisted Emanuel Ungaro halter dress in pale yellow watered silk. The dress belonged to Charlotte's mother, who had danced it to shreds before retiring it to a hanger in the mid-eighties. After more than two decades' worth of gravity and neglect, the delicate halter straps finally gave up and snapped; Charlotte spent Janie's twenty dollars on a length of black silk ribbon to replace them. The leftover ribbon she sewed into delicate rose buds, tying the ribbon over and over, pulling the loops into petals, feeding her needle into the base, securing hard knots. In the end, the ribbon produced six black roses, all in various stages of bloom. Charlotte sewed one to the end of one strap, two to the end of the other, and three in a cluster at the waist. The result was so beautiful, Charlotte herself couldn't resist trying it on. As she looked into the mirror, she came to the same sad conclusion she always did: she would never,

ever borrow her mother's clothes. She was just too short. Every dress Charlotte tried on made her look like the Wicked Witch of the West: "I'm melting! Melting! Ooohhhh . . . !"

But with Janie it was different. The buttery-yellow silk clung to her torso like a mold. The narrow skirt spilled from her nonexistent hips and cascaded to the floor, and the delicate halter straps showed her creamy shoulders to perfection. The dress transformed Janie from a pillar of low self-esteem to a high-performance fashion machine.

As the storm-gray Bentley pulled to the curb, Janie smiled at Charlotte for the eight millionth time. "Thank you so much," she said.

"Okay!" Charlotte cut her off. "Stop thanking me."

"Sorry," Janie whispered.

A crisply dressed valet opened the car door, and Janie lifted the skirt of her dress, presenting one long leg to the street. She turned, showing off the length of her slender, bare back. The silky black roses bounced between her delicate shoulder blades. *Thank you my ass,* Charlotte thought to herself. If Janie was so damn thankful, then why'd she dress Charlotte like a slap in the face? Charlotte glared into the lap of her "dress." It looked like Marilyn Manson had chewed up a British flag and yacked it all over her body. And the needlework! The needlework was appalling. Janie might as well have put it together with staples. (It never occurred to Charlotte that "messy needlework" was the whole point.) She fingered the chain of safety pins around her neck, her eyes bright with rage. Still, the angrier she got, the more amazing she looked. After all, nothing compliments a punk frock quite so well as a pissy mood.

"Are you guys coming?!" she demanded as Janie shut the door.

"In a minute!" Melissa and Petra yelled in unison. After all, they were as upset as Charlotte. Maybe even more.

"I refuse to go out in this." Melissa glowered into the lap of her Guatemalan-style peasant dress made of 100 percent natural hemp. The dress, which boasted no waistline whatsoever, billowed over her breasts and just sort of *floated*. Adding insult to injury, Petra had decorated the neckline, sleeves, and pockets with teeny-tiny painted peace signs. As a general rule, peace signs inspired Melissa toward violence.

"How could you possibly spend four hundred fifty dollars on *this*?" she choked out, smacking the window with her open palm.

"I didn't," Petra lashed back. "I made the dress and donated the change to PETA."

"What! How *much* change?"

"I don't know. Four hundred and thirty-eight dollars?"

"*What?!*"

"It's the least you could do for making me wear this!" Petra cried. She turned to the Bentley's dark, tinted window, mourning her new reflection. Melissa had put her in a baby pink Juicy Couture mini-shorts-attached-to-tube-top thing called a "romper." The romper's sole mission in life was to expose as much skin as possible. If Petra yanked it up to cover her cleavage, out came the bottom of her butt. As soon as she pulled it down, *pop!* went the cleavage. How was she supposed to move in this thing, let alone romp? How was she supposed to even *breathe*?

"You know you look good," Melissa quivered in defiance.

"Um . . . no!" Petra replied. "I look *naked*."

"Well, I *brought* you a jacket!"

"Made out of *rabbit fur!*"

"Do you even know?" Melissa clutched the jacket to her breast like a child. "This is Miu Miu bunny *bomber*."

"You think I give a crap?" Petra recoiled to the corner of her seat. "I told you. It's cruelty to animals!"

"Cruelty to *animals*?" Melissa repeated with a rueful laugh. "At least I'm not cruel to *human beings*."

Petra gasped. "Neither am I!"

"Oh yeah? Lemme let you in on something. *I* am a human being. And *as* a human being, I *personally* accuse you of cruelty."

"Me?!" Petra trembled with indignation. "I accuse you!"

"No, no . . . I accuse you!"

"Well, I accuse you!"

"Okay, shut the HELL up!!!" Charlotte screamed from the opposite side of the car. Melissa and Petra clamped their mouths shut and stared. Charlotte never, ever screamed. She sneered. She snipped. But screaming she regarded as a repugnant sign of weakness. Babies screamed. Crazy people. Charlotte cleared her throat. "This is our party," she continued calmly, "and we're totally missing it. Have either of you even looked outside?"

For the first time, the two others peered at the window for the view and not their own reflections. The face of Prada boasted a row of gleaming glass doors and an enormous, brushed-metal cube. The cube, which was lit from underneath, hovered over the guests like a UFO. The place was absolutely swarmed — a buzzing hive of flushed faces and bare shoulders, of giggling girls and gorgeous guys — some familiar, some deliciously unfamiliar. From east wall to west wall, East Coast to West Coast, anyone who was anyone was there: Marco, Deena, Kate, Laila, Jake, Evan, Don John, Bronywn, Christina, Theo, Joaquin, Tyler, Luke and Tim.... Plus there were Malibu High School kids, Brentwood kids, Harvard Westlake kids ... the striking sons and daughters of their parents' agents, managers, producers, personal trainers, their ex-model, ex–best friend's exes. Not to mention the cute guy from the Coffee Bean on Sunset, the even cuter guy from the Puma store on Melrose, and that one rock-star-hot assistant from the Endeavor Talent Agency.

And that wasn't even counting the mind-blowing hotties they'd all brought with them.

A girl who looked liked Kirsten Dunst sloshed a lemon-drop martini across her hand and squealed. She turned around, the light hit her in a new way, and suddenly it became clear: she *was* Kirsten Dunst. But then she bent to fix the strap of her strappy black heel and was back to being "the girl who looked like Kirsten Dunst." Not that you noticed. By then you were already staring at the guy who looked exactly like Justin Timberlake. Except, wait ... *was* that Justin Timberlake?

Melissa rolled down the window. A thumping smash-mix collided with the tide of overlapping voices. The sound swirled, filling the inside of the Bentley like a bubble bath. A flock of UCLA film students swooped in. Camera lights popped.

Everyone was having fun but them.

"I'm going in," Charlotte announced with a toss of her small chin. *"Je ne regrette rien."*

With that, she spiked the cement with her black satin platform pump and got out of the car. She slammed the door. She steamed into the crowd. She felt defiant. She felt badass. She felt a little insane. She hated to admit it, but she owed it to the Marilyn Manson yack-dress. For once, she didn't have to be the delicate flower.

For once, she could be the mushroom cloud.

Petra Greene

CHARLotte Beverwil

Don't they Look happy?

Melissa Moon

Janie Parrish

The Girl: Gretchen Sweet (aka "Naomi")
The Getup: Black cotton shirt, black short-shorts,
black "Sparkle and Fade" fishnets, black platform
Mary Janes, lizard-green eyeliner, silver
serving tray

Jake squeezed through the suffocating crowd until he located a
square foot of personal space. It took a minute to realize he was
standing on a window. The window was watermelon seed-shaped
and big as a bathtub. Under the glass, at the end of a short tunnel,
an impeccably dressed mannequin perched on a nest of purses.
Jake wished he could lift the glass and climb in next to her. She
looked tons more fun than the brainless people at this brainless
party. She was brainless, but she had a good excuse. She was a
mannequin. And she had no head.

"Sir?"

Jake looked up. A knock-out Naomi Watts look-alike smiled
from across a serving platter. The last thing he wanted to hear
from a Naomi Watts look-alike was the word "sir."

"Please," Jake insisted, holding up his hand. "Call me 'dude.'"

Naomi laughed, and her light-gray eyes sparkled. "Okay, *dude*.
Would you like a tuna tartar wasabi wafer?"

"Uh . . . ," he hesitated, spying the wafers. They looked a little
Fancy Feast.

"Come on," she pretended to beg. "I made them myself."

"Okay," he surrendered, pinching one from the small round tray. "Seeing as you slaved away in a hot kitchen. . . ."

"You have no idea." Naomi came one step closer. "How hot . . . my kitchen is. . . ."

Jake stared, the wasabi wafer hovering in front of his open mouth. Naomi tossed her peroxide-blond bob and smiled. "So . . ." She glanced around the packed lobby. "What's this ho-down about?"

"Uh . . ." (He hadn't quite recovered his ability to speak.) "It's a fashion thing. Like a label thing. For fashion. Thing."

"Really?" Naomi cocked a pencil-thin eyebrow. "I'm a fashion designer. Well, aspiring. *You* know the story."

Jake nodded. He was still thinking about her hot kitchen.

"You gonna eat that thing?" she asked, nodding to the appetizer in his hand.

"Oh yeah." He tossed the wafer thing into his mouth and felt a sharp tug on his arm.

"Holy sh-sh-tuh!" Jake squeaked, turning around. His eyes smarted with instant tears. Wasabi flashed across his tongue like a Malibu brush fire.

"What?" Charlotte pouted, her hands on her hips. "Do you think I look stupid?"

"No!" he huffed, waving his hand. "No, you look really h-hh-hot."

She beamed, smoothing the shredded folds of her deconstructed skirt. "Really?"

Jake grabbed a glass of champagne and downed it in two gulps.

"Hey-hey," Charlotte tsked, wresting the glass from his grip. "Don't waste yourself on this rot-gut." She plunked the glass on Naomi's tray, who narrowed her eyes and took off. "I brought along some private reserve," Charlotte explained, leaning toward Jake's ear. "Cristal..."

Jake raised his eyebrows. "Really?"

"Uh-huh," she murmured. "We need to celebrate."

"Celebrate what?"

Charlotte stepped back, grinning like a sly cat. "Gimme your hand," she ordered. She fished a mystery object from her vintage satin clutch and placed it in the middle of his palm. Jake peered down with a baffled smile. It was a small plastic water gun. Charlotte closed his fingers around it, one by one.

"There's a garden on the roof," she said, giving his belt buckle a surreptitious tug. "Meet me there in twenty minutes?"

At that, she walked away, raising her arm like a tango dancer. With a twirl of her wrist, Charlotte disappeared into the crowd. Jake watched after her, pressed the barrel of the water gun to his heart, and pulled the trigger: *click*.

He was starting to feel nervous again.

"Testing... ahem... hello?" At the sound of Melissa's voice, the volume of the crowd, which had swelled to maximum capacity, took a mild dip. Marco glanced to the top of the wide, polished wood staircase. His girlfriend held a mic to her lips. At least, he *thought* it was Melissa. For some reason, she was crouching behind a cube-shaped shoe display, hiding most of her body and face from view.

"LISTEN UP!" Marco yelled in support.

But the crowd lost interest and grew even louder. Melissa panicked. She never freaked out in front of an audience — she *lived* for an audience! What was wrong with her?

She grabbed Petra's hand as she walked by, pulling her down behind the shoe display.

"I can't do this," Melissa whispered into her ear. "I cannot make my speech dressed like this." She pushed a thin pack of index cards into Petra's hand. "You do it," she instructed. Charlotte and Janie were God knows where and Melissa wasn't about to search for them wearing this brown trash bag.

"Me?" Petra shook her head in terror. "I can't. I don't do speeches."

"Well, *I* don't hide behind shoe displays. But I am right now, and you wanna know why? 'Cause you dressed me like the kind of person who hides behind shoe displays!"

"You're still *you*," Petra reminded her. "I can't . . ."

"Yo-yo-yo-yo-yo-yo-yo-YOOOO!" Melissa belted into the mic, cutting short her colleague's protest. A hush fell over the crowd. Everyone knew eight consecutive yo's meant business.

"Go!" Melissa ordered, stabbing Petra's thigh with a fingernail. Petra yelped, bounding to her feet. She turned around. Three hundred expectant faces looked right at her. She swallowed, staring down at Melissa's first card.

"Congratulations," she read with all the passion of a robot. "Y'all have arrived to the ... OW!" Petra yelped a second time, glaring at Melissa and her evil death nail.

"Smile!" Melissa hissed like an overbearing stage mother. "Have fun! And *whatever* you do, *don't be yourself*!"

"*Fine.*" Petra smiled through clenched teeth. She whipped around to face the crowd. "WhaaaSUUPPP!!!" she called wildly into the mic.

"WHOOOOO!" the crowd screamed back. Marco bounced on his toes, waving his arms like a conductor.

"No need to introduce myself!" Petra grinned. "Y'all know my name ... the one and only ... *Melissa Moon*!"

Everyone exploded into laughter. All at once, Petra's out-of-character outfit made perfect sense. *Oh,* their faces seemed to say. *Now* we get it. Meanwhile, Melissa's death-nail continued to stab her like a scorpion. Petra didn't care.

"Yeah, baby!!!" She cupped a hand to her ghetto gold-hooped ear. "Tonight y'all have been *invited* to be *sighted* ... where? To the block to end all blocks. To the drive to end all *drives*! Y'all know what I'm talkin' about! Roh-DAYYOOOOOO!!! Give it up!"

The crowd whooped and whistled as Petra cracked her gum. Melissa sunk her face into her hands.

"As you may or may not have *heard*—my sisters Charlotte, Janie, Petra, and I have united the forces of style to create our very own fashion label. We are all very, *very* different people. But we do share *one* thing . . . clothes!" Petra lifted her lanky arms into the air and shook her baby-pink, romper-clad butt. A mass of half-drunk faces screamed in delight.

"But we also share something else!" Melissa snatched the mic from Petra's hand. Under the flashing lights, her light brown hippie bag-dress looked ten times worse. She looked like a hugely pregnant Oompa Loompa on her way to Woodstock.

"Omigawd-uh," Deena squawked in the distance. Marco's jaw dropped.

"You dirty hippie!" someone yelled to the crowd's tittering amusement. Melissa responded with an aggressive-looking peace sign.

"Yes, hello . . . my name is *Petra Greene*, and I am a dirty, dirty hippie."

The crowd reacted with a talk show caliber, "Oooo-OOHHH!!!"

"Cat fight!" another someone yelled.

"I would like to point out," Melissa continued, "that on this very special night — we share *much* more than clothes. We share a dream. A dream that one day, people of all colors, genders, and creeds will come together in support of life, liberty, and . . ."

Petra leaned into the mic. "The pursuit of kuh-*yoot*-ness!"

At that everyone went absolutely wild. Melissa stared at Petra in disbelief. "That was good," she admitted. Petra smiled, retrieving the mic.

"So now the question is . . . what to *name* that dream?" Petra added. The lights dimmed and an enormous clear plastic globe descended from the ceiling like a disco ball. Inside the globe, a built-in fan blew hundreds of tiny square tags around like snow.

"As you know, we need a name for our new label. Each of you received a blank tag in your invitation. We sent out one hundred and sixty-eight invitations and received *exactly* one hundred and sixty-eight tags in return." Melissa put her hand to her heart. "Your participation means *so much*."

"Even though we haven't read them yet," Petra said, "we know for a *fact* — every *one* of your suggestions is an act of pure genius."

"But we can only pick one!" Melissa reminded her audience.

"Sadness!" Petra fake-pouted.

"So we'll post the name of our wonderful, amazing, perfect-in-every-way winner on Monday."

"But until then have fun, 'cause . . ."

"*Tag!*" The two girls yelled in unison, pointing their fingers at the audience. "You're it!"

They threw their arms around one another's waists and bowed to the floor. The applause was deafening — like a million shining pennies falling on an old tin roof. Petra and Melissa turned to each other and smiled. They had to admit, it was a beautiful sound.

But only if the coins were lucky.

Janie ran up the small set of creaky stairs, praying the fragile hem of her dress wouldn't snag on a splinter or a nail. She stepped onstage, ducking the glare of stage lights, and tip-toed around intricate webs of wires and little flecks of glow-in-the-dark tape. Then she saw him. He was crouching next to an amplifier, twiddling a knob, and pressing his ear to the speaker. The bicycle chains around his narrow hips draped to the floor. His blue-tipped fauxhawk reached for the sky. The silver ring on his lower lip glinted like a fleck of drool.

Except Janie was the one drooling.

"Hey," she said. But the word got swallowed in a surge of feedback. She cleared her throat and prodded his shoulder. Paul Elliot Miller's shoulder. His threadbare black-sleeved baseball shirt was warm and damp with sweat.

Paul Elliot Miller's sweat.

He looked up, flicking his gaze along Janie's slender frame, his mismatched bluish-green, greenish-brown eyes smudged with black coal eyeliner. "You can't be here," he spoke at last, returning his focus to the speaker.

"Oh," Janie replied, crushed at his aloof demeanor. She finally got up the nerve to say hello and his response was "you can't be here"? What about "I love you"?

Didn't he know his lines?

"I need to see Amelia," Janie announced with as much confidence as she could muster.

"Wish I could help you," he muttered, then turned another knob, grunting with effort. Turning knobs, it seemed, was very hard work.

"Come on," she pressed, praying the tremor in her voice wasn't as obvious to him as it was to her. "Where is she?"

"Look," the beautiful mouth spat. "Amelia told me no one backstage. It's, like, no seeing the bride before the wedding—right?"

"She's not a bride."

"She's a lead singer, okay? Same rules apply."

"Well, I need to give her this," Janie insisted, lifting the Trader Joe's shopping bag in her hand. Paul peered down the length of his lightly freckled, aristocratic nose. He rolled a toothpick from one side of his lip to the other. "It's her *wedding dress,*" she explained, accepting his terms.

He sighed, spitting his half-digested toothpick to the floor. Janie stared. If he hadn't been right there, she would have swooped to the ground and cradled it in her hand. She would have taken it home and sealed it in a plastic bag. She would have handled it with sterilized tweezers. But he was right there, so she could do nothing but stare and say:

"You're disgusting."

Paul grinned, relishing Janie's response. And then, without

warning, he leaped offstage. He pushed his way through a throng of girls with leather bracelets and Bettie Page bangs, a bunch of guys in slouchy hoodies and studded belts. They watched Paul pass, sucking on their beers like grumpy babies. He turned around, staring at Janie with aggressive contempt.

"Are you coming or what?!"

"Oh," she startled, and obediently headed downstairs. Paul did not wait for her; in fact, he walked faster. Janie scrambled to catch up. She followed him behind the bar, past rows of glinting liquor bottles, the cat-pee smell of fresh beer and old vomit. She followed him through two saloon-style swinging doors. Black sheets were stapled to the ceiling. Graffiti webbed the walls. Music thudded like a distant heartbeat. Janie concentrated on the small of Paul Elliot Miller's back. *Take me,* she thought. *Push me against this greasy, gross wall and take me.*

"Meelia!" Paul called, pushing back a ragged black sheet. He stepped into a narrow hallway and pounded on a black door. "MeelYUH!"

"Hold on!" a female voice yelled.

Paul leaned against the wall and looked at Janie. She looked back at him, feeling the blood throb in her ears. His eyes lingered on the trio of black satin roses at her waist.

"What?" she asked, wrenching the word from the back of her throat.

In response, he pounded the door a second time. "Oi!" he yelled, sounding somewhere between Sid Vicious (punk rock

251

legend) and Sid Firestein (Janie's cranky grandfather). The door cracked open. Paul thrust his painted thumb in Janie's direction.

"Your prom date's here," he snickered.

Janie blushed, realizing exactly what he meant. She was Clashing with a capital C. Except, not only did the dress clash with *who* she was, it also clashed with *where* she was. She was Clashing with a capital C to the second power.

"Omigod!" Amelia gushed, opening the door wider. "You look so pretty!" Janie darted inside, slamming the door behind her. She couldn't handle the look on Paul's face—whatever it was. No doubt "pretty" was the last word he'd use to describe how she looked, assuming he looked at her, which he most definitely did not.

"Thanks," Janie whispered, once they were alone.

"Whatever," Amelia muttered, slamming the brakes on her initial friendliness. Amelia almost forgot: she and Janie were *in a fight,* which meant—head-over-heels happy as she was to see her—she had to act the opposite.

"So, what are you doing here?" Amelia asked, digging through her white leather hobo. "I thought you had that, like, 'Pop Your Zit' party to go to."

"I do," Janie replied, noticing two bloated cigarette butts in the toilet bowl. "If they find out I left, I'm pretty much dead."

"So go." Amelia shrugged, heading for the door.

"No, wait!" Janie insisted. She presented Amelia with the

brown paper shopping bag, much like the one she presented Charlotte hours before. "I had to give you this."

"What is it?" Amelia asked, melting a little. She was a sucker for presents.

"Open it."

Amelia hesitated, turning to the water-spotted mirror. "We're going on in, like, two minutes," she announced, applying an extra coat of dark red lipstick. Janie noticed it was NARS, a brand Amelia definitely could not afford. Not that it mattered. Her best friend was an expert shoplifter, an act she jokingly referred to as "coming down with a case of the Winonas." Sometimes Janie thought it was funny. Sometimes she didn't.

She pressed her lips together and blotted on the wall. "I'll open it after the show," she said with a hard look. "Now, if you'll excuse me."

She whisked outside, slamming the door behind her. Janie stood in the center of the bathroom, stunned. So stunned she didn't hear the click of the door handle, or the sound of Amelia stepping back inside.

"Ew!" Amelia cringed, wringing her hands like she'd stepped in something gross. "That was so bitchy!"

As she flung her arms around her, Janie laughed with relief. "Never let me be that horrible again," Amelia whispered into her ear. "I'm, like, traumatized."

"MMMEEEEELLLLLLIIIAAAA!" Paul bellowed down the hall.

Amelia rolled her eyes. For a supposed anarchist, Paul sure was a stickler for starting on time.

"I've gotta go," she apologized. Janie blocked the door.

"Not until you open this thing!" she demanded, swinging the shopping bag by its paper handles.

"Okay," Amelia surrendered, snatching the bag from the air. She tore apart layers of tissue paper like a crazed animal. "Omigod." She gasped in disbelief. "Is this what I think it is?"

Janie laughed, clapping her hands.

Amelia immediately tore off her navy blue baby-doll dress and slipped into Janie's creation. Charlotte's budget had bought enough material for not one, but two dresses. The first dress served as a learning exercise; Janie dropped some stitches, misjudged a couple of pleats. But she learned from her mistakes, and so the second dress was perfect.

"The London Vampire Milkmaid Dress," Amelia whispered as Janie zipped the back. "I can't believe it."

In the distance, their drummer, Max, commenced an execution-style drum roll. The message was clear: either Amelia showed up in three seconds, or it was off with her head.

"Okay." She gasped again, hugging Janie one last time. Janie watched her bound breathlessly down the hall. A moment later, Amelia's audience screamed in appreciation. Amelia leaned into the mic and cleared her throat.

"Shut up," she murmured. The crowd rumbled with laughter.

"You ungrateful slobs. You disgusting leeches. Isn't it time you cleaned your freakin' rooms? Don't you *realize* we're..."

"CREATURES OF HABIT!" the crowd exploded, right on cue. Amelia laughed, twanging a string on her bass.

"Thank you," she smiled, shaking her hair back. "Thank you so much."

Backstage, Janie smiled, hiding her grin behind the stage curtain. Amelia never thanked an audience. And she wasn't thanking them then.

She was thanking Janie.

She still couldn't believe she'd asked Evan Beverwil for a ride, but what choice did she have? Jake, who promised he'd take her to Spaceland, seemed to have disappeared. And just as her brother was nowhere to be found, Evan was just about *everywhere*. All Janie had to do was turn around and he appeared: at the bar, on the stage, behind the staircase, by the bouquets, on the dance floor, in the lobby. He was even outside the girls' bathroom. But she never saw him look at her, that is, until she tapped him on the elbow. At the moment of her touch, Evan, who'd been chatting with Bronwyn Spencer, stopped mid-sentence and snapped to attention. Janie noticed his car keys in one hand. (She tried not to notice the beer in the other.)

The London Vampire Milkmaid Dress

off-shoulder collar cropped t-shirt

Safety pin & red bead necklace

Safety pin & red bead detail

union jack tiered skirt

exposed stitching

taffeta petticoat for MILKMAID EFFECT

← Guitar = sheep

"Do you know where Spaceland is?"

When he agreed to drive her, she was unbelievably relieved. And it was her relief that had occupied her thoughts as they sped from Beverly Hills in the direction of Silverlake. Of course, by the time they headed *back* to Beverly Hills, Janie's relief had dissipated, and her mind was free to think about other things.

Like the fact that she'd accepted a ride from a *beer drinker*.

All at once, Evan's red Porsche 911 convertible seemed uncomfortably low to the ground. Janie could see the individual bumps of gravel in the road. Then he changed gears. In a matter of seconds, the bumps became streaking comets. Janie's heart leaped into her throat.

"We're going kind of fast," she squeaked, glancing at the beer in his cup holder.

"Come on," Evan replied, following her gaze. "I've had one beer all night. Besides, this is a *nine-eleven*."

"Right." She grimaced, gripping the sides of her seat. She tried to block out the image of her brains splattered across the road.

"So," he said, zipping through a yellow light, "did your friend like his present?"

"You mean *her* present," she corrected.

"Wait . . ." Evan looked confused. "Who was that dude you were talking to?"

"You mean Paul?" she asked, blushing the color of the convertible.

"I don't know." He shrugged, dropping his arm across the back of Janie's seat. He glanced at her. "He seemed kinda gay."

"He is *not* gay."

"He was wearing eyeliner."

Janie recoiled against the passenger door, appalled. *"So?"*

Evan caught a glimpse of her expression and sighed, returning his hand to the black leather wheel. "Can I ask you a question," he said. Janie watched him clench and unclench his jaw. "Do you, like, hate me in *particular?* Or do you just, like, ooze with general hate."

Janie's jaw dropped. "Excuse me?"

He didn't respond. They headed down Sunset Boulevard and made a right on La Brea. Janie looked out the window. They passed by Mashti Malone's, the store with the legendary saffron-and-rosewater ice cream. They passed the Volvo mechanic on Santa Monica Boulevard, the mega-Target, and the Starbucks. And then they passed by Jet Rag, with its skyscraping red neon sign. All but three letters were burned out. Together they read: TAG.

Evan pulled to the side of the road, the Porsche growling as he shut off the engine.

"I'll be right back," he announced. And then he got out of the car.

Janie craned around in her bucket seat, watching him saunter down the dimly lit sidewalk. Was he just going to leave her there? She fidgeted for a few seconds before opening the car door. As much as she hated Evan's company, she hated her own more.

She got out of the Porsche, floating around the car like an aimless raft tied to a dock. She waited for him to turn around—waited for him to see her waiting. But he didn't. He just hung onto a chain-link fence, his face close enough to smell the rust.

What was he looking at?

Janie surrendered and started walking toward him. She was curious. And she was lonely. Sometimes she wondered if every choice she made came down to those two feelings.

"Hey," she said, hugging herself with her arms.

"I just needed some air," he replied, looking straight ahead. "Sorry."

A streetlight lit up the crown of his head, casting his face in shadow. Janie pressed her forehead to the chain-link fence.

"Oh . . . ," she murmured, hugging herself tighter.

The elephant looked different at night, illuminated by murky green lights and criss-crossed with grassy shadows. Janie couldn't see the tar, but she could smell it. She could hear it, too—bubbling like a witch's brew.

"I used to have nightmares about this elephant," Evan said.

"Yeah?"

Evan nodded. "We took this field trip in, like, second grade? And our guide told us the elephant was really alive, but trying really hard to be still, so she wouldn't sink into the tar, or whatever."

"Omigod," Janie blurted with disbelief. "I totally had that same guide!"

Evan shook his head and laughed. "That guy seriously messed with my head."

"Me too!"

"He should be, like, jailed or something."

"Or thrown into the tar pit," she suggested.

"I *like* it." He smiled. "Poetic justice."

Janie smiled back, allowing their eyes to lock. Her heart rose and fluttered in her throat. *This makes no sense.* How could Charlotte's older brother have the same elephant issues she had? Of all the people in the world, Evan Beverwil *understood.*

"Can I ask you something?" he asked.

"Okay," Janie whispered, holding her breath.

"Did that guy, that eyeliner dude . . ."

"Paul," Janie responded, feeling sick. How could she have something in common with a guy who thought Paul Elliot Miller, the god of her idolatry, was *gay*?

Evan cleared his throat. "Did he tell you how unbelievably pretty you look tonight?"

"Oh," Janie replied with a blush fierce enough to cause temporary blindness. "No."

Janie could feel him looking at her. She could not bring herself to look back. She just stood there, rooted to the sidewalk, absolutely still.

She was stuck.

Evan nodded and let go of the fence. The chain-link jingled like a spur. "Just checking."

Jake was beginning to understand why Accutane and alcohol didn't mix. All he'd had was, like, two glasses of champagne and — *five seconds later* — *bam*. He was stumbling around like Tara Reid. Through a combination of luck and pure willpower, he'd managed to direct his stumbling toward a cantaloupe rind–shaped chair. Fifteen minutes later, he was still there, head in his hands, waiting for the world to stop spinning.

But it just spun faster.

"Hi, Jake!"

He looked up. A cute blonde in a slinky purple dress peered down at him, her face a blur of pinks and whites and blues. Jake squinted until the pinks relocated to her lips and cheeks, the whites to her inexpertly powdered forehead, and the blues to her eager, shining eyes.

"It's me, Nikki! I like your tie!"

He stared at the frosted glass of clear liquid in her hand. "Is that water?" he croaked.

"Oh." She rolled her eyes. "My friend asked me to hold this for her. She's telling everyone it's straight vodka but it's actually water. *So* lame."

"Can I have some?"

"Sure!" she trilled, handing him the glass. Jake drank like a desert wanderer, swallowing in loud, eager gulps. Nikki watched the rise and fall of his Adam's apple, transfixed.

"So . . ." She sat next to him with a klutzy *thump.* "You look really nice," she whispered. "Can I tell you that?"

"Um . . . okay." He smiled. "You look nice too."

"Really?" Nikki breathed. She leaned her head toward his shoulder, but missed completely and fell into his lap.

"Hey . . . ," Jake said, sliding his hand under her cheek. He spatula'd her face from his lap like a pancake. "Are you okay?"

"This is so much fun!" she squealed. And that's when Jake realized — Nikki wasn't exactly sober herself.

"Come on." He tried lifting her to her feet. "Let's get you some air."

"No." She pouted, grabbing onto the collar of his shirt.

"Hey." Jake gently wrested her grip from his only good button-down. Nikki grabbed his hand, and he allowed her to drag him around to the other side of a freestanding wall. The wall looked like one of those foam egg-crate mattress pads, except instead of bright yellow, it was avocado green.

"Where are you taking me?" Jake laughed. A row of glass fitting rooms glinted under the light.

"You wanna see something?" Nikki asked, wavering in the hall.

"What?" Jake hesitated, looking around him. He was starting to feel guilty, but he didn't know why. He followed her inside a fitting room. "What," he said again, as she slid the glass door shut.

"Look outside." Nikki pointed. Jake looked through the glass door. The crowd churned under the disco lights, colliding into each other, shrieking like they were being boiled alive. The DJ was blasting Daft Punk's "Harder, Better, Faster, Stronger." Everyone danced their hardest, bestest, fastest, strongest. Jake felt like he was a little kid, pointing a kaleidoscope at the sun.

And then, all at once, the glass door transformed into an opaque white wall. The party disappeared.

"Whoa," he exclaimed, stepping back. Nikki giggled. Jake stared as the opaque wall faded back into a transparent, glass door.

"Look." She pointed again. A silver dome sat on the slate-gray floor like a mushroom. The word PRIVACY was engraved across the top. "Press it," Nikki instructed, like a character from Alice in Wonderland.

He tapped the silver dome with the toe of his shoe. Sure enough, the glass door transformed back into a wall. "Holy shit," he laughed, tapping the dome a few times in a row. The glass door flickered like a ghost. Jake beamed. "It's like the future!"

Nikki giggled, stepping on his foot. Jake held his breath. The pressure of her foot on his was nice. So nice, he let her push further—until the silver dome sank into the floor, the glass became a wall, and, just like that, they were alone.

"I should go," Jake said. She whipped her foot away and nodded, staring at the floor.

"Sorry," she whispered.

"Hey." He suddenly felt bad and jostled Nikki's shoulder. "Hey," he said again, this time with surprise. He held onto her shoulder and tried to get used to it. She was totally *shaking*.

"Listen," Jake murmured, hooking a lock of Nikki's hair behind her ear. And then, without thinking, he leaned in and kissed her. He kissed her as a token of charity — because she liked him so much and, well, *he felt bad*. Except, once they started kissing, it felt good. And then it felt really good. Which is exactly when Jake stopped feeling bad for Nikki, and started feeling bad for someone else.

"I can't do this," he declared, pulling back. "I'm sorry." Jake closed his eyes to the spinning room. "That was really stupid."

When he opened his eyes, he expected Nikki to be looking right at him, crushed. But she wasn't looking at him. She was looking through the door, which, to both of their confusion, had changed back to see-through glass.

They must have *stepped on the dome* while they were kissing.

When she finally looked at Jake, she didn't look crushed. She looked terrified. About twenty feet away, in a weird, haphazard frock, Charlotte stood like the Angel of Vengeance. She clutched a bottle of Cristal like a medieval weapon. Strobe lights flashed across her face like lightning.

"Charlotte!" Jake called. "Wait!"

He pushed Nikki aside and exploded from the dressing room, weaving through the crowd. A clot of grinding dancers blocked Charlotte's path long enough for him to catch up. "Charlotte!" He reached for her arm.

"Don't *touch* me!" The bottle of chilled champagne slipped through her fingers, smashing across the floor.

"Charlotte," he pleaded. "It was an accident!"

"No!" She shook her head. "I *saw* you!"

"I know, but you've got to believe me. I don't even know what happened. I just got really drunk and . . ."

"You had one glass of champagne!" Tears began to stream down her cheeks.

"I think it's the Accutane."

"The what?!"

"It's this medication . . ."

"Is it for multiple personalities?" She trembled, wiping the hot tears from her face. "Because it's *not working*!"

"It's for my skin. For my acne," Jake pleaded again, feeling miserable. The last thing Jake wanted to do was remind Charlotte of who he used to be, and who, in his darker moments, he believed he still was: a zit-encrusted, pus-infested loser. Charlotte's silence was deafening. With all the courage he could muster, Jake looked into her cold, pool-green eyes. He couldn't tell what she was thinking.

Charlotte thought about the garden upstairs, about the lemon trees in their terracotta pots, the small manicured Cyprus, the lavender, the rambling rose. She thought about the night jasmine blooming on the trellis and the checked blanket under it, the careful way she'd spread it out, pinning the corners with bowls of blueberries and raspberries. She thought about her straw picnic basket, which she'd packed to the point of bursting: baguettes and cheese, quiche and apples, figs and chocolate-covered almonds. There were pears in gold foil and petite Madeleines. The tiniest pots of caviar. She'd lit the way with flickering tea lights and, last but not least, sprinkled the path with Sweet Tarts. She tossed them by the handful, like bird feed — like wedding rice. She made sure every single Sweet Tart was green.

"Omigod," she breathed with a chilling little laugh. "I can't believe I've been so stupid."

"Charlotte," Jake pleaded again, this time reaching for her hand. She writhed from his grasp like a fish, escaping in a flash. He stood in the middle of the dance floor. The broken champagne bottle glinted at his feet. Five minutes ago, that bottle was worth over 7,000 dollars. But Jake didn't know that.

All he knew was that it was worth nothing now.

His stomach surged with something sour.

Melissa staggered out of the Prada store with the heavy clear globe in her hands. The built-in fan was turned off and all the white tags had settled to the bottom. She lowered it to the ground, slipping off Petra's hideous Bjorn clogs to pin the globe in place. The last thing she wanted was to see it rolling down the street — yet another departed guest. Except "departed" was the wrong word.

"Kicked out" was more like it.

"Well, it's official," Charlotte sighed, joining her on the street. "We're banned from Prada for life."

Melissa closed her eyes. Vivien was going to *love* this. "I can't believe it." She shook her head. "This is so unfair!"

"Ah well," Charlotte sighed. *"C'est la vie."*

"Easy for you to say." Melissa narrowed her eyes. "It wasn't *my* boyfriend who vomited all over the dance floor."

"He is *not* my boyfriend! Anymore!" Charlotte warbled, turning pale.

As if that's the important detail, Melissa thought. And not that Jake Farrish's vomit caused a stampede of epic proportions. Poor Jake. After Charlotte dumped him, he couldn't hold it together. And once he couldn't hold it together, he realized he couldn't hold it down. The vomit came up like a geyser, spewing a distance of at least ten feet. At first no one noticed. But then Kate Joliet slipped, landing smack in middle of the acrid swamp of barf. She shrieked at the top of her lungs.

And then all havoc broke loose.

Melissa could still hear the sounds of their screams, the thousand flailing hands clawing for the exit. They weren't sure why they were running, just that everyone else was running, which was reason enough to run. But then Bronwyn Spencer's Sergio Rossi heel spiked the train of Deena Yazdi's floor-length midnight blue gown, sending Deena into a full-on frontal free-fall — right into the crotch of a female mannequin. A conga line of mannequins toppled like dominoes, crashing their way toward the last mannequin in line: a gigantic man mannequin. He was ten feet tall and absolutely ripped. The female mannequins collapsed at his feet like hysterical groupies. Man Mannequin teetered back and forth; then he toppled to the floor, mere inches away from Laila Pikser's beloved black alligator Dior pumps. Laila screamed as Man Mannequin came apart on impact, his gigantic limbs rolling downstairs like renegade logs. His giant torso came last, thudding downstairs like the world's angriest parent. Then came the horrible, inevitable sound of shattering glass. The party was over.

So, it seemed, were their lives.

Imagine Janie's confusion when, at around 12:15 a.m., she and Evan rolled up to find the once raucous Prada store empty, dark, and still as a tomb. As Evan eased on the brakes, Melissa, Charlotte, and Petra stepped toward the street, lining at the curb like ducks in a row. Janie sunk down in her seat.

The ducks looked angry.

"Well, if it isn't the Fast and the Furious," Melissa scoffed, sucking in her cheeks. "Nice of you to show up," she added. All eyes were on Janie, which Petra seized as an opportunity to spark up a joint.

"Come on," Evan replied, his hand on the gear shift. "We just went for a ride."

"Oh, I bet you did," Charlotte sneered, eyeing Janie's disheveled hair. Their eyes met. "Keep your hands off my brother," Charlotte snapped.

Evan gritted his teeth. "Shut up, Charlotte."

"Oh, whatever, Evan," Charlotte retorted. "I just don't want you to make the same mistake I did."

"What are you talking about?" Janie got out of the car and slammed the door. "Where's Jake?"

"Jake had to call a cab," Petra replied, exhaling a thin stream of smoke.

"Why?" Janie asked, whirling on Charlotte. "What did you do?"

Charlotte's eyes flashed. "What did *I* do?!"

"Thanks to your *brother*," Melissa announced, "we're banned from Prada for *at least* the next three years."

"Oh, who cares about Prada!" Charlotte snapped, her eyes growing glassy. *"Prada n'existe pas!"*

Melissa gasped. She didn't have to understand French to know blasphemy when she heard it.

While the girls continued to bicker, Petra slipped out of Melissa's excruciating crystal-beaded stilettos and into the comfy Bjorn clogs stranded on the sidewalk. She felt numb with relief, so numb it took her seconds to register the clear globe rolling down the street. She stood there and stared, then, using all the energy she had left, she said: "Um . . . you guys?"

The three girls followed her pointed finger and peered down

the street. In an instant, they were off, neck and neck, like a pack of Saratoga racehorses.

"Who are you betting on?" Evan joked, joining Petra on the sidewalk. She sucked on her dwindling joint and looked pensive.

"No one." She inhaled and held her breath. "They're all losers."

"Not Janie," Evan insisted. Even in high heels, Janie was yards ahead of Melissa and his sister. Evan watched the leaping shadows of her perfect legs through the thin gauze of her pale yellow dress. A familiar tightening in his stomach cued him to look at something else. He stared at a gray wad of gum on the street.

"Not Janie?" Petra teased, watching his somber face. "Guess you guys *did* touch each other."

Evan shook his head. "Why do girls think everything's so *sexual*? It's so annoying."

Petra blushed, averting his gaze. At the other end of the street, Janie, Charlotte, and Melissa continued to scramble. The clear plastic globe had cracked against the gutter and split into two perfect halves.

"That's just great!" Melissa yelled as a few Ferraris whooshed by. Hundreds of white tags lifted into the air and scattered across the street. Janie, Charlotte, and Melissa darted around, scooping up as many as possible. Another car sailed by, horn blaring.

"I should probably...help them," Petra muttered. Evan's Porsche responded with a guttural purr. Petra looked up as he zoomed down the street. She sighed, heading toward the girls.

One of the white tags floated down the sidewalk. She leaned over to pick it up, unfolding it as she walked. A single word was written inside:

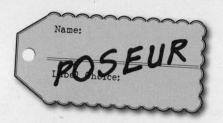

Melissa sat on the sidewalk, going through the tags one by one. She shook her head in disbelief, and her heart began to beat faster.

"What the hell *is* this?" The stiff, white tag trembled between her fingers. "Some kind of joke?"

"They all say the same thing," Charlotte realized, unfolding another tag. Janie nodded in stunned agreement.

"'Poseur,'" she read out loud, lowering a tag to her lap.

"Someone did this." Melissa trembled. "Someone broke into the ball and did this."

"Or everyone just happens to think one of us is a poseur," Petra suggested.

"It's 'cause we dressed in each other's clothes," Melissa glared at Janie. "I *knew* that was a bad idea!"

"Right," Janie bristled. "But we'd be less poseury if we did nothing."

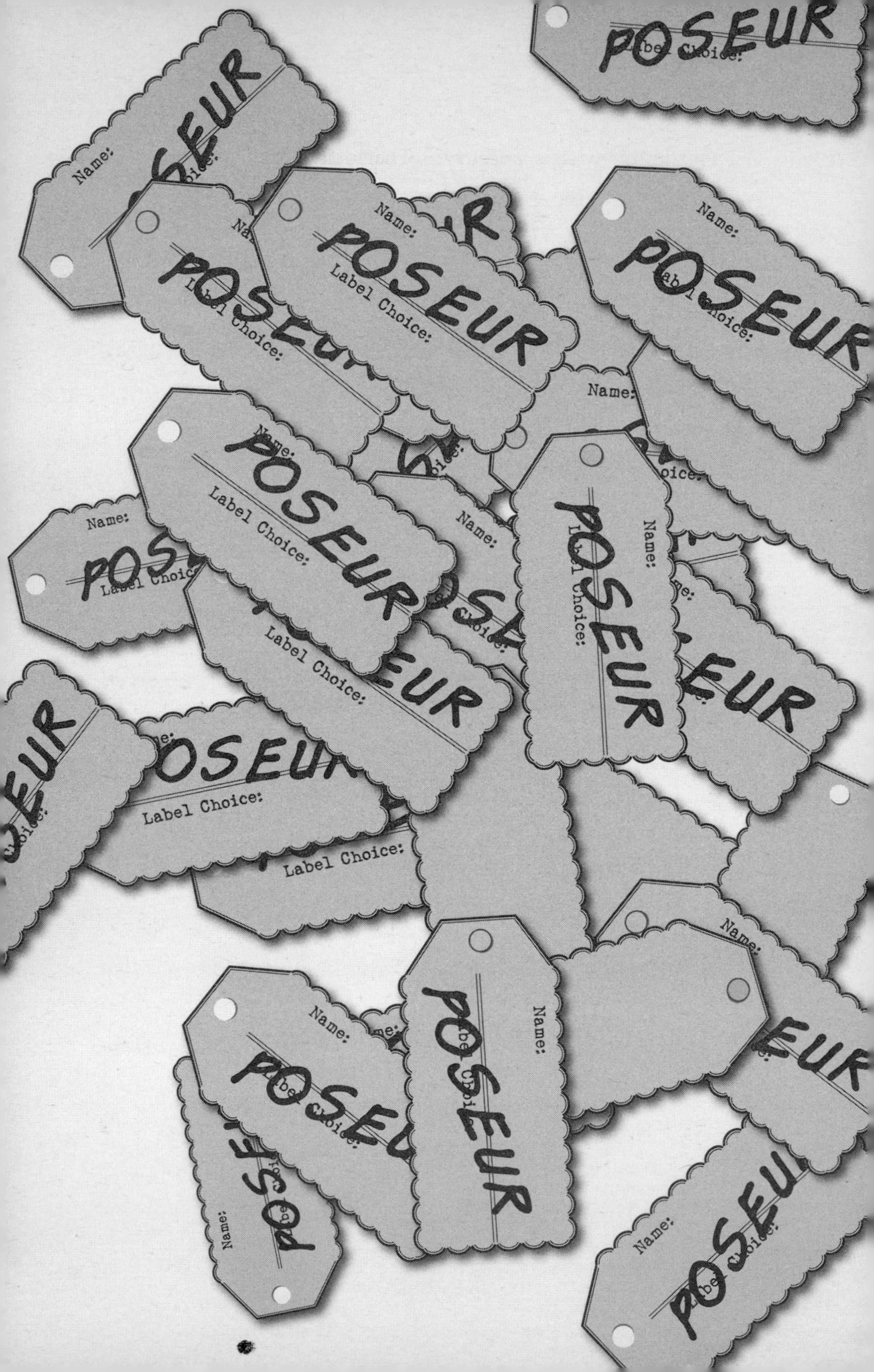

Name:
POSEUR
Label Choice:

"You know what's poseury?" Charlotte raised an eyebrow. "Valley rats who hang out in Beverly Hills."

"Ha!" Janie huffed. "What about acting French when you're *obviously American*?!" At that, Melissa stifled a laugh. Charlotte's eyes shot darts of pure evil.

"Like pretending to be some ghetto chick when you grew up in *Bel Air* is any better?" she seethed. Melissa's face froze, but Charlotte persisted. "Or what about acting like you're famous when you're *nobody*?"

"Oh lord." Petra shook her head. "This is sooo immature."

"Oh *please*!" Melissa erupted. "You're, like, the worst poseur ever!"

Petra folded her arms and frowned. "Really."

"Come on," Charlotte agreed with a roll of her eyes. "You act all *natural* when, chances are, you've had plastic surgery. You're really rich, but you dress like a beggar. And you go around like this nice person, when, you know what? You're just too *stoned* to be mean."

"And *we're* the immature ones," Melissa snorted.

"Okay," Petra countered. "All of you know *nothing* about my life. But go ahead! Act like you do! 'Cause that makes you the *worst* kind of poseur there is."

"Oh boo!" Charlotte wiped away a pretend tear.

"Petra . . ." Janie reached for her hand. Without thinking, Petra slapped it away.

"No, I'm out!" she announced, tearing down the street. "I can't believe I ever got involved with you . . . you . . . *people*!"

"Here, here." Charlotte folded her arms.

"Good riddance!" Melissa headed in the opposite direction. "I cannot *wait* to be on my own!"

"WAIT!" Janie refused to be left alone with Charlotte. "Don't we still have to share a ride home?"

The two girls stopped in their tracks.

Five minutes later, The Trend Set sat in the cab of the Beverwils' storm gray Bentley, arms folded across their chests. "After this— I'm out," Petra muttered.

"Me too."

"Threesome."

"Foursome."

Charlotte's driver, Julius, started the car and pulled out onto North Rodeo. The four girls stared out their separate tinted windows. Outside, the white tags flipped along the asphalt, picking up dirt and grime.

Tomorrow they'd be gray as ashes.

After a few tearful sessions on her forest-creature couch, Miss Pal-etsky agreed to dissolve The Trend Set. But, she pointed out, Winston was too far along in the semester for the girls to sign up for something else. She reinstated their Wednesday block of time as a one-hour study period. The girls were ecstatic—until Miss Paletsky explained study periods were a) not opportunities to socialize, and b) strictly "in house." In other words, no off-campus privileges allowed.

How quickly ecstasy turns to ick.

The off-campus ban was a pain in the ass, but socializing, it turned out, wasn't hard to resist. The only kids who weren't in class were twenty random seventh graders who happened to have a free period. It wasn't like the Four Formerly Known as The Trend Set were going to talk to *them*.

At the same time, they *definitely* weren't going to talk to each other.

By the time Wednesday arrived, the girls had resigned themselves. They studied. Melissa planted herself on a bench by Doggie Daycare. While Emilio Poochie slobbered away on a dried pig's ear, she thumbed through the library copy of *When Bunnies Brood: The Emotional Lives of Animals*. Charlotte found a tranquil windowsill where she could read *Frock and Roll: The ABCs of Dressing like a Rock Star*. Janie stretched out in the shade of the Winston weeping willows, secured her headphones, and pressed PLAY. "*Écoute et répète,*" a recorded voice said in enunciated French. "I love my friends. . . . *J'adore mes amies.*"

"*J'adore mes amies,*" she repeated to the trees.

Only Petra crawled to her usual spot on the hill behind the gym, where she dug through her bag and pulled out her most illicit stash to date. . . .

The latest issue of *W*. The latest issue of *Allure*. And, of course, the latest issue of *Vogue*.

The bell rang and Janie stuffed her iPod contraband out of sight. She headed for her locker, careful to avoid Petra's gaze. She brushed past Charlotte without a word. She ignored Melissa and her circle of shrieking friends. Janie slammed her locker shut and headed for Spanish IV. It wasn't until she'd achieved a safe distance that she allowed herself to look the way she felt: pathetic. She missed The Trend Set, but she was the only one. That much she knew for sure.

Petra, Melissa, and Charlotte felt the exact same way.

Petra's parents left for Date Night (which Petra renamed "Hate Night"), leaving her in charge of Sofia and Isabel. Despite their older sibling's protests, the two sisters always insisted on playing Barbie. When Petra tried to explain the dangers of Barbie in a post-feminist world, the little girls gasped for air and pretended to die. When Petra noticed their dolls were uniformly blond and blue-eyed, she went out of her way to secure them Asian Barbie alternatives.

"THESE ARE DUMB!" her sisters had cried. The next day Petra found Island Fun Miko and Flying Hero Kira decapitated on the lawn.

But that evening, Petra tried not to worry about Sofia's and

Isabel's developing self-image. They played "Going Shopping," and Petra painted a delicate snowflake on her south wall. She reserved one wall for each of the four seasons, but her favorite wall was winter. As she dabbed her brush into a blob of silver paint, her cell phone chirped to life.

"Can I get it?!" Isabel panted with excitement.

Petra put down her paintbrush and nodded.

"Hello, Greene residence?" Isabel answered like a hotel concierge. "May I ask who's calling, please? Yes . . . *just* a moment."

"Who is it?" Petra whispered, taking the phone. Isabel shrugged, returning to Malibu Fun Whitney.

"I don't remember," she said. Her older sister sighed, pressing the phone to her ear.

"Hello?"

"Hi, Petra. I was looking for my fuschia disco skirt, which is the only thing that goes with my black cashmere tank, and I realized you still have it."

A long call-waiting beep interrupted Charlotte's voice. It was Melissa. Petra glanced at the pirate's chest in the corner of her room. She'd forgotten all about it.

"Can you hold on for a sec?" she asked, clicking to the other line.

"You have my strawberry-print t-shirt," Melissa answered, cutting to the chase. "You need to bring the chest to school on Monday."

"Can you hold on?" Petra said, clicking over to Charlotte. "Hey. I'm just gonna bring the chest to school on —"

"Are you kidding me?" Charlotte interrupted. "I refuse to be seen with a pirate's chest at school."

"Hold on," Petra sighed, clicking back to Melissa.

"Fine," Melissa sighed. "I'll just come over to your house."

"You can't," Petra panicked. Her parents were due home from Hate Night, which meant they were bound to be fighting.

"Well, what am I supposed to do?" Charlotte sighed a second later. "I have a date at Chinois tomorrow night. That skirt is *crucial* to the whole aesthetic."

"Bring the chest to my house," Melissa replied once Petra relayed Charlotte's complaint. "Tell Charlotte and Janie to be here at eight-thirty."

"Okay," Petra sighed, snapping her phone shut. She sent Isabel a stern look. "I'm hiring a new secretary."

"I'm not your secretary," Isabel replied. "I'm your boss."

"Yeah," Sofia echoed.

Petra smiled. "My mistake," she apologized. Then she shook her head and dialed Janie's number.

Janie told Petra she'd pick her up, and no — she didn't mind if her little sisters came along. Sofia and Isabel sat in the backseat, their faces frozen into masks of dismay. Why didn't Janie's car have a mini-fridge? Where was her DVD player? Why was there silver tape on the door?

What was that weird noise?

By the time they pulled up to Melissa's massive gold-embossed gates, Sofia and Isabel were brimming with questions.

"Hey," Melissa greeted them at the front door. She was wearing Baby Phat cargo knickers with a pink mesh top over a white tube top. On her feet were white plastic platform mules to match her glossy white Chanel sunglasses to match the white square tips of her French manicured nails.

"Charlotte's already here," she said. Sofia and Isabel stayed behind to pat Emilio Poochie's slumbering body. Petra and Janie carried the pirate's chest by its ornate brass handles and followed Melissa into a grand wood-paneled hallway. A long row of glossy photographs and platinum records glinted behind thick panes of glass. Melissa kicked a pink Pilates ball out of the way and led them into a sunken, shag-carpeted "meet and greet" room. Charlotte waited by Seedy's gleaming white Steinway Grand, her delicate hand resting on the music stand. She looked like she was posing for a society portrait.

"Okay." Petra nodded, lowering the mahogany chest to the floor. She paused, noticing with horror the white shag carpeting, which, upon closer examination, looked like fur.

"Relax," Melissa assured her. "It's fake."

The girls crowded around the chest, fitting the locks with their four keys. Petra lifted the lid. Gone were the neat, folded stacks they remembered. During the journey, the perfect piles had toppled. Clothes tangled together in chaos, like something washed up on the beach.

As Charlotte pulled out her fuchsia disco skirt, Janie's red t-shirt clung to the silk ribbon.

"Sorry," Charlotte apologized, detaching the tank and handing it to Janie.

"Oh wait," Melissa said, handing Petra her jeans. "These are yours."

"Wait," Petra reached inside the waist and pulled out a sock.

"That's mine," Janie remarked, retrieving the stowaway.

Once the clothes were separated and returned to their rightful owners, the four girls folded them again. But they seemed to be taking their time. Several minutes later, when Seedy Moon shuffled into his living room for a relaxing round of Extreme Chess, they were only halfway done.

"Well, hello there!" he beamed in greeting. At the sound of his voice, Charlotte, Petra, and Janie dropped their clothes and froze. Seedy Moon was one of the fiercest voices in rap. And yet here he was, greeting them like Mister Rogers.

"I'm Melissa's dad," he explained to them, then winked at his daughter. "I suppose these are your *colleagues*?"

The girls looked at each other.

"We're sort of *former* colleagues," Charlotte explained after a moment's hesitation.

"Former?" Seedy waited for an explanation.

"The band broke up, Daddy," clarified Melissa.

"I see," he replied, taking a seat on his Louis Boy. He folded his strong hands in his lap and frowned. His Bugs Bunny slippers stared their one-eyed button stares. "Anyone wanna tell me what happened?"

"We don't have anything in common," Janie offered, checking with the other girls. They nodded their approval. "We fight, like, all the time."

"We're just really different people," Petra explained. "We . . ." She looked to Charlotte for assistance.

"We *clash*," Charlotte offered. The other girls murmured in agreement. "Clash" was exactly the word.

Seedy drummed his bejeweled fingers on his knees. "Clash, huh?" He pressed his lips together and nodded.

"Oh no." Melissa shook her head with dawning comprehension. "Daddy . . . don't."

"Don't what?" Seedy feigned innocence. He smiled at Janie, lifting his chin to the corner of the sweeping room. "See those two bamboo sticks over there?"

"Daddy!" Melissa slapped the shag carpet with her hand. "No!"

Seedy ignored his daughter. "Will you bring them over here?" he asked Janie. Janie got to her feet, sending Melissa a quick, trepid glance. What was going on?

She handed Seedy the two bamboo sticks.

"Great," Melissa muttered.

Her father clutched the bamboo sticks in either hand. "Here we have two bamboo sticks. Both exactly the same." After a pause, he hit the sticks together. "This is the sound they make. Let's try it again." He hit the sticks together a second time. "Look at that. Same sound. Same sticks. Everything *exactly the same*. Do you girls find that interesting?"

The girls stared in perplexed silence.

Melissa balled her strawberry shirt into her face and whimpered. "You're supposed to say *no*."

"No," the three other girls chanted.

"Good." Seedy nodded, lowering one stick to the floor. "Now," he continued, still holding the other, "pick something in this room. Anything you want."

After some hesitation, Charlotte pointed at his Grammy.

"*No,* not that!" He winced. "Something else."

Petra pointed out the white porcelain tiger in the middle of the long glass coffee table. Seedy nodded his approval. He paced a slow circle around the tiger, the bamboo stick behind his back. And then, before anyone knew what was happening, he whipped the stick through the air. There was a sudden slicing noise followed by an explosive crash. The girls gasped and ducked for cover.

The tiny tiger smashed to smithereens.

"NOW!" Seedy's voice boomed. "Is that tiger the same as he was before?! No he is NOT! When similar objects come together, what happens? Nothing. But when *different* objects come into contact, what happens? CHANGE happens! Things are destroyed and things are created! So!" He began pacing the room. "How does this relate to you?"

No one spoke.

"Y'all say you don't get along?! You think Eminem would be *half as good* if he and Kim *got along*? You think my platinum album *Mo'tel* would have been the indisputable masterpiece it is, if me and Slick Willi hadn't experienced a few . . . *creative differences?*"

In one lightning-quick move, Seedy unzipped his black Adidas tracksuit jacket and revealed his bare chest. The liner notes to *Mo'tel* weren't exaggerating. Slick Willi *had* shanked Seedy with the dull edge of a can opener during a quarrel over the cello track on "Kim Chee Killa." The scar arced across Seedy's rock-hard abdomen like an angry comet.

"You girls need to *cherish* this fight!" he bellowed. "You need to *love the hate*! You need to clash and clash and clash *again*. Why? Because it is out of *conflict* that *creativity* is born!"

At that, Seedy re-zipped his jacket, concealing his chest (and past) from view. "All great art," he concluded with a long, stern look, "is born of conflict."

"Totally," Petra whispered after an awkward pause.

"That was" — Charlotte cleared her throat — "moving."

"Yeah," Janie agreed.

"Are you *done?*" Melissa flared.

"Yes," her father replied. "But just one more thing." Seedy frowned at the floor, choosing his words carefully. "Conflict," he paused, "doesn't always mean you hate each other. Sometimes . . . deep down? It means you love each other."

The girls looked at each other for the first time since arriving at Melissa's door. A meaningful silence passed between them.

"No," Charlotte confessed at last, "I'm almost a hundred percent sure we hate each other."

"Definitely," the three girls concurred.

"Okay," Seedy conceded. "But just 'cause you hate each other, doesn't mean you have to give up on The Trend Set. Right?"

"I guess not." Charlotte shrugged. The other girls nodded in bewildered agreement.

"You won't regret it." He smiled, then shuffled toward the wall and punched the button on the intercom.

"Yes, Mr. Seedy," a nasal voice crackled from the speaker.

"Yo, Zelda, whassup," he replied, scratching the back of his head. "Uh . . . we got something broken in the living room? I know. Yeah. No idea how it happened, no. Aw, come on, Z . . . would I lie to you?"

While Sofia and Isabel played in the living room with Emilio Poochie, the members of the newly restored Trend Set decided to meet in the Moons' kitchen and discuss the future of their fashion label. First, they created specific positions based on their strengths. After some discussion, Melissa drew up an official chart.

NAME, POSITION	DEFINITION OF RESPONSIBILITIES
Janie Farrish, Art Director	Oversees all fashion drawings. Responsible for four professional-level fashion drawings per month (one per meeting) according to the collective vision of THE TREND SET. Conducts one drawing class the first Wednesday of every month.
Charlotte Beverwil, Head Seamstress	Oversees all needlework, including sewing, embroidery and mending. Responsible for turning one fashion drawing (to be determined by THE TREND SET) into a fully executed, industry-standard (read: wearable) garment. Conducts one sewing class the third Wednesday of every month.
Petra Greene, Secretary of the Interior	"Interior" refers to the collective soul, conscience, and moral integrity of THE TREND SET. The Secretary of the Interior conducts all research, background checks, and charity work. THE TREND SET vows to maintain cruelty-free standards.
Melissa Moon, Executive Officer Public Relations	Oversees the organization and execution of: Press Releases Party Planning Fashion Shows Travel (?)

Once the positions were official, the girls decided to make a meal to celebrate. Petra sliced up every vegetable in the house: red, green, and yellow bell peppers, bright baby carrots, fresh cucumbers, and crisp jicama. Janie whipped up a special yogurt-dill dip. Melissa air-popped an enormous bowl of popcorn, and Charlotte made her dessert du jour: crêpe and nutella "sushi" rolls. The four girls stared at the banquet in front of them, salivating for a taste. They were starving! But the rule was: no eating until they came up with a name for their label. After all, they couldn't just call it THE TREND SET forever.

"Okay," Janie said after five minutes of serious thought. "This might sound a little crazy. But what if we just go ahead and name the label . . . "Poseur"?

"What?" Melissa almost choked.

"I don't know," Petra considered, shrugging her shoulders in consent.

"You don't know?" Melissa gasped. "That word is an insult! I mean — it makes us look bad."

"I know." Janie nodded. "But, you know, if someone uses a word to insult you, you can't let it *get* to you. You gotta, like, take that word as your own. Once you *own* your enemy's word and act like it's something to be proud of — you take away its power."

"Beautiful speech," Charlotte oozed. "Bravo, *Pompidou.*"

At the sound of that word, Janie flushed with the old, familiar anger. But then she realized: Charlotte was only testing her point. If her theory about "Poseur" had any merit, then it would have to apply to "Pompidou" too. She turned to face Charlotte, her supposed greatest enemy, and smiled. For the first time, Charlotte hadn't intended Pompidou as an insult. She intended the word as a gift.

"Okay, okay . . ." Janie laughed, pumping her fist in mock-triumph. "I am Pompidou!" And that was all it took. At last the word belonged to her.

"I guess I'm *Harlotte,*" Charlotte announced with a celebratory finger-swirl.

"I am Petrafried!" Petra joined in. The three girls laughed, turning their dancing eyes toward Melissa.

"And I am not participating." She frowned. "*That* said: Janie . . . I see your point. My dad calls what you're talking about, um . . . he's calls it . . ."

"Appropriating the language of the oppressor!" Seedy's voice echoed down the hall.

"*Thank* you, Daddy!" Melissa replied in a teasing lilt.

"So then" — Janie smiled — "are we down?"

Everybody waited as Melissa unsnapped the smooth Tiffany blue leather case that contained her Tiffany gavel. She raised the small hammer into the air.

"All for sticking it to those who dare call us names!" The silver flashed. "Say here!"

"Here, here!"

"All for taking *their* word and making it *ours,* say here!"

"Here, here!"

"All for naming our label *POSEUR* because we don't give a frying duck!"

"Frying *duck?*"

"Just say 'here'!"

"Here, here!"

Melissa brought the gavel down, tapping it four times — one tap for each girl.

"Wait," Janie interjected the ensuing whistles and cheers. "Does this mean we have to make t-shirts with POSEUR across the chest?"

The four girls looked at each other and collapsed into gasping guffaws. "Totally!" Melissa shrieked.

"What kinda noise was that?" Seedy Moon popped his head into the kitchen. At the sight of his mock-stern face, The Trend Set tried to contain their laughter. But they couldn't.

"You ladies are *getting along!*" Seedy shook his head in faux dismay. "After *everything* I told you!"

"No, Daddy." Melissa covered her smile and shook her head.

"We are *not* getting along," Charlotte added.

"We hate each other," Petra whispered.

"To the *core,*" Janie squeaked.

"Yeah, excellent work, ladies." Melissa's father continued shaking his head. "Keep it up."

At that, Seedy Moon headed down the hall, leaving the girls alone. Melissa looked at Janie. Janie looked at Petra. Petra looked at Charlotte. All four of them were smiling. They smiled because they understood what they didn't have the nerve to say: how you look can be the opposite of who you are. What you say can be the opposite of what you mean. And who you think you can't *stand*... can turn out to be exactly who you need.

They smiled because, knowing this, they could admit what no one else could:

They were just a bunch of poseurs.

October 4, 10:13 p.m.

Fellow Winstonians, Fashionistas, and Fabulazzi:

Okay, so it's official. Our grand experiment in over-the-topness, our daring exercise in 'til-you-can't-stopness (aka the "Tag—You're It" party), has come to its inevitable tragic end. No doubt some of y'all are lying in bed, staring at the ceiling, wondering what more there is to life. Well, to you we say: chillax. There are more parties on the horizon, bashes so bananas they make yellow the new black. Why? Our up-and-coming label has a brand-new name. What is that name, you ask?

POSEUR.

Yeah, you read that right.

We chose POSEUR 'cause (admit it!)—it's hard to always "be yourself." How're we supposed to be ourselves when we're still figuring out who that is? So, if you think you're one thing one day, but change your mind the next, we at POSEUR say: that's cool. And maybe even chic.

Yours with a cherry on top,

Melissa, Janie, Charlotte, Petra

P.S. Our wonderful but VERY SHY label name winner is currently anonymous. So, if you or anyone you know has any leads to who this person is, please let us know. We'd hate for this amazingly perfect person to wander around without receiving their due reward....

In the words of William H. Shakespeare,
"all the world's a runway,"
and it's high time you played your part.

So who are you, anyway?

You can be a Janie, a Charlotte, a Petra, or a Melissa . . .
or even a crazy combination of all four. (Hmm . . . are
you a Petrottemelanie?)

Whatever you decide, turn the page and make their
looks your own. New York City fashion label Compai
shows you how. It's easier than one, two, um . . . spree!

DISCO SKIRT

You'll need: 1 long curtain (at least 5 ft. wide and 7 ft. long) or any fun fabric
Time: 30 min.

1. Cut a 5-in.-wide strip from edge of the curtain.

2. Cut out a circle from remaining fabric. The wider the diameter of the circle, the longer your skirt.

3. Cut a slit in center of skirt (about 12 in. across for a medium size).

4. Zigzag stitch around all raw edges.

5. Sew the strip all the way around the slit of the circle (zigzag edges facing inward), leaving enough fabric on the ends to tie shut.

SEXY RAGS TANK

You'll need: 1 big, comfy old T-shirt
Time: 12 min.

1. Cut off sleeves to tank, leaving the collar intact as indicated.

2. Cut hems off of the sleeves and put aside for later.

3. Cut off back to racer back as indicated.

4. Sew previously cut sleeve hems onto either side of tank at waist and tie in back.

TERRY TUBE

You'll need: 1 piece of stretchy terry cloth (length should equal the circumference of your bust plus 4 in.)
Time: 28 Min.

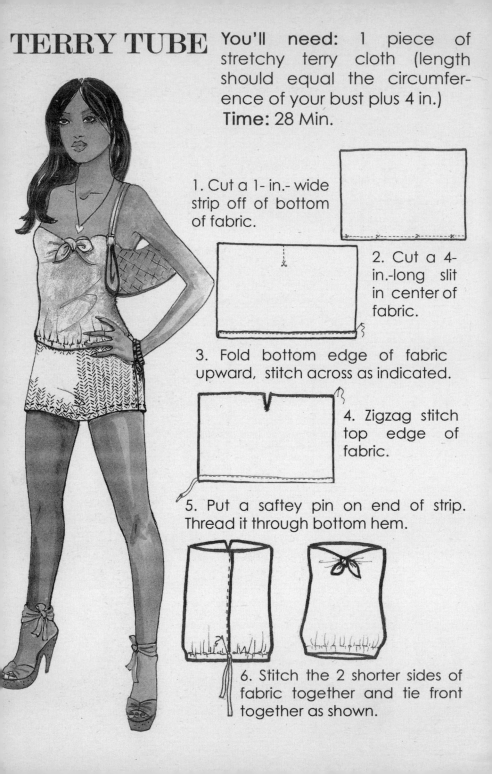

1. Cut a 1- in.- wide strip off of bottom of fabric.

2. Cut a 4- in.-long slit in center of fabric.

3. Fold bottom edge of fabric upward, stitch across as indicated.

4. Zigzag stitch top edge of fabric.

5. Put a saftey pin on end of strip. Thread it through bottom hem.

6. Stitch the 2 shorter sides of fabric together and tie front together as shown.

BOHO BAG

You'll need: 1 long thin scarf and 1 large square scarf
Time: 16 min.

1. Tie knots in long scarf.

2. Fold square scarf in half and iron the crease.

3. Tie the corners of each side together, in two tight knots.

4. Take one bottom corner of the scarf and pull it upward. Tie it together with the existing knot. Repeat on other side. The result should be a "bananna" shaped pouch.

5. Sew knotted scarf to each end of pouch to complete the purse.

Welcome to Poppy.

A poppy is a beautiful blooming red flower
(like the one on the spine of this book). It is also
the name of the new home of your favorite series.

Poppy takes the real world and makes it
a little funnier, a little more fabulous.

Poppy novels are wild, witty, and inspiring.
They were written just for you.

So sit back, get comfy, and pick a Poppy.

poppy
www.pickapoppy.com

gossip girl

THE A-LIST   THE CLIQUE

POSEUR